WRONG KIND OF PAPER

CYNTHIA SIMMONS

BROWN POSEY PRESS

an imprint of Sunbury Press, Inc.
Mechanicsburg, PA USA

an imprint of Sunbury Press, Inc.
Mechanicsburg, PA USA

For information about special discounts for bulk purchases, please contact Sunbury Press Orders Dept. at (855) 338-8359 or orders@sunburypress.com.

To request one of our authors for speaking engagements or book signings, please contact Sunbury Press Publicity Dept. at publicity@sunburypress.com.

FIRST BROWN POSEY PRESS EDITION: July 2021

Set in Adobe Garamond | Interior design by Crystal Devine | Cover design by Victoria Mitchell | Edited by Jennifer Cappello.

Publisher's Cataloging-in-Publication Data
Names: Simmons, Cynthia, author.
Title: Wrong kind of paper / Cynthia Simmons.
Description: First trade paperback edition. | Mechanicsburg, PA : Brown Posey Press, 2021.
Summary: Hallie Linden wants to write for the *New York Times*, but the only job she can find is at a sleepy Midwestern town's daily paper. She resolves to dig until she finds a story that will be her ticket to a better job. Soon she discovers that things are a little off at the Green Meadow Police Department. With help from some surprising allies, Hallie uncovers frightening truths that have only been whispered about for years.
Identifiers: ISBN : 978-1-62006-494-8 (softcover).
Subjects: FICTION / Feminist | FICTION / Small Town & Rural | FICTION / Romance / Firefighters | FICTION / Family Life / Marriage & Divorce | FICTION / Indigenous | FICTION / Political.

Product of the United States of America
0 1 1 2 3 5 8 13 21 34 55

Continue the Enlightenment!

To B and C. And for P, especially for P.

Acknowledgments

The author would like to thank the hundreds of people who contributed, in ways large and small, to the creation of this book. Facebook friends who remembered the 80s, suggested names for boots and were so very supportive through this long process; Penn State grads Rachel Weaner and Kellyn Holmes; Mo Palko, Sarah DeHart Crisp, Margaret Simmons, Elisabeth Monaghan, Sarah Cypher, Jaquelyn Mitchard, Amy Scattebo, Karen Carlton, Karen Beriss, Cate McQuaid, Jen Rand, Danielle Crowe, Amy Altmire Hendricks, Pam Monk, Jan Levine Thal, Stacie Chandler, Curt Chandler, Le'a Kent, Terry Ayers, John Gastil, Stuart Horwitz, Christine Day, Matt Katinsky, Andy Lau, Babs Griswold, Bobbi Jo Deardorff, Anne Hoag, Steve Sampsell, Marie Hardin, Russ Eshleman, Megan Moore, Elisha Halpin, Siri Newman, Whitney Polakowski, Elle Morgan, Meghan Sweeney, June Ramsay, Marisa Eichman, Tara Caimi, Helen Marie Graves, Carolyn Turgeon, Mark Simmons, Brian Satrom, Anthony Varallo, Pattie Beem, Kelly Spencer, Pearl Gluck, Billy Toy, Luciano Sormani, Jeff Knapp, Theresa Heaton, Andy Benjamin, Phyllis Fletcher, and the late Jane Eiseley

Chapter 1

It means a lot to me that you, a judge, want to know how it happened. I will tell you. But before I do, I want you to know that I see there were missteps on my part. Lapses. I admit that.

I guess it all started with the first story I covered for the Green Meadow *Daily-Observer*. It was that fire on April 16, 1989, a one-story house on River Road.

You never get used to covering fatalities. It doesn't matter if it's a three-car pileup or a little house fire like that one, it's not the smoke that makes you choke up when you ask, "Anybody killed?"

Firefighters hate that moment, the moment they have to admit they didn't get there soon enough, didn't rush in fast enough. Or that they work for a town that won't pay for the right equipment.

When I got to the River Road house, I saw a firefighter shaking his head as he pulled a hose back out of the front door. I was walking over to interview him when the police chief, almost as if he wanted to save the firefighter the pain of having to answer my questions, stepped right into my path. "One fatality," he said, his voice gravelly. "The victim must have worked the night shift at Trojan Truck. He was smokin' in bed."

House fires were nothing when I interned at the *Saint Paul Pioneer-Press*. A single-fatality fire rarely got more than two paragraphs in the B section unless it was something really unusual that started the fire. But I was just an intern at the *Pioneer-Press*, and none of the interns got hired that year. So, I had to adjust my news values for what was important in Green Meadow, Indiana.

I tried to think of something that would make the story interesting as I wrote down what the police chief said. Behind him I could see the firefighter, who I would later learn was nicknamed Blue, make a series of grimaces as he walked down to the river.

Firefighters mourn, just like crows do. It does not matter that they did not know the deceased. Firefighters hate losing somebody. They carry it, like Blue did, as a personal failure.

Perhaps you're wondering how I wound up at the *Daily-Observer* in the first place. It wasn't the kind of paper I had envisioned when I decided to major in journalism. Actually, I was a double major, journalism and women's studies, with a minor in anthropology, at Macalester College. But I get ahead of myself.

My college roommate, Amber, and I got an apartment in Minneapolis after graduation. I freelanced for the *City Paper* while I looked for a full-time job. I applied to more than a hundred papers, sending clips from my *Pioneer-Press* internship and stories from the *City Paper*, but no one called me for an interview.

Freelancing is all glory, not much pay. I was writing cover stories but still coming up short when the rent was due.

The first time it happened, Amber sweet-talked the landlord and he let it slide. That didn't work the second time, so Amber called her dad and he bailed us out.

I don't have that kind of relationship with my dad. People think if you're an only child you're really close with your parents. But my senior year at Macalester, my parents informed me that they were joining the Peace Corps. They're somewhere in Africa, smugly preaching neoliberalism to people with no shoes, let alone bootstraps.

I'm not bitter. They don't owe me anything. But I was eyeball-deep in student loan debt, just barely getting by.

My old journalism professor, Norm Wassle, was more like a father to me than my dad was. We used to call him Wassle the Fossil behind his back. One time he heard us. He didn't get mad, he ran with it. "I'm not saying the ice age is coming," Wassle said, "but journalism is changing, and not in a good way."

That second month that I couldn't make the rent, I called Wassle and we met for coffee. When Wassle asked where I had applied since graduation, I ticked off the *Chicago Tribune*, the Cleveland *Plain Dealer*, the *Providence Journal*.

He said, "You're going to have to shoot lower."

So, I started applying to really small papers, anything with a circulation above 5,000. They often called themselves "community" newspapers in the ads in *Editor & Publisher*. When I asked Wassle what they meant by that, he said, "You're getting stale, kid. Just get a job."

The *Daily-Observer*, a chain paper that published six days a week, was the only one to respond. Their ad said they were the newspaper of record in Green Meadow, Indiana, looking for a gunner to cover cops, courts, and schools. On the conference call, Frank Brierly, the managing editor, explained in a high, screechy voice that switching to only publishing six days a week had allowed them to cut their circulation department.

"We don't have delivery boys anymore. We place our product in the reliable hands of the US Postal Service."

Kim Joseph, the assistant editor, jumped in. "There's still plenty of room for features." I heard a lot of enthusiasm in her voice, a sharp contrast to Frank.

They hardly asked me any questions. At the end of the interview, they put the phone on mute for a minute, then Kim came back on.

"We'd like to meet you in person."

I had no idea what round-trip airfare would cost, but I was certain it was more than I had in the bank. Heart pounding, I asked, "Will you pay for my ticket?"

Frank whispered something to Kim that I could not hear. Then Kim said, "We really like your clips. We just need to know, are you serious about us?" Her voice was still megawatt cheerful, but there was something uncomfortable in the question. "We understand that you have made other applications. But if we make you an offer, are you likely to—"

I said, word-for-word, what Wassle had told me an editor at a small-town paper would want to hear: "I am looking for a place where I can put down roots and really get to know the community."

"So, you would take the job?"

"I would not have applied if I was not interested in joining your team."

Kim gave a relieved sigh. "Okay, we can fly you to Chicago."

"Will you also cover a rental car?"

Frank huffed.

"Don't grunt like that when we go back on," Kim said, "the microphone picks up everything."

Indeed, and apparently Kim had forgotten to press mute.

Frank told her, "Costs are starting to pile up. If she says no, I'll have to go back to corporate for money to run another ad."

Kim said, "If she doesn't take it, we can interview one of the local applicants."

"Which one?" Frank shot back, "The one who can't spell or the one who won't work weekends?"

Kim said, "Aw, shoot, I forgot—" and the hold music came on.

When they returned, Kim said, "We'll do the interview in Chicago. Frank's got a little sports car that he loves to drive, and really, it's just a hop and a skip to get there."

Chapter 2

As soon as I got off the phone, I yelled, "I've got an interview!" and Amber came running.

"What are you going to wear?"

The only dress clothes I owned were the wraparound skirt and tunic I had worn to graduation. Amber straight-up laughed when I removed them from the closet.

"I'll loan you my suit on one condition," Amber said and pulled up one leg of my sweatpants. "Will you shave?"

I did not own a razor. Shaving was equivalent to bowing down every morning to put on the shackles of the patriarchy. I'd written those very words in a paper for Race, Class and Gender Theory.

"You're going to have to wear pantyhose," she said. "It's a job interview."

She found a lipstick in a drawer in the bathroom and handed it to me, then sized me up in the mirror. "Your chin is too strong."

Kim met me at the gate. She had curly red hair and big glasses. She looked like she was in her early thirties, wearing a gauzy yellow kaftan and a navy suit jacket with David Byrne shoulder pads.

We went to a Denny's near the airport. Kim did most of the talking.

Frank I could not figure out. He wore smoky pink aviators and he never smiled. When he handed me the buff-colored folder with the Green Meadow Chamber of Commerce seal, he said, "We are a forward-looking town." He said *we* the way editorials say *we*. And then, I kid you not, he asked me what my worst fault was.

I said, "I've been working with a counselor on my kleptomania."

Frank ripped his glasses off and squinted at me.

Kim said, "You might want to go to the ladies room." As if Frank could not hear her, she stage whispered, "You've got lipstick on your teeth."

In the bathroom mirror, an unfamiliar face stared back at me. The hair Amber had fussed over fell to my shoulders in compliant brown curls. The pale makeup made my chin seem open to compromise.

I wiped the pink smear off my teeth, then fumbled with the lipstick, drawing a girly smile on my anything-but-girly face.

I did not like Frank. I did not like the way he referred to the paper as a "product." He said, "I think we put out a good product, comparatively." What kind of editor ends a sentence like that?

"You have to start somewhere," I said to the face in the mirror.

My new patent leather flats pinched as I walked back to the table. I could see the smoke from Frank's cigarette curling above his head while Kim pointed at my last front-page story in the *City Paper*.

Kim saw me and cleared her throat.

The lipstick felt like latex paint on my mouth, but I smiled it right at Frank. As I slid into the booth, I said, "I think you were about to ask about my *best* quality."

Frank cocked his head, "I hope it's not sarcasm."

I said, "I'm a workaholic. I'm frequently told by editors to take some time off, but I can't. I love writing on deadline. I get in contests with other reporters to see who can write the most stories in a week."

Frank perked up.

"You see from the *City Paper* how many times I've had stories on the cover. Keep in mind, I'm not a staff writer there. It caused considerable grumbling in the newsroom that someone just out of college had the cover story twice in one month."

"Your writing is strong," Kim said, looking to Frank for agreement.

"The writing's fine, but how's she going to fit in? It's a small town."

I said, "There's news everywhere and I love a challenge. If part of the challenge is finding the news, I'll find the news."

Frank wrote a figure on a napkin.

"That's per week?"

"No, monthly."

My mouth dropped. I could feel the lipstick drying and cracking. The pay was barely half what I would need once I started my student loan payments.

Frank's eyes narrowed. He turned to Kim. "I told you this was a waste of time." His voice was scratchy in a way I've only ever heard in Southerners, irritated, I suppose, by his smoking. But also irritated as a way to make people do what he wanted.

Kim reached to me across the table. "The cost of living is very low in Green Meadow. And," she looked to Frank, "we've got an apartment you can live in above the office."

Frank blinked about ten times.

I quickly did the math. If rent wasn't part of the equation, I'd have $400 left over each month. Not a lot, but it was doable.

I asked, "Can I sleep on it?"

Frank rolled his eyes. I think he always held it against me, that I thought I was too good for the job.

I carried six recent editions of the *Daily-Observer* onto the plane. They were extra-small tabloids. The first one led with a hospital board meeting story that Kim had written. *On April 6, the board of the Green Meadow Hospital met to discuss . . .*

I had started a story with a date exactly once in Intro to Newswriting. Professor Wassle marked it with an F and I never did it again.

As soon as I got off the plane, I found a pay phone and called Wassle. "I don't think I'm going to make it."

"Look, kid, you've got to give me some context. Is this a suicide call, or are you thinking about doing something really stupid, like going into PR?"

He agreed to pick me up at the airport. "You clean up good," he said when he saw me in the atrium. "Who wouldn't want to hire you?"

"These are the only people who do," I said and held out the *Daily-Observer*.

Wassle took the paper and read Kim's hospital board story, shaking his head the whole time.

When he was done, he spoke so quietly I had to lean in to hear him. "In a different year, Hallie, a student who writes as well as you do would have had a job offer from the *Baltimore Sun* or the *Chicago Tribune* before graduation."

The problem was all the newspaper mergers in the last year, he explained. The major dailies were cutting staff. "You're the only one from your class to get a full-time offer."

I think he was going to say I should take the job, but he couldn't get the words out; he just started coughing and couldn't stop.

I got a cup of water for him from the airport bar. When he took it, I noticed his hands shaking.

"I always thought you were destined for the *New York Times*," Wassle said. "There are no guarantees in this business, but if you do your best, people will notice. I think the Pulitzer and Silverton committees will be looking for good work from smaller papers just to spank the chains."

When I got home, a blue envelope from the student loan company was waiting for me: I had used up all the forbearances.

I didn't tell Amber. I just dialed Kim's number. "I'll take it."

Chapter 3

From the start, there were signs it was not the right paper for me. For instance, on the first day, Kim told me Frank was having a barbecue the Saturday after Memorial Day. I looked around the newsroom. Kim had a bag of pork rinds open on her desk. Charles, the business reporter, smoked nonstop. It seemed a pretty safe bet that I was the only vegetarian.

I started to decline, but Kim said, "Frank barbecues like a Black man." Then Charles echoed her, only he didn't use the word Black.

I should have walked out then. I don't like what it says about me that I didn't. Instead, I said, "What do you mean?"

Kim said, "You know, Black people really know how to barbecue."

"All of them?"

Kim shifted uncomfortably on her task chair. She was a big woman and could only fit in a chair with no armrests. If I was going to last in the job, I was going to have to find a way to fit in, too. My noncommittal "Thanks for the invitation," was a start.

Green Meadow was a town of ten thousand. Kim told me on an impromptu tour that unemployment was high. Most of the people who still had jobs, including Kim's husband, worked at the Trojan Truck factory on the edge of town. The factory that used to make peanut butter had closed. Kim pointed out big pots of petunias hanging on its chained doors. "The Ladies Garden Club put them up," she said, "to attract new business tenants."

The tour ended when Frank zoomed up in his convertible.

"House fire on River Road," he yelled.

We raced back to the newsroom. Kim worked the phones. I grabbed a map, but really, all I had to do was drive toward the sirens.

That was the single-fatality house fire I told you about covering on my first day.

The sirens were still shrieking in my head when I got back to the newsroom. Who? What? When? Where? Why? You have to impose a story with situations like that, even though all you've got are the five Ws.

They were withholding the name of the victim until the man's next of kin was notified, but the police chief had said he was a night worker at Trojan Truck. That would have to suffice for Who. What, When, and Where were in my notes. The question I could not answer was Why? In 1989, why would anyone smoke in bed? Was Green Meadow such a backwater that people didn't know it's dangerous to fall asleep smoking? I wondered if maybe the guy was drunk, but the police chief had said they wouldn't order toxicology tests since the cause of death was obvious.

Kim liked the story and put it on the front page. "That's a real accomplishment on your first day," she enthused.

Frank jumped the second part of my story to page six so it would line up next to an editorial he wrote about personal responsibility.

In the paste-up room at ten p.m., my eyes still itching from the smoke at the fire scene, I proofed my story, then stuck around to make sure the typos I had marked on the galleys were corrected.

I was still buzzy with adrenaline, so I ventured to the back of the building. In the hall past the restrooms, you could look in on the press through a long window. The newsprint came off rolls so big it took a forklift to move them. I watched the paper, pulled taut, running between rotating metal cylinders. Then I moved down to see the complicated machinery cut and collate the newspapers.

In a dim area near the loading dock, the production crew waited. Their job was to stuff, fold and address the papers, then bundle them by ZIP code and load them onto pallets to be taken to the post office.

During the building tour earlier that day, Kim had pointed out the "stuffers" with an exhale that suggested they were more trouble than they were worth. Apparently the company hadn't been able to figure out a way to end their insurance benefits and still require them to work six days a week. So, Frank switched them all to private contractor status and paid them piece rate.

"They wound up giving us no savings at all," Kim had complained. "We can't make them take out the trash or do maintenance on their down time. Corporate's lawyer said if we told them to do one thing, they could make a minimum wage claim. One called in sick three days in a row and there was nothing we could do about it."

"Didn't stuffers call in sick before?" I asked.

"Sure, but we still had a circulation crew then. If a stuffer was sick, we'd pull one of the guys off the route sort to sub." Her tone had turned sharp when she added, "I told the one who kept calling in sick, 'This is a newspaper. We get sick days in theory, but everybody knows that if someone is gone unexpectedly, we can't function.' Don't you think that goes without saying?"

She'd gestured then to the quartet of workers whose hands were flying over stacks of national ad inserts. "These guys, if something goes wrong with a babysitter or if one of their kids is afraid of a thunderstorm, they've got no compunction about calling in sick. The post office waits for no one. If we miss that deadline, the paper doesn't go out."

"Didn't Frank consider that when he eliminated the circulation department?"

"The newsboys made twenty cents a paper. Our bulk permit lets us mail for less than two cents."

Since the stuffers were standing right there during the tour, I hadn't asked then what the piece rate was. But looking at them again as they waited for the press run to finish, I surmised it wasn't much.

There were four stuffers, a man and three women. Their clothes were nearly identical, black aprons, dark T-shirts, and inked-up jeans. The women wore Kmart sneakers. The heels of the male stuffer's orthopedic shoes were worn down to a slant.

I hung back that first night, not knowing if editorial employees and production workers socialized. They didn't in the Twin Cities, but in the Twin Cities, there were hundreds of bars open after midnight. Here there was only the Top Hat Lounge, which Kim had told me was the unofficial VFW, and a country-western bar that looked too vile to enter.

"Are you the new reporter?" asked one of the stuffers, a dark-haired woman who looked like she was in her late twenties.

"That's me. Hallie Linden."

She told me her name was Sandra. "Interesting story about the fire."

I wondered how she'd seen it already. The press was still pounding in the other room.

"Did any of you know the man who died?"

Sandra's hand went to the cross on her necklace. "My brother-in-law knew him," she said. "It's a cryin' shame."

"That he was smoking in bed?"

I felt Sandra's eyes on me too long. She asked, "Do you really think it was his fault?"

I said, "The police chief said he was smoking in bed." That didn't seem to satisfy her. "People make mistakes," I allowed, not sure why I felt the need to defend the victim.

A buzzer sounded and Sandra and the other stuffers jumped into place along the river of black-and-white papers that emerged on the conveyor belt.

Outside, I made my way up the fire escape on the back of the building, the only stairs to my new apartment.

The door opened into the kitchen. In the next room there was a dining table. Then in the front room, an arc lamp hovered above an Ultrasuede couch. I didn't turn on the lamp. Instead, I spied on my new town through the window, watched the slow parade of hot rods and trucks on oversized tires. The same vehicles passed again and again.

I couldn't sleep, so I put all the chairs on top of the table and vacuumed. Try as I might, I could not make the apartment feel like home. Its only decoration was one of those generic teamwork posters.

I stared at the image: rowers silhouetted against a blazing dawn.

I tried to picture the faces of my new team. Kim, the assistant editor, seemed earnest under her wet-look perm. Frank's eyes were obscured behind his pink glasses. Both Kim and Frank had deep furrows between their eyebrows. Probably from squinting into computer monitors all day. They say you're not supposed to look at screens up close for very long.

The business reporter, Charles, just looked old. I remember thinking when I met him that he resembled a garden gnome. He was tricky, too. When I had first gotten to the newsroom, I asked him to introduce me to the publisher.

"You met him at your job interview," Charles said, as if he were telling a riddle. "It's Frank! He was promoted a while back. He's editor *and* publisher."

I guess Charles could see the shock on my face because he quickly added, "It's really streamlined decision-making."

So, Frank had the publisher's office but also a desk in the newsroom as the managing editor.

Trying to stop myself from analyzing the situation, I said out loud my own version of an inspirational slogan. "The paper doesn't have to be the best; I just have to do my best." That's what I was repeating as I fell asleep on the couch.

Chapter 4

The *Daily-Observer* didn't offer a formal training program. My second day Charles just walked me over to the police department to show me how to do a beat check there.

It seemed like an enormous responsibility. The *Daily-Observer*, as a newspaper of record, listed every car crash, arrest, and fire call. It was my job to get all the facts from the incident reports, then figure out which of them merited full stories.

When I interned at the *St. Paul Pioneer-Press*, I had occasionally done police blotter stories. In one of them, a masked gunman held up a convenience store. In Saint Paul, something like that would usually only make page six of the B section, if that. But when *I* had a masked robber assignment, I added the detail that the gunman wore a Ronald Reagan mask, and it was page A-1. My *Pioneer-Press* editor loved the fact that I had interviewed the clerk, a Vietnamese man, who said he didn't press his alarm because he thought the real Ronald Reagan was shopping in his store. "The hair, it was very realistic." That was the quote that moved the story to the front page.

I wanted to have all the background information I would need to get the police to open up to me, give me the details that would land my police stories on the front page of the *Daily-Observer*. So, on the walk over, I asked Charles about the force's organizational hierarchy.

"Is the police chief elected or appointed?"

Charles had to think.

"The sheriff is elected, but the mayor appoints the police chief. Doesn't matter who's mayor though. Conrad Kellan is always chief."

"Why's that?"

Charles squinted. "It just is."

"Does the police reporter have to monitor the police frequency all the time on the scanner? This afternoon, one of the officers was talking about a welfare check. Should I follow up on that?"

Charles looked at me as if he were doubting whether I could do the job. "That was probably nothing—they have calls like that all the time. You might not have noticed, but nothing ever happens around here. Makes a reporter's job pretty easy."

When we arrived at the low cinder block building, we were buzzed in. I saw the police dispatcher, a man who looked like Archie Bunker, hunched over a wastebasket, shelling peanuts. Beyond the dispatch center, through a partially closed door marked "Chief," I could see a rack of deer antlers mounted on a plaque.

"Who is it?" the man behind the door demanded. His voice was hoarse. A low haze of smoke told me why.

"It's just Charles," the dispatcher called back. "He's got a girl with him."

I winced, but Charles squeezed my arm. "I'd like to introduce you to the reporter who's going to be taking over the police beat," he called.

The chief leaned forward to peer out through his doorway. "Another brunette," he muttered, apparently not remembering that we had met at the fire on my first day.

"I'm Hallie Linden," I called. "We'll be seeing a lot of each other."

The chief did not get up.

Charles waded into the silence. "She'll be coming over for news releases—" Charles looked to me. "Every week?"

I said, "I'll do a beat check here every day."

Charles chuckled. "A real go-getter!"

I stepped back to take in the scene. Everything in the room was centered around the dispatch console. They had a tabletop model, so the microphone and transmitter sat on an ordinary wooden desk. It looked as if a child had set up a police station kit, the way kids get chemistry and erector sets.

Charles made a sweeping gesture with his arm. "So, this is the dispatch room. The incident reports are in the tray."

That was it. No training on the state's open records laws. No protocol for requesting files.

"Shouldn't there be a shift log?" I asked.

The dispatcher removed a clipboard that was hanging from a nail on the side of the desk and pushed it toward me. The single sheet of notebook paper on it was blank.

"I heard something on the scanner around one-thirty today," I said, "about a welfare check. What was that call?"

"Dunno," the dispatcher grunted.

I said, "Don't you have to log every time an officer radios? In St. Paul, they log calls immediately. Actually, they've got a computer that does it automatically."

"City council didn't see fit to get us one of them computers," the dispatcher said.

Charles said, "The new cruiser was expensive. You've got to remember that."

The dispatcher told me, "We write them by hand, miss."

"Hallie. You can call me Hallie."

Charles looked at his watch. As if an afterthought, he tapped the short stack of incident reports in the tray. "Nothin' here, right?"

Charles didn't pick up a single report. *That's a mistake*, I thought. The stories are in the details, and you don't know the details if you don't read the reports. I made a mental note to allow more time than Charles took when I covered the cop shop myself.

Just as we were getting ready to leave, the second-shift dispatcher came steaming in. She was blond, maybe a couple years younger than me. She had a giant plastic soda cup with an accordion straw sticking out through the lid.

"Hi, sugar," the man at the console said.

I'm sure my jaw dropped. I watched the new dispatcher settle in behind the console. She was heavy, hair bleached to an even shade of yellow. *She's my in*, I thought as I watched the a.m. dispatcher hand her the clipboard with the empty shift log sheet.

I told Charles to go back without me.

When he left, I positioned myself against the wall to get a read on the p.m. dispatcher. Archie Bunker told her there had been some trouble earlier, but no arrests.

"What was the trouble?" I asked.

"You're interrupting."

I matched his tone. "What was the problem?"

"We don't have a report."

"When will the report be done?"

"It was nothing," he insisted. "There may not be a report."

"Who was the officer that responded?"

The a.m. dispatcher shook his head. "I'm clocking out."

Chapter 5

Kim was quite a picture when I got in at two the next day. And it wasn't a Norman Rockwell tribute to freedom of the press. She was alone in the office pounding the top of a silver machine about the size of a Rubik's Cube. Every time she hit it, the wad of cords that dangled from the contraption flapped and its computer voice gave the Greenwich Mean Time.

"I don't care about the GMT, you stupid piece of shit!"

I cleared my throat.

"Sorry. I thought I was alone."

"Fuck a duck, Kim. You can cuss around me. For Christ's sake, it's one of the two benefits of being a reporter."

"I know the other one isn't the state-of-the-art equipment we work with."

"What is that thing?"

"It's a weather radio. It's supposed to give the current temperature and the forecast from the National Weather Service, but it's on the fritz. I've pressed that button forty times and all it gives me is the Greenwich Mean Time. You know what's ironic? Every time I ask Frank about replacing the weather radio, he won't give me the time of day."

Kim had been an English major. I figured she was lonely in Green Meadow.

"Do you want to come up to the apartment for dinner?" I asked her. "I'd love to show you what I've done with the place."

Kim's eyebrows shot up. "It's just an informal arrangement. You can't paint or anything. Don't make any changes up there. We didn't have permission from corporate to sweeten the deal for you. We could all get fired if HR finds out you're living upstairs."

I shook my head in disbelief.

Kim said, "Frank says we shouldn't have given it to you."

"But you did. You shook on it."

Kim made a straight-lipped smile. "You shook *my* hand. The way Frank sees it, that's not legally binding. He's the boss."

"I moved all the way from Minneapolis, and now you're telling me I don't have a roof over my head?"

Kim held up her hands. "Heavens, no. We're not reneging on the deal."

"Is that a royal *we* or are you speaking for Frank, too?"

"The apartment's a sore spot for Frank. Could you just not rub it in his face? Don't move furniture until after he leaves work."

"At four p.m.? I'm working at four."

"It's already set up with everything you need. Come to think of it, use of all that stuff wasn't in the job offer. What you've got up there is a *fully furnished* apartment stocked with dishes and linens and light bulbs and toilet paper."

I quickly calculated that it would take more than a thousand dollars to replace the furniture, kitchenware, sheets, and towels. I wasn't going to have a spare thousand dollars for months. I needed that stuff or I was going to have to default on my student loans. So, I tried to make myself fit. "What are you suggesting?"

"Don't mention the apartment. Frank will get used to the arrangement. And don't decorate."

"Are you telling me not to hang any posters?"

"Exactly."

"There's already a poster up there."

"A poster is okay. A nice Georgia O'Keeffe poppy or something. But don't put up any hippie wall hangings. And you know the windows front to the street. Don't put anything close to the windows. It shouldn't look lived in."

⚐

When I got to the police station for my beat check, the second shift dispatcher was on a folding chair at the dispatch console.

It was my goal to make her like me, so I searched for commonalities. We were about the same age, both female in a town that was stuck in the '50s. That was a start.

"Yesterday when I was in here, the other dispatcher called you 'sugar.' Didn't that bother you?"

"What?"

"The a.m. dispatcher. Yesterday, he called you 'sugar.' Do you have to put up with that all the time?"

"Honey, that's my name." She extended her hand and did the half shake thing, bent her fingers so I could not really get a grip. "Sugar Jane Ecclesiastes Johnson."

I didn't know what to say, so I repeated, "Sugar Jane Ecclesiastes Johnson."

"Mommy named me Sugar because I was so sweet. Daddy said I had to have a regular name, too, for school."

"And Ecclesiastes?"

Sugar lowered her eyelids. "Oh honey, that's how I got here in the first place. You see, my daddy was real religious. He was saving himself for marriage. But Mommy wanted him something fierce."

"She told you this?"

"He was holding out for a girl he'd want to marry, but Mommy quoted him Ecclesiastes four-eleven: 'If two lie down together, they will keep warm.'"

"They kept warm?"

"Four kids in four years."

"So, did you go by Jane or Sugar in school?"

"Daddy runnoft when I was six. Found a girl he wanted to marry. He had his bags packed and was loading them in the car down at the end of the driveway when bam! A test truck from Trojan hit him. So there's Daddy, flat as a pancake. Sixty-four broken bones."

Sugar told this as if she were talking about a crash at the Indy 500.

"He was three months in the hospital, but they couldn't save his legs. Mommy said that was God smiting him down. She called the woman whose name was in his note. Home wrecker didn't want nothin' more to do with Daddy. So when he got out of the hospital, it was Mommy set him up on a bed in the living room. She fed him and bathed him right in front of the TV, turned him over every six hours so his bedsores wouldn't be too bad. Whenever she turned him, she said, 'You don't want to leave me now, do you?' She quoted him Ecclesiastes four-ten: 'Pity anyone who falls and has no one to help them up.'"

"That's a lot to carry in a name."

"Daddy's face was taped up. He couldn't talk for the longest time. So Jane? Might as well have been erased from my birth certificate. From then on I was just Sugar."

Back in college, we had this saying, *too much information*. I didn't know where to go with the conversation, so I asked how the reporter before me had done beat checks.

"Allison? Boy, I miss her. We'd visit for a half hour or so every day, then I'd give her the incident reports and the arrest reports."

"Do you have investigation reports, too?"

"We don't give you those," Sugar said, all the sweetness drained from her voice.

"They're public record."

"Not if it's a ongoing investigation."

"Noise complaints?"

"Ongoing investigation."

"Gunshots heard?"

"That's just huntin' season."

"But if it's not hunting season?"

Sugar tapped her badge. "This is how it works. You come in and we visit, talk about all the fascinating things going on in this town. Then, if I like you, I pull out what looks interesting from the reports."

"And if you don't like me?"

"I give you a stack of papers once a week with every cat in a tree, every elderly fall, every car that backfired and scared the neighbors."

"You're going to like me."

⚓

For my dinner break in the apartment at eight, I plopped down a bowl of noodles on the dining table and stared at the teamwork poster.

Teamwork is the ability to work together toward a common vision. The ability to direct individual accomplishment toward organizational objectives. It is the fuel that allows common people to attain uncommon results.

I could not see the faces of the rowers silhouetted on the river, but eight oars were in the water.

What would success look like for me? I tried to visualize rowing, moving in unison with my *Daily-Observer* coworkers, then breaking off, a boat unto myself, going faster and farther.

No, I told myself, *stay with your team*. How could I do that?

I was trying to visualize holding my nose and rowing with just one hand when I heard clanging on the fire escape, then three cheerful knocks.

Damn. I'd forgotten that I'd invited Kim for dinner.

This is where you start, I told myself as I pushed the paltry bowl of noodles to the center of the table. Kim was the only person in the newsroom who didn't make me want to gag. I had to try to develop a good working relationship with her.

I poured some tomato sauce into the pan I had used for the pasta, then opened the door.

With a sly smile, Kim pulled a jug of Carlo Rossi Chianti from her bag, presenting it the way one would unwrap some precious contraband. Then she came in and started rummaging in my cupboard.

Kim settled on a mug with the chain's corporate logo and filled it to the top.

"I met Sugar Johnson today," I told her, eager for her take on the dispatcher.

"Now there's a real Green Meadow girl. Her mother's a cousin of the police chief. Her father was nearly killed in a terrible accident."

"She told me."

Kim said, "Her mother is a saint, taking care of him all those years. I don't know that I'd stick around if I had to change Norton's diapers. With a baby, you have to tolerate it. But once is enough with that kind of shit, pardon my French—"

"I told you before, swearing is one of the two benefits of being a reporter—"

"And I know the other one is not the high pay," Kim laughed, the sparkle back in her eyes. "Listen, about earlier. I want you to know how much we want you here."

"The apartment makes this doable for me. Not paying rent is the only way I can make my student loan payments on this salary."

Kim moved to the kitchen window. "It wasn't easy being the only woman in the newsroom."

"Why did the last reporter leave?"

"Allison ran off with the prosecutor. Never came in for her last paycheck."

"I suppose she couldn't cover courts if she was involved with him."

"Nope. But the kicker is he was married with two kids."

"A pillar of the community."

"Up until then, we thought he was."

I said, "There seems to be a lot of friendliness between reporters and the people they cover."

"We're a small town."

"But sometimes it's an adversarial relationship."

Kim shook her head. "Not really. Haven't you noticed nothing ever happens here?"

I turned off the flame under the sauce. "There was a fatal house fire my first day."

"That guy was smoking in bed. Stupid happens here, same as the next town."

"But on that question of friendliness with sources, Charles seemed awfully chummy with the morning police dispatcher when he introduced me at the cop shop."

"Charles is the business reporter. It's not a conflict. Those guys are in the same lodge. Frank's in it, too. I wish we had something like that for women. Maybe you and I could start a chapter of the American Association of University Women. It'd be pretty exclusive, just you and me and the superintendent's wife!"

I said, "About the apartment."

Kim held out her mug. "Give me a refill and let's take a tour. I haven't been in here since we had to carry the regional director up." She seemed to take great delight in relaying this detail. "He comes for site visits a couple times a year. Unannounced, of course."

When we got to the dining table, Kim eyed the bowl of pasta. "Is that it?"

"No, there's sauce on the stove."

"Hallie, this is barely enough for one person."

I didn't have any more noodles, so I went back to the kitchen and put two slices of bread on a plate. When I brought them out with the sauce, Kim was already in a chair. I said, "I can't spend a lot on groceries. My student loans will take half my pay."

Kim said, "I got a partial scholarship at Hamilton College."

"I got a partial scholarship, too. But the place I went was damn expensive."

"Then why did you go there?"

That was a good question. Prestige? Had I really believed Macalester was the Harvard of the Midwest? No. But Wassle—I wouldn't trade my years with Professor Wassle for anything. He made me a journalist. That's what I thought, but what I said was, "It was one kind of economy when I was choosing a college, a completely different one when I got out."

I passed Kim the noodles. She was careful to only take half.

"Did you know you wanted to be a journalist from the beginning?" she asked.

"I edited my high school newspaper. So yeah, I guess I knew."

Kim said, "Ink gets in your blood."

"How about you?" I asked.

Kim gave a world-weary laugh. "I wanted to be a novelist. Science fiction. I thought I would invent worlds where the women were in charge."

"Kind of post–Margaret Atwood?"

"I never read her."

"Don't start with *The Handmaid's Tale*. You'll slit your wrists."

"You've read a lot. I like that. Not a lot of people in Green Meadow read books."

"Why are you in Green Meadow, Kim?"

Kim seemed surprised, as if she'd never asked herself that. "I'm married. We've got a house here."

"Why'd you get married?"

Kim's easy smile vanished.

I said, "You've got to be bored here."

Kim looked down, then wiped her bread inside the saucepan. "I really don't see Norton that much. He works when I sleep. He sleeps in the day when I'm with Misty."

"You didn't answer my question."

Kim's mouth gaped, as if she didn't have words, then she looked at her hands. Her fingertips were red with marinara.

"It doesn't make sense," I pushed.

Kim composed her face. "He was my high school sweetheart, okay?"

"And?"

"How much wine do you think I've had?"

"And?"

"I was pregnant."

If I had been interviewing Kim, I would have known from the way her voice cracked on the word pregnant that she had a lot of emotion pent up behind that fact. Without even thinking about it, she had made herself vulnerable to me. If this had been an interview, so long as I could keep her in that emotional state, I could count on her answering honestly, even against her own interests.

But it was not an interview.

"Now you," Kim said, finding her napkin. "Why did you choose the *Daily-Observer*?"

My voice didn't crack. "I'd never lived in a small town before. And I just liked you."

She grabbed my hand. "I'm so glad you joined our team."

"It's funny that you use the word 'team.'" I pointed to the poster of the rowers. "I want to take that down."

Kim read it out loud: "Teamwork is the ability to work together toward a common vision. The ability to direct individual accomplishment toward organizational objectives." She scrunched up her nose. "That's not a complete sentence."

"So I can take it down?"

"Better not."

Chapter 6

The next day, Charles walked me to the courthouse. I already knew he had grown up in Green Meadow and still lived in a Victorian house downtown with his elderly mother. We had pretty much run out of small talk, so I asked, "What do you think our common vision should be? What should our organizational objectives be?"

"I made a business plan for the paper a few years ago," he said, a little bounce in his step. "You know how there are the three Rs in education? Reading, Writing and Arithmetic?"

"That's one R, a W, and an A."

"I know that," he said, annoyed. "In my plan, I had three Ps for the *Daily-Observer*: pride, progress, and public records. The problem with reporters is reactivity. News happens, we write about it. News drives our content. But nobody ever asks our customers—"

"You mean our readers."

"No," Charles said, "our advertisers are our primary customers. Subscriptions are an important revenue stream, but they're not even close to what we get from display ads and classifieds. What I was saying is, our mission, if we're to have a really good product, is to know what our advertisers want in the paper and deliver that every day."

"What do our advertisers want?"

"First, they want a paper that shows civic pride."

I pointed to a row of vacant storefronts across the street.

"The retail core is a problem, yes," Charles said. "But we've got growth with the water park. That brings thousands of tourists to our area, hungry people who need gas and lodging, sunscreen and swimsuits."

Charles said he had freelanced a special report on business growth for the Chamber of Commerce.

"And that's what you found," I asked, "the water park, Sir Splash-A-Lot's?"

"Green Meadow is in a post-manufacturing phase. Trojan is really the only large manufacturer left."

"They make semis?"

"Just the trailers. Unions killed off engine manufacturing here in the seventies. Now Trojan imports the tractors from Japan. Like I said, we're in a post-manufacturing era. Sir Splash-A-Lot's got it right. Tourism is our future. So, my second P is progress. The *Daily-Observer* needs to be a leader in promoting tourism since that's the only growth sector."

"And the third P?"

"That's your job. Public records. In the last reader survey, people said the main reason they subscribe is that they don't want to miss any of the Vital Records news."

"Car crashes? Fires?"

"Police and fire calls are part of it, but only part. You see, this is a small town, but not that small. Not everybody gets invited to every wedding, but everybody wants to know about every wedding. The girl who covers cops and fires also covers courts, and all the birth, death, marriage, and divorce certificates filed at the courthouse."

"No one mentioned that in my job interview."

"If you do it once a week it doesn't take much time."

"Did you do it while my position was vacant?"

"No, I'm the business reporter."

"Who did it?"

"Frank and I disagree on this. He says nobody reads those. We have to run them to keep our eligibility to run legal ads, but he let your predecessor and the girl before her get way behind. I think our circulation proves my point. We dipped to six thousand this year. Our circulation never went that low before the chain gave Frank the publisher duties."

"You don't like Frank?" I asked.

"Didn't say that. Frank is a lodge brother of mine. A good man. He just lacks connection to our readership. He's only been here four years. I think he's like you, thinking of this as a steppingstone."

"A steppingstone?"

Charles rocked back on his heels. "You should get an Academy Award."

"You think this is just a steppingstone for me?"

"It is for all of you. Nobody lasts in your beat."

"Why not?"

Charles thought for a minute. "For a young person, it's hard to cover what really matters in Green Meadow."

"What really matters here?"

"I just told you: Business. Progress. Achievements. And weddings and funerals. We used to cover those. Now Frank only runs paid wedding announcements and obituaries."

"Who used to cover them?"

"The girl always does that."

I bit my tongue and looked away.

"What's wrong?"

I told myself that part of teamwork is saying what you need so people don't keep making you mad. So I said, "I don't think of myself as a 'girl.' And it would go a long way with me if you didn't call me a girl. I'm an adult. I'm twenty-two."

"So you are." Charles smiled and held the courthouse door for me.

Inside, men in suits moved between the white marble columns as Charles led me to the clerk's office. Charles seemed to know everyone. "This is a young *lady* I'd like to introduce you to," he said to each person we passed. His voice bounced off the stone walls as he explained that I would be picking up where the last reporter left off. One man snickered at that and Charles said, "Not literally, of course."

We walked right behind the counter in the clerk's office.

"Is she going to do the Vital Records column?" the clerk asked.

I jumped in. "Not right away. I've got so much to learn about the progress of this city, the things people here take pride in."

"First things first," Charles allowed.

He asked the elderly clerk to show me how to request files.

She said, "I don't move so fast anymore, so you can pull the files yourself. I just ask that you put them back in order."

"Where are the criminal files?" I asked.

"We don't have murders here, dearie, or any other interesting crime. Whatever you're used to in the Twin City or wherever you said you're from, dial it back."

I said, "Thanks for that insight, ma'am." But I knew I would prove her wrong.

Chapter 7

Kim posted the schedule for the last week of May. Normally I had Saturday off, worked Sunday and Monday, got Tuesday off, and then worked Wednesday through Friday. But this week, she had me off Monday, then working from Tuesday through to the following Sunday.

"You'll work Memorial Day, too, of course. That's the following Monday. But both Saturday and Sunday we'll go home early unless something big happens."

"Why isn't Charles on the schedule for Friday or Saturday or Sunday?" I asked.

"He's got to get his boat in the water. Frank's got his convertible, Charles has his boat. You know what they say, 'Boys need their toys.'"

"That's not a saying."

"It'll be fun. I'll buy pizza from petty cash."

⚓

Walking to my beat checks, the truants cruising Main Street seemed to have multiplied. One had a wad of cassette tape caught on the tip of his antenna. The end of it licked the wind as he sped by.

At the cop shop, Sugar asked if I had plans for the long weekend.

"I'll be covering you guys."

"By yourself?" she clucked.

"Kim will be in the office. Why?"

"Things heat up when the weather gets warm. Lordy, lordy. Your first three-day."

As if on cue, Darnell Kellan, the young cop, walked in. "Did you say you want your first three-way? I'm here for you, girls."

Sugar put her finger to her mouth and said to Darnell, "If you convince Ricky, I'll see if I can't get Dora to cover for me on dispatch."

Officer Kellan made a great show of shuddering. "I'm only in if it's two girls on me."

I made a quick exit.

⊿⌄⌄

The Friday before Memorial Day weekend, the scanner on my desk never shut up. Most of the calls were for speeding, noisy parties, and DUIs.

"We'll get a fatal crash before the weekend is through," Kim predicted.

We did.

On Saturday, a teenager going the wrong way near the I-65 interchange slammed into a sedan driven by an elderly man. I got there after the police and ambulance. The teen in the pickup was fine, but the old guy broke his neck.

"Better'n living in a nursin' home waiting to croak," Darnell Kellan said at the scene.

I walked over to the teenager, wobbly in cowboy boots. Darnell didn't have him in cuffs.

"Didn't you see the other car?" I asked.

The teen looked drunk and scared, so I went for a television reporter approach. "How do you feel?"

Boots just spat on the ground.

"I'll take that to mean no comment."

The kid glared at me, but the expression didn't fit his face. It was like he was putting on a tough-guy act, which, if he had been at as many accident scenes as I had, he would know was not normal.

⊿⌄⌄

Later that day, I went out to report on two more crashes, plus a house fire. I saw Darnell again at the fire. He said, "Looks like they forgot the 'out' part of 'grillin' out.'"

I saw the woman whose house was gutted standing behind him. Her features moved from shock to anger. She seemed to want to override Darnell, to not let his voice be the one that spoke for her in the paper. But there had already been two fatalities, so her fire, though it changed her life completely, would only be a line in the list of fire calls.

Since there would be no story, I didn't interview her. I think I was getting numb.

⟋▸▵▴

Sunday was more of the same: a drunk driver in a Chrysler LeBaron T-boned a station wagon on Dunphy Street. A mother and her seven-year-old daughter were killed. When I arrived, the preteen son, who had been sitting in the front passenger seat, was screaming hysterically and refusing to get into the ambulance. There wasn't a scratch on him.

When I saw that, I remembered how both Charles and Kim always said nothing ever happens in Green Meadow. *They don't get out of the newsroom much*, I thought.

⟋▸▵▴

When my head hit the pillow Sunday night, I had a hard time getting to sleep. If I closed my eyes I saw police lights flashing. So, I stared at the ceiling and tried to put the dead in order of descending news value. The seven-year-old, of course, was first. The fact that she died with her mom cinched it. But what would have made the crash with the teen driver more compelling? What if he had been an honor student? Would that have topped the seven-year-old? No. What if the man he killed was his own grandfather? Maybe. What if, instead of an old man, it was the teen's pregnant girlfriend that died in the other car? Definitely. What if he only learned at the accident scene that she was pregnant? Even at the *Pioneer-Press*, that would be front-page news.

⟋▸▵▴

When I arrived for work on Monday, Kim told me a reader had phoned in a tip that there had been a suicide at Hillcrest.

Hillcrest was a retirement complex just west of downtown. When I got there, residents were grouped in the clubhouse.

"We knew she was feeling down, but no one thought she was that depressed," one of them told me.

A sixty-ish woman wearing a sundress and sneakers said, "She was a lovely person. She kept birds. Sometimes she had one on her finger when she came to the door."

I led with that. It seemed like a way to humanize the victim. Edna Buchanan, my heroine at the *Miami Herald*, could do better, but I wasn't competing for a Pulitzer that day. I just wanted to get the story done so we could leave.

"Quote lead?" Kim called from behind her computer. "Are you sure you want to blow your one quote lead of the year on a suicide?"

"She was a person, Kim. Suicide is just how she stopped being a person."

Kim read a little farther. "I'll allow it. How did she do the deed?"

"Gun in the mouth, just like Hemingway. Her neighbor said she found *For Whom the Bell Tolls* on the couch next to her."

"Did she use a shotgun or a pistol?"

"Pistol."

"It's a close call, but I don't think we can put it on the front page." Kim looked up and grinned at me. "I hope she wasn't wearing white shoes."

I hadn't seen the suicide victim's shoes, but I imagined they were canvas Keds like her friend was wearing and I had to bolt for the restroom. "Just breathe," I said in the mirror as I steeled myself to return to the newsroom.

On the page mock-up, Kim had written, "Mom and daughter perish," as a headline, then added a subhead: "Twelve-year-old son walks away from crash unscathed."

I said, "I don't think he was unscathed."

"The cop you quoted said he sustained no injuries."

"He saw his mother and his sister die. He was scathed."

"But you see the irony?"

"That's not irony. That's dumb luck. And believe me, the kid is not feeling lucky."

"It's late. I'm just going to pull rank on you."

Kim decided Saturday's teen driver crash could be added at the end of the mother-daughter fatal. She was going to roll in the suicide, too, but then decided she liked my quote lead after all, so she kept it as a separate story on page three.

"Hillcrest suicide leaves residents shocked" was her headline.

I said, "They knew she was depressed."

"What do you want for a headline? 'Friends of suicide victim somewhat surprised, thought she'd never do it?' Why are you so difficult tonight?"

The paste-up guy had Memorial Day off, so Kim and I went through the swinging doors to the layout room.

Kim made the mother-daughter fatal the lead story even though it was a day old. She put a teaser for the suicide story on the front page above the masthead, "Apparent Memorial Day suicide mars start of summer for Hillcrest residents, see page 3" with a yearbook photo of the dead woman. The suicide victim had been an English teacher at the high school until 1983, but Kim chose a photo from ten years before that.

To my tired eyes, the page glowing on the light table made no sense. When I asked Kim why she used the old photo, she said she thought the cat-eye glasses the woman was still wearing in the early seventies made a strong visual statement.

"And it adds a little mystery," Kim said. "It suggests she was out of step with the times."

"We don't know that, Kim. We don't know why she killed herself. She didn't leave a note."

"She committed suicide. You don't get to check out and then not like the way people talk about you."

A phone rang in the newsroom. Probably Frank checking up on us.

As soon as Kim was out of the paste-up room, a stuffer came in through the newsroom's back door.

"I'm Sandra. You probably don't remember me."

"You asked me what I thought about the smoking-in-bed fire. I remember you."

"Your first three-day?" Sandra asked. As she read the front-page layout, she fingered her necklace and whistled "Sunday, Bloody Sunday."

I said, "Today was pretty bad, too. There was a suicide at Hillcrest. You might have known her. She taught at the high school."

Sandra looked away, then bent down to get a close look at the layout.

"Why are you running this old picture?"

I told her Kim thought it added a note of mystery.

"No," Sandra said. With her ink-stained fingers, she pulled the picture off and ripped it in half. Then she repositioned Kim's teaser, cutting the words apart with an X-Acto knife and spacing them out to fill the place where the photo had been.

I was shocked, but we were running late. There was no time to get another photo. "That looks better than the way Kim had it," was all I said.

Sandra asked, "After I get off work, do you want to have a beer?"

She explained that she had a kid to get home to, but if I wanted to go to her place, we could talk there. Thirty minutes later, I followed her back to a white farmhouse a few miles out of town.

We went in through the back door. "There's beer in the fridge. Help yourself," she said. "I've got to run upstairs and tell my mother-in-law she's off duty."

The refrigerator door was covered with drawings of spaceships. I grabbed a Schaeffer and went into the living room.

On the mantel above the fireplace there were bronzed baby shoes, a wedding picture, a praying hands sculpture, and a portrait of a Marine. Next to that was a folded flag in a triangular glass box. If I had been there for an interview, that would have been enough to spark an hour's worth of questions. But this evening I had only one.

"Why did you take off the suicide photo?"

"You've heard of Indian Canyon?" she asked.

"It's more of a ravine."

Sandra shook her head. "It's rocky enough. That's where my mother jumped about a month after my wedding."

I said, "How awful," but Sandra didn't seem to want sympathy.

"Things must seem pretty dull here," she said, "compared to the Twin Cities. But that's no reason to spice up the news using old photos."

"I didn't choose the photo," I reminded her.

"No, you didn't. There's hope for you."

I said, "You read the paper every day, what do you think of my stories?"

As a reporter, you become sensitive to how long someone takes to answer your questions. A long pause can mean the person is trying to decide how much to tell. Sandra's silence dragged on, but what came next suggested she wanted to trust me.

"It seems like the paper goes through police reporters faster than toilet paper."

"It is a small town," I explained, "and nothing ever happens here."

"Who says that?"

"My editor, and Charles," I said.

"Charles can't report his way out of a paper bag. Or won't. He may have gone away to business school, but he's Old Green Meadow. The good ol' boys who run this town have him right in their pocket."

I said, "He's bully on the Chamber of Commerce, that's for sure, and Sir Splash-A-Lot's."

Sandra said, "That damn water park is an abomination," which I thought was a strange thing for a mother to say since there wasn't much else for kids to do in Green Meadow. But the revulsion in Sandra's voice also reminded me of her tone when she had questioned me about the fatal fire on my first day.

"You said your brother-in-law knew the fire victim, the man who was smoking in bed."

"Are you going to do a follow-up story?"

That must have been why she had invited me over. "What's to follow up?"

"I could ask Luke to talk to you. That's my brother-in-law, Luke. But it would have to be off the record."

Off the record! Those three words are the bane of a reporter's existence, from people who want to give you some hot, or, more often, useless tip, but only if you don't use their name. Verifiability is a reporter's stock in trade. No one can verify a quote from an unnamed source.

I knew I would not call Sandra's brother-in-law, but I took Luke's phone number anyway.

Chapter 8

That next week flew by. Summer had officially started, and the denizens of Green Meadow were doing more of the things that made people the subjects of police and fire calls. Some days when I finally got up to the apartment, I was too tired to eat, which was good, since I had almost nothing in the cupboards. When you move, you forget how much staples like flour and baking powder cost. I had to prioritize, and priority one was protein that wasn't from some poor murdered chicken or cow.

I woke up at ten on Saturday morning with one goal: making tofu. If I could get some soybeans, I could make a big batch and freeze enough for a month.

I found soybeans at the farm supply store in Shelton, but only in a fifty-pound bag. They cost nearly all the money I had until I got paid on Friday.

Once I got the unwieldy bag into my car, I saw my gas was low. Maybe it hadn't been such a smart purchase after all. It made me mad that I was employed full time and still had to choose: gas or food.

Food was the right choice, I told myself as I rooted around in the cupboards for a pot big enough to soak the soybeans in. I couldn't find a stockpot. So I scrubbed out the tub and rinsed it with bleach. I'd soak them there.

It felt really good to be getting a handle on my nutrition. With this one day off, I could finally return to my normal habits.

I got out *The New Joy of Soy*. It said it was best to soak the beans overnight, but if they were cracked, the soak time could be reduced to six hours.

I wanted tofu for dinner, so I got out a big serving spoon and mashed the soybeans against the side of the tub. It took an hour to get them all cracked. When I was done, my arms were dotted with soybeans.

I rinsed them off in the sink, which left a big mess, but I decided I'd clean it later when I cleaned the tub. I had six luxurious hours to do absolutely nothing.

I climbed back in bed with the Sunday *New York Times* I had brought with me when I drove down from the Twin Cities. In the week in review and the travel section, I studied the leads and nut grafs, the artful transitions from anecdote to summary. "I'll be there someday," I said as I drifted off to sleep.

When I woke up, the soybeans had doubled in size. Time to run them through the blender and rig up my "cheesecloth."

I will say one thing for myself: I am resourceful. When I saw that I did not have enough dishtowels for the project, I started looking for other suitable fabric and found a spare sheet in the linen closet. The apartment didn't have a sieve, so I turned a dining chair upside down on the table. Using the square made by the foot rungs as a frame, I set up a new garbage bag on the four chair legs, then I draped the sheet loosely across the rungs. I ran the soaked soybeans through the blender in batches and poured the mash into my jerry-rigged cheesecloth. I could only get about a third of the beans in, so I repeated the set-up with the remaining length of sheet and two more chairs.

It would be a long wait, so I called Amber, glad to have time for a real conversation. I tried not to think about how much each long-distance minute cost.

"When are you coming to visit?" she asked.

I said I only got one day off at a time, Saturday and Tuesday.

"Then Monday holidays should be great. If you get Tuesday off, that means you get a four-day weekend."

"That's not how it worked for Memorial Day. Charles got four days off. I worked ten days straight."

"How come Charles is the only one who got the holiday off?"

"Frank got four days off, too," I said, putting words to something I had not allowed myself to think about. "It wasn't so bad working the three-day, though. When it's just me and Kim, we can get out early."

"What's her story?"

"Kim and her husband have a daughter. He works at the truck factory. Isn't it weird? We learned at Mac about the modern proletariat, but I've never actually known anyone who worked in a factory."

Amber said, "Can you imagine? Marrying someone you met in high school? I mean, I'm a completely different person than I was then. Wouldn't they just feel like an anchor after a while?"

"Maybe she likes feeling anchored."

I stretched the phone cord so I could survey my handiwork: three perfect milk bags propped on the chair bottoms. The end of the sheet dangled down to the floor.

I was just starting to describe my soybean milking set-up to Amber when I heard a sharp clang.

Someone was coming up my stairs.

I turned to find out who it was, and the sheet went taut. A torrent of precious soymilk swept across the carpet. My toe had caught in the sheet!

"No," I shrieked as the first and then the second chair fell to the floor.

I could hear Amber yelling, "What's happening?" from the receiver swinging against the wall. Someone was knocking on the door, but my focus narrowed to the one milking station still upright. I had to make sure that chair stayed on the table.

I unhooked the sheet from my toe. Soybeans sloshed everywhere.

Heart racing, I sprang to secure the chair still on the table. Soybean muck mashed under my feet.

Three more terse raps on the door. Then a key slid into the lock.

Kim pushed into my apartment.

"What in the blazes is going on here?" she demanded. "Frank called. Why aren't you at his barbecue?"

"I don't eat meat."

Kim stalked through the kitchen like she owned the place.

I said, "I'm busy."

"I told you about the barbecue on your first day."

Kim looked at the mounds of soybean mush in the flaccid bags on the carpet.

"Accident with a home cooking project," I said. "I'm going to be working on this for a while."

"No, you're going to Frank's barbecue. And you should know, the regional director has dropped in for another of his surprise visits."

I didn't like the way she was talking to me, as if I had no say in how I spent my Saturday off. She got a reporter pad out of her purse and started to draw a map to Frank's house. He lived way out in the golf course community past Sir Splash-A-Lot's. I told her I couldn't go: I didn't have enough gas.

Kim looked at her watch. "Neither of the gas stations is open this late. I'll drop you off, but we've got to hurry if I am going to get back to the newsroom in time to get the baseball box scores."

Kim eyed my cut-offs. "Get cleaned up and meet me at my car."

As soon as Kim was out of the door, I retrieved the phone. "Amber?"

"Does she always yell at you like that?"

"She's usually great," I said. "Sorry, I've got to go find out what this is about."

I needed a shower, but all the soybean debris would stop up the tub. As I threw on a clean T-shirt and my wrap-around skirt, I told myself that everyone at the barbecue would already have a few beers in them and would not notice.

We rode in silence. When Kim finally stopped at Frank's ranch-style house, she sized up my clothes.

"You look like a hippie."

She was talking to me like she was my mother. It wasn't easy to keep anger out of my response. "I did not know this was a required function."

"Listen, when you factor in the apartment, we are paying you more than we've ever paid any reporter. I pushed for you because you can write. But you've got to play the game, girl."

She didn't mean 'girl' to be diminishing, I told myself, she meant it like 'sister.' The air was heavy for a minute. I reminded myself that, for Kim, because she was so big, a career did not come easily. She had to combat sexism *and* sizeism. I tried to take that into account.

Kim grabbed my hand and squeezed it so tight my knuckles cracked. "Don't blow it."

I walked around the double garage to Frank's backyard.

There were about fifteen people there, everybody from ad sales, Charles, and the sports reporter. Frank had roasted a pig. It sat there on a tarp, parts of its sides gone. The whole scene was, in a word, disgusting.

Charles saw me and rushed over. "Did you have a problem?"

I said no.

"You've got to have a piece of cake," Charles insisted, pulling me over to the dessert table. Next to the now-empty ice cream carton was a white sheet cake with the words, "Welcome Hallie" in pink frosting.

"It's all right, she's here, everybody," Charles announced. A relieved sigh moved through the group. A man in a white shirt and red tie came up to me and introduced himself. Jed Stevens, the regional director from the corporate headquarters.

"You've made quite an impression in the short time you've been here."

I wondered what Frank had told him.

"We were lucky to get you," Corporate continued.

Frank's wife came over with a cake knife. Charles pulled out a camera. I thanked everyone. I said, "You shouldn't have."

Frank just stood there glowering.

When Kim made it to the party two hours later, she pulled me aside.

"What happened in the apartment?" she demanded.

"I'm making tofu. I had a spill. It'll probably take me two hours to clean it up."

"I cleaned it up. You must have had forty pounds of soybeans."

"What do you mean you cleaned it up?"

"I threw that mess out. Jed Stevens stays in the apartment when he's here."

"That's *my* apartment. Those are *my* soybeans."

"We'll revisit this after Jed's gone."

"Is this a joke?"

"No. You'll stay at my house until Jed's gone. We've got an air mattress."

This couldn't be normal. If an apartment was part of your pay, it was supposed to be your apartment all of the time. And my soybeans! I wouldn't have another dime for food until Friday.

It was hard to like Kim at that moment. Still, I tried to play it cool. She was my boss.

"I'm going to need to go back and get some clothes."

"Already got them. They're in a paper bag on my back seat." Kim smiled as if she had done me a big favor.

When we joined the group, Frank was holding forth on the inevitable fall of communism in China, given how many students were protesting in Tiananmen Square. His wife stared at Kim, who was scraping together a dinner from what was left in the serving bowls: plenty of pig, but not much coleslaw, potato salad, or Jell-O. I watched Mrs. Brierly's face as she read down the buttons straining to keep Kim's shirt closed.

The remaining women all had the kind of hair Elizabeth Dole wears. Frank had lit tiki torches, and in their flickering light, every lipsticked smile seemed bigger than what was called for.

It was like those other guests didn't see Kim. Although both of her hands were full, none of them offered to help her. I found a lawn chair for her and pulled it over. When she finished eating, we collected all the plates and carried them into the kitchen.

Kim asked, "Did you meet the regional director?"

"Jed? The corporate guy who's stealing my apartment? Yes."

"Good news is he likes you. We won't tell him what you did, just that the carpet had to be shampooed. It'll be dry before he wakes up tomorrow."

Chapter 9

"Good mornin', Miss Hallie."

A small person was jumping on the end of the air mattress.

I said, "You're going to pop it, kiddo."

"Misty, get out of there." The grumbly voice was Norton, Kim's husband. If he was home from work, it had to be at least 8:30.

"It's okay. I'm awake," I called. Norton didn't respond.

I made a monster face. Misty shrieked and hid behind the curtains.

"Get out of there!" Norton bellowed.

"It's okay," I repeated. "She's not bothering me."

"NOW!" Norton exploded.

"Whoa, Norton, take a Prozac."

Norton appeared in the archway, still in his work coveralls. His name was embroidered on a patch on the right side of his chest. "Trojan Truck, only the best for America's highway freight," was on the other side. I imagined that the uniform had started out indigo but had faded like a pair of jeans. The knees were nearly white.

"We need some ground rules," he said.

"Yes. I like to sleep until ten."

"*My* ground rules. You get up by seven-thirty. I want you out of the bathroom before I get home. You can watch Misty from eight to nine if Kim's not here. She should practice her spelling words before breakfast."

"I didn't sign up for childcare."

"You may be a guest in my house, but we weren't expecting you."

"Kim packed my clothes without even asking me, Norton. I'm supposed to be in the apartment above the newspaper."

This seemed to make Norton even madder. "Kim's worked for the *Daily-Observer* for five years," he said. "She don't get free housing. She's on the schedule from two to ten tonight. She probably won't get home until eleven or eleven-thirty, but they still had to have her in at eight-thirty this morning to chat with Jed Stevens. That's when I *sleep*."

I'm not saying I started to like Norton, far from it, but I could see that, until Jed was gone, things were going to be tough for both of us.

When I got out of the shower, Norton was frying bacon. It smelled like death, sweet and wrong at the same time. I edged past him and found a box of Shredded Wheat in Kim's pantry. I took it with me when I left.

In the car, I calculated that I could buy half a tank of gas with a reimbursement I was owed from petty cash. Payday was six days away. Until then I had only four dollars and twenty-eight cents. I felt around in the crack in my back seat for change. I didn't find any, but I did find a Ziploc bag of raisins from my drive down. I allowed myself to eat a third of them.

I went in to work the back way. Someone had parked in my spot. There was an orange smear the color of Frank's barbecue sauce on the fire escape railing.

I went into the ad department's copy room, which was also the break room, to get a petty cash form. A red, white, and blue poster informed me of the federal minimum wage and what to do if I was injured on the job.

As I was filling out the form, Jed came in, crisp white shirt and striped tie.

"I was hoping to see you," he said. He was carrying a bakery box. "Nobody wanted the bran muffin, but they said you might." He opened the box to reveal evidence of a donut frenzy and one huge brown muffin. "Don't make me throw it out."

My instinct at that moment was to not let Jed know how hungry I was. Jed was my boss's boss's boss. For some reason he liked me. That gave me power, but I didn't know how much.

"Why'd you get it if you didn't want to eat it?"

"I like an assortment," Jed said. "I like that in my newsrooms, too. All kinds of people. All kinds of tastes."

I said, "I'll eat it if nobody else will. It's wrong to waste food."

I broke the top off the muffin, turned it upside down, and ate it like a cookie. I made a point of trying to look indifferent, to not let him know how delicious that carby sweetness exploding on my tongue was.

"What are you doing here so early?" Jed asked. "Has Frank got you on days?"

"Don't worry, I won't put in for overtime. I just came in to—"

Jed stopped me. "It's okay, I like enterprise. You've already got some extra thing you're working on that can't fit into your shift. The chain values your kind of fire. I've got my eye on you," he said, moving his finger from his eye to point at me. "Shoot me a line when you've got a good story."

I won't need to shoot you a line, I thought. When I get going, the AP will put my stories on the wire.

I decided to go for a walk. The only park on my map was a narrow strip in front of Sir Splash-A-Lot's. I thought it might have swings or something I could sit on, but when I got there, I saw it was just a place for people to wait to get into the water park.

The Splash-A-Lot's gates weren't open yet, so it was crowded. I went over to a large koi pond to the left of the gates.

The water was murky, but I could still see shocks of orange and yellow as the fish moiled near the pond's plastic liner.

Someone behind me threw fish pellets into the water and the submerged creatures rushed to the surface, mouths gaping.

"They're all yes-men," I said.

"Who are you talking to?" a woman behind me said.

"You, I guess." I said, "This is so wrong. There's no natural way for these koi to get food. So, every fish is dependent on whatever tourist happens to throw in fish pellets or a crust of bread. They swim right over each other. Look at them. They're attacking the food like they're starving, but every one of them is unnaturally fat. That's the way you get when everything you eat is artificial."

The woman's toddler said something about fishies that I could not understand.

"We'll come back later," the woman said, the barbs in her voice all for me.

I scooped up some of the gravel at the side of the pond. When I threw it, the fish rushed to the places where the ripples started, just as they had for the pellets.

"Cut that out," a man behind me snapped.

"What?"

"Don't throw rocks in the pond."

He was a pimply teenager in a Splash-a-Lot's uniform. He tapped a sign on a three-foot pole: *Do not throw rocks.*

"They're so dumb," I said, "they go after the rocks like they're food."

"I can make change for you if you'd like to buy some pellets," the teen said.

I declined. "It's unnatural. I mean, look at that bizarre color of orange. Pylons aren't that bright."

"You're not from here, are you?"

"Why does everybody keep asking me that?"

"The man who built this water park put in the koi pond as a gift to the town. Even when Splash-A-Lot is closed, people bring their kids to feed the fish. Some of those fish cost more than a hundred dollars."

"Those fish cost a hundred dollars each?"

The teen took a step back. "Well, one of them did."

"Which one?"

"The white one. The owner collects them. He had it flown over from Japan."

The teen left to impose order on the crowd now surging to the turnstiles.

As I headed back to my car, I thought about how awful it would be to be one of the moms, chained to a kid for 18 years, looking forward to the day they would start kindergarten. "I like time alone," I told myself, which is true, but as the words entered my mind, I was also aware that I was lonely.

I had no way to call Amber, so I went to work early.

Misty must have spilled the beans about Norton's hospitality. As soon as I got in, Kim said, "I heard Norton was his charming morning self."

I shrugged.

"Here's the good news: Jed likes your writing and wants to figure out what you're doing so he can make a protocol to implement company-wide."

Secretly I was pleased that my work was already getting noticed, but I said, "It's not rocket science. I interview people and write stories based on what they say."

"Frank thinks Jed came down to do ad reconnaissance. Frank is pretty sure he's convinced Jed that circulation can't go any higher, so they're trying to figure out if there's any way to get more ads. The only growth in this economy is the water park."

The lines between Kim's eyebrows deepened. "The company already bought our only competitor. There's no one left to merge with."

You'd think that not having a competing newspaper would have made Kim's job easier. But Kim said it had not worked out that way.

"It's a corporation. It's not about news or this town's businesses promoting themselves. It's about profit. When we had competition, Frank and Jed were always talking about how we could get the ads that were running in the Shelton paper. But since the chain bought that paper, Jed sees there isn't much money to be made here."

Kim looked like those mothers in the line for the water park. There was an anxious hunger in her voice.

Chapter 10

When I woke up on Monday morning, I was on the floor, perpendicular to the air mattress.

I had been dreaming about the physics class I took at Mac. Dr. Wong had spent a lot of time explaining the path of least resistance. I remember waking up and thinking, "I'm at least as smart as an atom," and indeed, in the night I had found that the path of least resistance was not to pad the air mattress with blankets but rather to admit the thing was not a mattress at all and move onto the floor. My back felt better for it.

The clock flipped to 7:30. Might as well get up. I found a note taped to the bathroom mirror: "Had to leave early to buy pantyhose for 8 a.m. meeting with Jed. Misty won't wake up until Norton gets home. Sorry to saddle you with childcare, but I thought that was better than waking you. CALL if there's an emergency."

The condensation on the mirror reminded me of how Kim was always sweating.

I found Kim's Magic Marker on the vanity. I wrote, "Norton—I'm up. If you want to sleep, I'll do spelling words with Misty and get her ready for school." It was the path of least resistance.

Kim looked frazzled when I walked in that afternoon. With Jed visiting, Frank was in publisher mode. Kim said Frank and Jed had meetings with the Sir Splash-A-Lot's marketing people and half the Chamber of Commerce members.

"It's not like I can't do the editor's job," Kim said, "but working eight to four and six to eleven every day is totally disrupting my home life."

Before I could say I understood, the scanner started squawking.

Kim turned up the volume. "That's the second time they've come on. I can't tell what it is. Something out at the old bridge."

"Do you think it's a fire?"

"No, it's at the old bridge," Kim said, as if that explained everything.

They said stuff like that a lot. Old bridge, new bridge. Old main street, new Route 22. The town had existed since the 1840s. But in the 1930s, the river that ran through it had been dammed north of town, creating Long Lake. A few months back, the power company upped the generation at the dam, which meant a lot more water passed through.

I unfolded my map. "Nothing's labeled 'old bridge.'"

Kim stabbed her ballpoint through the place where a road just stopped at the river.

"Take the camera," she said, handing me an SLR I had never been trained to use. "It's auto-focus. Just get the faces more or less in the middle."

I drove so fast that I beat the rescue workers. I parked at the top of the hill and walked down to the river so my car wouldn't be in the way when the ambulance came.

As I approached the bottom of the hill, nothing looked amiss. The sun glinted off the water. Fallen tree branches raced by in the current. There was a chain-link fence where the bridge entered the river; it sagged so low in the middle that the top was actually underwater.

I stopped and took a picture. Beyond the cottonwoods on the other side, the sky stretched out forever. A man, who I could see from behind, was the only figure.

"Can I talk to you?" I called. "I'm from the *Daily-Observer*."

He was gray-haired, dressed in overalls, no shirt. When he turned, I saw he had a fishing lure hooked to his baseball cap.

"Where's EMS?" he snapped.

I said I was sure the paramedics would arrive in a minute.

He dug his hands into the pockets of his overalls. "There's two of them down there."

"Down where?"

"Down there," he yelled, flinging his hands at the river. "Two boys—"

"How old?"

"I don't know, sixteen or seventeen. They were fishing."

"Do you know them?"

"No, they were just kids playing hooky. I was fishing under the new bridge when I heard one scream."

"What did he scream?"

"Jeez, lady, what do you think? He screamed 'Help.'"

"Is that all?"

The fisherman looked very annoyed, but he kept answering my questions. "The kid said that his buddy had gone under and asked how long a person can stay underwater."

"How long ago was that?"

There was a long silence during which his face went from angry to grim. "Too long."

I got the fisherman's name. He started talking so fast that it was hard to get every word.

"Everybody knows not to walk on the old bridge, there." He pointed an accusing finger at a sign. It read *Danger: Fast-Moving Current. Keep Out.*

I said, "It looks like the fence has been pulled down."

"They hopped the fence to get to the old fishing hole. They were too dang lazy to walk up to the new bridge and then walk back down on the other side. Can't they read? No! They're truants."

I was doing my best to keep my cool. It wasn't my job to calm him, but it was my job to get every detail he could remember. Once the police arrived, there was no telling how long they might take to interview him. I had to get all the facts for this story and still get to the courthouse by 4:20 to do the beat check there.

"So, they hopped the fence?"

"Are you DEAF? I just said—"

"Sorry. I'm trying to get the context here. I'm new."

"No kidding."

Patience is one of the virtues you've got to turn on when you're a reporter. Patience and ignoring people insulting you.

"Tell me exactly what happened."

"I told you: I hear screaming, so I yell, 'Shut up, you're scaring away my fish,' and the kid screams that his buddy's fell in and ain't come up."

"Was he panicked?"

"Wouldn't you be!"

The man said, "He kept saying steel-toed boots, his buddy was wearing steel-toed boots. He thought maybe he couldn't swim in them. He asks me how long a person can stay under water and I say, I don't know, but you better jump in and pull out your friend or he's going to spend eternity in Davey Jones's locker. But he doesn't dive in. He says, 'Do you know CPR?' and I say no, and he says, 'Then call an ambulance.' So I go back and prop my rod on a stick and go up and call from the gas station."

"Which gas station?"

"There's only one gas station this side of the river! It's right up there." He pointed up the hill to an Arco station I had not noticed in my rush to get to the bridge.

"I told you, I'm new. How long did it take to get there?"

"I got a bum knee. I can walk fine, but I can't climb. The kid's yelling 'Go! Go! Go!' and I shout back, 'You gotta save your buddy. I'm going as fast as I can, but you gotta dive in and get him.'"

"Do you know if they could swim?"

"Apparently not very well."

I ignored his tone. "How long ago was that?"

The man looked at his watch. A long crack split the crystal. "It's supposed to be waterproof, but it's not."

I repeated my question, and when the silence got too long, I said, "So you don't know how long?"

"Two minutes?" His face seized up. "Three? I went as fast as I could. I really did."

I think the man wanted me to tell him that it was okay, that it wasn't his fault. I could read on his face what he was thinking. I was thinking it, too.

I had covered fatal accidents, shootings, and even murders back in the Twin Cities. But the bodies were always safely tucked in at the morgue by the time I was on the story. Now there were two kids underwater, and I very much wanted it to be a non-story. I wanted to get back to the office and have to say, "Sorry, they turned up kicking downstream."

The fisherman was blaming his bum knee. He said he saw a police car driving away from the Arco station as he made his way up the hill, but he couldn't run to flag down the officer.

I could not help remembering that Amber had played water polo our freshman year. She practiced holding her breath so she could stay underwater as long as possible, but she never got past a minute and a half.

A siren split the air, then a police cruiser crested the hill and sped down, kicking up rocks. The cop who got out left his door open.

"What's the problem?" he barked.

"Where's the rescuers?" the fisherman shouted, incredulous.

More sirens. Two more cruisers, an ambulance, and a fire truck.

"Move your squad," somebody yelled.

I looked at my watch. I figured I'd been there two minutes. Somebody needed to track how long those kids had been under. The police officer, checking every pocket for his keys, didn't seem up to the task.

When the cop finally moved his squad car, it took another full minute for the fire truck to park parallel to the river. Two divers got out. They donned flippers and scuba tanks and goose-stepped to the water. The captain clipped tethers on them and they dove under.

While this was going on, people started arriving; mothers, cousins, neighbors. It seemed that everyone who knew one of those kids was standing there holding their breath.

Even though the radios and the lights were going on all the emergency vehicles, the scene felt oddly still. I moved through the crowd and saw a woman rubbing the arm of one of the moms.

"It's going to be okay," she kept saying. "He's a good swimmer."

When the first diver was winched up, everyone stood stock still. He had one of the kids strapped to a backboard. There was a cheer when it popped out of the water, and then the crowd went silent. "Come on, come on, come on," the mother yelled.

Two paramedics ran over and grabbed the kid. He had one boot on and one boot off.

"Why would you wear boots like that to go fishin'?" an older man next to me asked. "Cock of the walk, that's not a boot for any kind of work."

Someone elbowed him.

"I'm just sayin'."

Whatever he was saying, the man had the sense to stop.

The crowd went silent as the paramedics laid the boy on the ground, his head turned to the side, and started CPR. His head jolted, and water gushed out of his mouth. Then all the movement stopped. One of the paramedics slapped the boy's face. The print of his hand stayed there, red against blue.

The mother rushed up and two police officers literally had to hold her back. She let out this cry, the most unearthly sound I have ever heard, and then it was as if all the women figured it out at the same time and started wailing.

I had never seen a dead person before. The kid was only a few years younger than me. My deadline was coming up. I had to get the story and get out of there, go do the courthouse.

I tried to focus on the light glinting off the water, the unreal sound coming out of all those people, how it rose and fell. They weren't crying—it was another sound entirely, raw anguish.

One woman was praying. *That's a picture*, I thought.

I pulled out the camera. I got the woman's head in the middle of the frame and pressed the button halfway to focus, then all the way. The mechanism made a reassuring click.

I clicked away as they brought the second boy out in a black bag. When the relatives saw that, the wailing became louder and I had to step back.

Keep it together, I said to myself. You did not know these kids. What's the story here? What do you still have to find out? I ticked off the five Ws in my head. Who? I had to get the names of both the kids. What? Jumping a fence to take a shortcut. That's what they were doing, walking across the submerged bridge. But why did they drown? Did the first kid get stuck on something? I could hear some men behind me speculating that it was the steel-toed boots. Nausea moved through my belly like the northern lights. *Keep it together*, I repeated. *Find the real story.*

The tall diver had his mask off and was moving away from the crowd. It was the same firefighter I had seen at the River Road house fire.

I went over to him. "Was it the boots?" I asked.

He looked at the sky and tried to smile. He said no, it wasn't the kid's boots, and then explained that water released at the dam came through really fast, but the structure under the bridge supports was solid—meaning that on the downstream side of the bridge, the water didn't move at all.

"If you get too low, the water from the top curls down and makes a downward pressure that pins things against the bridge base."

"You said things. They were people."

He shook his head as if it was all he could do not to walk away. Then he said, "It's not like the deep end of the pool." I could tell that was the quote he wanted in the paper. "It's not that the water is deep, it's that the pressure is almost impossible to swim against. You can't tell which way is up. You don't float up."

I said, "Hence the fence and the warning signs."

"Don't say that in the paper. These families have lost so much to the dam—to the river." There was a hitch in his voice. He seemed to be trying to remain professional, but he, like everyone else, was looking for something to blame.

He shook his head, turned so I couldn't see his face, and walked away. From a distance, I watched him join the other firefighters, then peel off the top part of his dive suit.

I got enough from that interview. I had the What, I had the Why. I only needed Who—the names and ages of the kids and where they went to school.

I was back about forty feet from the crowd. I didn't want to interview one of the relatives, interrupt a grief so new. I asked myself if there was an easier way to get the names. And there was: A police officer was walking up on the gravel at the side of the road.

Relieved, I smiled and started to ask for the kids' IDs.

"Don't put a picture of the body in the paper."

He didn't have to say that. No American newspaper runs photos of dead bodies.

I couldn't think straight. "First Amendment," I said and put the camera to my face. I clicked off three more shots without even focusing. "Give me their names and ages so I don't have to ask the families."

He sneered, but he gave me the information. Then he spit on the ground an inch from my foot.

I went in the back entrance and gave my film to the darkroom guy.

When I swung into the newsroom, Kim wanted to know what took so long. "You still have to do the beat check at the courthouse."

I wanted to slow down. I couldn't get that first kid's face out of my mind, the water pouring out of his mouth. *Focus on the story,* I told myself. *What's the story? Is it that they disobeyed clear warning signs? Or is it just a sad victims' story?*

I waved Kim off and pounded out the standard accident story. It was generic in every way except that I led with the mother wailing. I wanted to emphasize her loss, what the kids left behind by choosing an underwater shortcut.

My beat checks were a blur.

When photo brought the contact sheets for my drowning story, Kim chose a picture that clearly showed the keep-out sign.

"I don't think we should run that."

Kim said, "It pretty much tells the whole story."

Normally that would be the end of the discussion. That's the purpose of photojournalism, to tell the story. But Kim hadn't been there. She hadn't seen the relatives of those kids doubled over with grief. I wanted to protect them, just like that firefighter on the dive team.

I said, "Think about how that's going to feel to the families."

Kim shot me a cockeyed look and asked Charles to be the tiebreaker. Unfortunately, the only other photo that looked good and didn't have a body in it was of the futile attempt at prayer.

Charles looked at the contact sheet. "I have to side with Kim."

◆▲▲

I hammered out my remaining stories and got done early. I did not want to go back to Kim's house, and there wasn't a bar that I wanted to go to alone. So, I went back behind paste-up, where the newspapers came out on the conveyor belt from the press room.

The run hadn't started yet, but the stuffers were already at the belt. They were taking up a collection for the families of the two boys when I walked in.

"Did you hear about the kids that drowned?" the woman with the envelope asked me. "It's a crying shame."

"I was there when they pulled them out."

Sandra came over from the belt and put her arm around me. "How awful."

That was actually the first time anyone had acknowledged my feelings about what I had witnessed.

"I don't know how to get that scene out of my head," I said, trusting Sandra for no reason except that she appeared to care. I remember feeling my shoulders relax for the first time that day.

There were two other women who were probably in their forties, plus Sandra and the man who wore orthopedic shoes. I heard Sandra whisper, "I think she just needs to be with people," and they huddled around me. The man explained to me what would happen when the newspapers started coming on the conveyor belt. Each of them had their own role, he said, "But we help each other out."

The buzzer for the conveyor belt sounded and the stuffers flew to squares of masking tape on the floor. Each set of hands moved as fast as a boxer working out with a punching bag.

Chapter 11

Kim asked me to work Tuesday even though I wasn't on the schedule.

"Jed's leaving this evening, so you can have the apartment back, but he's going to have Frank and me in meetings half the day. He seems to forget we've got a newspaper to put out."

I went in early, secretly hoping no one else had drowned, burned, choked to death, or otherwise perished since my last deadline. I suppose I started at the firehouse instead of the cop shop because it was easier. Firefighters just tell you what you need to know. They don't bat you around like a cat playing with a mouse before giving you an incident report.

The smell of frying onions hit me as soon as I opened the door and started the climb to the second-story roost where most of the firefighters hung out between calls. At the top of the narrow stairs, the tall diver who had given me the quote about the deep end of the swimming pool blocked the entrance.

"Do you really think you should come up here?"

There can be blowback when you do beat checks in person. If somebody doesn't like something in a story, they let you know.

I wasn't in the mood for it, but this guy didn't scare me. He was a firefighter. They're not bullies. Even towering over me at the top of the stairs, his posture suggested he was unsure of how this game was played.

"You printed the 'They were idiots' photo." When he shook his head, as if he couldn't believe someone could be so cruel, his hair caught the light, glints of blue in the black that reminded me of the sun on the water that had swept so quickly over those boys.

I stared at him. That often works with a hostile source. You just take the stronger position with your eyes.

Everyone, when confronted with direct conflict, will look for a way to restore social niceties. The key to winning is to know that everyone blinks.

He blinked, then ushered me in with a wary sweep of his arm.

I said, "My editor chose the photo. It wasn't my call."

"It's not easy working for monkeys," he allowed.

In the brief period I had been in town, I had picked up that the *Daily-Observer* was not highly regarded. Of course, I couldn't say that I agreed, so I just said, "There were reasons to go with the photo she chose."

He wasn't satisfied. His eyes were green and brown, and they flashed with a need to know more.

"Did you agree?"

I had no stomach for it, but I knew if I laid out our decision-making heuristics, he would shut up. "In every newsroom, from the *New York Times* right down to this local paper—"

"Big gap there."

"Do you want me to explain this or not?"

He said he was sorry, and the sincerity in his voice caught me by surprise.

"The rule of thumb is a photo that tells the story beats any other photo."

"But don't you agree, running that photo was cruel to the families?"

"The circumstances were that two kids died." My heart started pounding. My hands were sweating, but I was freezing cold. "We can't really think about how people might react to photos."

The firefighter pointed to a plaid recliner. "Have a seat. There's no chili yet, but I'll get you a glass of water."

I sat. I drank. He sat on the footstool close to me and looked at me with professional concern.

"I'm okay. It just weirds me out a little."

He was searching my face with his eyes. I wanted to reset the balance. I said, "I'm sorry that I said that you called the first victim a thing yesterday."

"You were in shock. People say stupid things when they're in shock."

"I wasn't in shock."

"Had you ever seen a dead body before?"

"No."

"Then you were in shock."

He was looking at me with such complete compassion that I felt utterly protected. I suppose that gaze was how he could get kids to confess that they were playing with matches, get arsonists to tell if anyone was inside a burning building. Maybe it was something that was taught in firefighting school, like medical students are taught to exude concern.

I said, "You're very good. I work on my listening face, but you're amazing."

He gave me a quizzical look. Apparently he had no idea what I was talking about. "You're new. Are you even old enough to drink?"

I said, "I'm twenty-two," with perhaps more assertiveness than was required.

"Twenty-two?" He stretched it out long, like he was playing with the number in his mind. "I'm very glad to make your acquaintance. My name is Blue. Twenty-two might be a very good year for you."

He was so close, I could smell the cayenne pepper on him, the onions and garlic. I craved that chili. I had to remind myself it was probably full of meat.

When I made it to the cop shop, Sugar wasn't there. But the incident reports were stacked neatly in the tray. A small pink envelope with my name on it sat on top.

I put the envelope in my back pocket and went through the reports. Nothing good, but they had been ordered from most newsworthy to least, least being a cat in a tree, best being a deer that crashed through somebody's sliding glass door.

Back outside, I opened the envelope. On the front of the card, a bee buzzing over six daisies spelled out "You're invited" in a dotted line. Inside, the dotted lines for time, date, and place were filled out in pencil. It was signed, "Sugar J. E. Johnson."

When I got back to the office, I showed it to Kim.

She said, "Isn't that sweet?"

"Then you think I should go?"

Kim said, "You've got a source in the police department who wants to be friends with you."

"I know, it's gold. And yet I hesitate."

"Sugar's tricky. I wish I knew how to reach the reporter who had your job before Allison. She and Sugar were pretty tight. She would have some pointers for you."

"But you're saying you'd go if you were me?"

"Heck yeah. Why not?"

"She seems to want to be more than a source."

"This is a really small town, Hallie. When somebody new moves here, that's exciting."

"But she's so—"

"You know her father was nearly killed by a test truck from Trojan."

"She told me."

"And her mother was kind of a—" the smile on Kim's face suggested it was something juicy.

"What?"

Kim didn't say anything for a few seconds, like maybe she wasn't going to tell me, but I knew she would. "Have you ever heard the expression, 'town pump'?" Her lips curled around the question. "Mrs. Johnson was more like the town waterworks. Sugar's father was lying there in a body cast and every Tom, Dick, and Harry just let himself in."

"How can you know this?"

"I can't know for sure. I've just heard it a lot of times. And it kind of explains why Sugar is the way she is. Not a lot of quality parenting in that household."

My feminist disdain for Sugar was starting to share room with something else: a realization that she had gotten a raw deal.

Chapter 12

"That's a wrap," Kim said as she handed the galleys to the lead press operator. It was past eleven, but there had been a lot of news and I could tell that she was more energized than tired. "Do you want to grab a beer?" she asked.

"Don't you have to get home to take care of your daughter?"

"Norton's got the night off."

I hesitated.

Kim said, "I'll buy." She probably just meant that she would buy the first round, but I knew how to nurse a beer. Nobody expects you to buy a round if your own glass is more than half full.

We went in Kim's car. It was a Chevette, like mine, and I could see the problems my little car would have a few years down the road without proper maintenance.

"What kind of bar are we going to?"

Kim laughed. "We've only got two bars. The cops drink at the Top Hat, so I prefer Dusty's A-OK Corral. I don't enjoy running into Sugar when she's drunk."

Kim turned into the parking lot of a low building sided with brick shingles. A half dozen pickups lined the lot.

The bouncer took a long time examining my ID.

"Minneapolis, huh? You're a long way from home."

"I work here now," I told him.

"You've got to get that changed," Kim whispered. "You've got to let people know you are here permanently. How did you say it in your interview?"

"Putting down roots?"

Kim beamed. "You can't imagine what a relief it was to hear that you wanted to put down roots here. It's been almost a year since Allison left."

The bar had a Western motif. There were decorative spurs cut from a Spam can. The name of the bar was spelled out in rope on a plywood sign above the top liquor shelf.

The bartender gave us a nod, but other than that, no one registered our arrival. Most of the other patrons were sitting alone, but even the ones in pairs were staring in opposite directions. They wore caps with John Deere and seed company logos.

I asked for a Leinenkugel.

Kim laughed. "It's Schlitz or Stroh's, city girl." And then to the bartender, "We'll have a pitcher of Schlitz."

When the beer came, she offered a toast: "To your long tenure at the *Daily-Observer*."

I didn't know what to say, so I went into interview mode.

Kim said she had been an English major at Hamilton College. I think at that point I had counted that Kim had told me she went to Hamilton College at least fourteen times. It wasn't the Hamilton College on the East Coast. It was a small religious school for women somewhere north of Green Meadow.

"I was on the dean's list seven semesters in a row," she said, lifting another toast, this one to herself.

"What did you do that last year?" I teased. "Bad case of senioritis?"

Kim's eyes went to a place far beyond the walls. She seemed both to not want to answer my question but also to need to answer it. "You get right to the kill."

"It's just like on *Sesame Street*. You know, 'One of these things is not like the others.'"

A shadow moved across Kim's brow. She took a long drag on her beer and then motioned to the bartender. He seemed to know without asking that she wanted to switch to shots.

"I loved it at Hamilton," Kim said. "I did well in my classes. I had smart friends like you who read and went to the foreign movies they showed on campus. We'd stay up all night, just talking about what we were going to do with our lives, how we were going to change the world."

"But?"

"But Norton." Kim slammed the shot.

"Norton went to college with you?"

Kim looked at me as if I had missed something obvious. "Hamilton is a women's college. Norton never went to college. We dated in high school. He gave me a promise ring when I left for Hamilton."

"Is that some sort of pre-engagement ring?"

Kim rubbed the back of her neck. "We hadn't talked about getting married, so it surprised me. The ring was so small, I couldn't even get it on my pinky. But I wore it on a chain and stayed true."

"Does true mean you never slept with anyone? It was the late seventies, right?"

"My dad was a pastor. He's pretty conservative. My whole town was."

I didn't want to know about Kim's sex life. I don't know why I was questioning her, except out of boredom. I was doing the interview equivalent of wind sprints, trying to see how much I could get out of her in one sitting.

"My senior year, instead of my dad driving up to bring me home for Thanksgiving, Norton came. I introduced him to a few of my friends while he was on campus and I could tell they didn't like him. I started trying to look at him the way they saw him."

The bartender returned with the bottle.

"Norton's family and my family did Thanksgiving together. His parents were real active in the church. The dinner was at our house that year, and I remember Norton was a real boor."

"What did he do?"

Kim was deep in the memory. "I remember I started talking about one of the professors I admired, and he cut me off. He said, 'Do you know why college professors have the letters P-H-D after their names? It's for piled high and deep.'"

I didn't need to encourage her to go on.

"All weekend long, he was saying things like that and making little jabs at me. He said I was getting as pointy-headed as the Coneheads on *Saturday Night Live*. He said I had better watch out, or I wasn't going to fit in when I moved back home. Of course, by that time I had no intention of moving back home. What was I going to do? Wait for a job to open at my old high school? They only had one English teacher."

"That's a small town."

Kim said, "I had been back for summers and holidays, but it was that last Thanksgiving when it really struck me that I had no future there."

Kim went on, "From all my classes at Hamilton, I was really aware that I hadn't seen the world yet. I'd never even lived on my own.

"What I noticed that Thanksgiving was how presumptuous Norton was. I hadn't told him that I wasn't moving back. I hadn't told my family, either. What I was going to do was travel to Europe with one of my girlfriends from Hamilton. We were going to stay a whole month, see London, Paris, and Rome. Then we were going to go to New York and try for jobs as editorial assistants at a ladies' magazine. There was a good chance we could do it. She had an aunt who worked at *McCall's*. She thought they might hire us both."

"You worked at *McCall's*?"

"No." Kim emptied her shot glass, then shook her head as if it burned more than she remembered.

"Norton drove me back to Hamilton after Thanksgiving. In the car, we had nothing to talk about. If I mentioned one of my friends, Norton said, 'I don't like that girl.' If I mentioned a class, he said, 'Get out of your head.'

"It was a three-hour drive, and by the second hour I wanted out of the car. I wanted nothing more to do with him, ever."

"What happened?"

"We get to my dorm and he carries my suitcase into the lobby on the first floor where people study. He offers to carry it upstairs to my room. I said, 'No thanks,' and that I'd been doing some thinking, and I really thought it would be best if we cooled things down and didn't make plans.

"He didn't understand my meaning, or maybe he chose not to understand. He picked up my suitcase and said, 'Cooling things down is for people who don't love each other, and I love you, Kim.' He said it really loud. Everyone looked up. Everyone saw him grab my suitcase out of my hand and march upstairs like he owned the place.

"I followed him up. I said, 'You're not allowed in my room,' but he grabbed my keys from my hand. He opened the door and threw the suitcase on my roommate's bed. I was standing in the hall. I could not believe what I was seeing. He walked back out and picked me up, literally picked me up, and carried me in."

"He carried you over the threshold? Was that supposed to be romantic?"

"It wasn't romantic. He kicked the door shut. When we were alone in the room, he took off his belt. He said he could feel a distance between the two of us and he thought it was because we'd waited too long. He proposed. I said, 'You're supposed to be down on one knee, and you're supposed to have a ring.'

"He grabbed the promise ring on the chain around my neck. He pulled it so hard the chain broke. He said, 'You've had my ring three years.' And then—" Kim's voice cracked.

"He raped you?"

"You can't call it rape if you're engaged."

Whatever distance I had enforced because of my anger about the apartment moved into the background. I wanted to punch Norton's face in for Kim. But words had to suffice. I said, "Rape is rape."

"It wasn't rape," Kim said, as if she were trying to convince herself, "but it was awful. My roommate walked in. Norton yelled at her to get out of her own room! She came back with the resident assistant. By then Norton was finished. The RA wanted to call the police. She kept asking me, 'Did you want this to happen?' I couldn't say anything."

"Was that the first time you—"

"I was a good girl. I was a Christian." She said it more to herself than to me. "The RA got Norton's name from my roommate and then kicked him out. He was yelling all the way down the stairs, 'Tell them I'm your fiancé. Tell them you love me.' But I couldn't speak. I couldn't say anything. I was going to have to marry him."

"Why? You were raped."

Kim shook her head. "I told my mother what happened when I was home at Christmas. By then I knew I was pregnant."

"What did your mom say?"

"She said it wasn't rape. She said we had to get married. I said not on your life. I don't know what I thought I was going to do. But one of my so-called friends ratted me out and I got kicked out of the dorm. My parents wouldn't loan me money to rent an apartment."

"What did you do?" I asked.

I thought she was going to cry right there in the bar. She said, "My family wouldn't take my calls. My friends didn't want to have anything to do with me. I sat alone in that dining hall and ate all the things you're supposed to eat when you're pregnant. I just got bigger and bigger and more and more alone. So, I asked Norton to marry me."

"Why would you do that?" I asked.

Kim didn't seem to have words to answer. "He was a known quantity," is what she finally settled on.

"The devil you know."

"He was still a kid when all this happened. Well, nineteen. We never talk about it."

I finished my beer.

Kim said, "My father was mortified that I was pregnant at the wedding. He refused to come."

"In retrospect?" I asked. It was something Wassle had taught me, to just trail off a question, as if the subject is assumed. It's a way to find out what the interviewee is thinking.

Kim's eyes were back in the bar. She was living in the present, with its dim light and limited beer selection. She said, "I love my daughter. But nothing about having her made it right with Norton. I knew it never would be, even as I said my vows."

The pitcher was empty.

"Do you need another round?" I asked.

"Nope."

When I got home, there was a message from Amber on my answering machine.

"Birthday countdown starts now!"

My birthday was ten days away. Amber thought she could get someone to cover her shift at the restaurant. She was driving down to see me!

The next morning, I ran down and found Kim in the newsroom. She did not acknowledge our conversation at the A-OK Corral, so I didn't either.

"I need Friday of next week off."

"I've never seen anyone so excited about the rhubarb festival," Kim chuckled. She said Charles liked to have every Friday off in the summer.

"But I'm owed two comp days."

"You still believe in the Tooth Fairy, don't you?"

"It's my birthday."

Kim smiled. "If you work this Saturday, I think we can swing it."

Chapter 13

I had a gnawing fear that something big was going to happen at one of the schools and I wouldn't know. I decided to start going in at eight in the morning to focus on schools.

I tried to think of how Jontha Karasaki at the *Pioneer-Press* had cracked the school beat. The thing I remember Jontha saying was that most people on the education beat did top-down reporting. They went to school board meetings, but they never spent time in the schools themselves, unless it was to watch a special program.

I didn't want to be a top-down education reporter.

Frank scowled when he came in and saw me already at my desk. "Your shift starts at two. I'm not approving any overtime."

I said, "How can I cover education if I'm never working when school is in session?"

"The last girl did fine just going to school board meetings."

I said, "That *woman* had the benefit of source relationships she had already developed. Even if I had those, the best reporting entails in-person observation, kind of like an anthropologist going to live with a Native American tribe."

Frank said school kids were not Indians, and it did not make sense to waste the *Daily-Observer*'s money observing them.

I pulled my copy of Jontha's Pulitzer story from my backpack and showed it to him. It was one of those stories that had gone unnoticed for years: homeless children hiding the fact that they had no address so they could stay in school. Jontha only got the story because she'd made friends with a bus driver while doing participant observation at a middle school.

Frank blinked and blinked. He said, "This is a *community* newspaper," as if that settled it.

But it didn't. My job was impossible. My beats were cops, courts, and schools. I had to be there at night because that's when most of the fires and car crashes happened. Courts I could usually do late in the afternoon by catching the attorneys as the courthouse was closing. But the schools? The actual day-to-day part of education? I had no idea what things were like in the classrooms.

I picked up Jontha's story and looked at that magnificent front page. Most of the space above the fold was given to a photo of two kids bundled tight in a single sleeping bag. The picture, the headline, everything worked together. I compared it to the disjointed offerings on the front pages of old *Daily-Observers* piled around the newsroom.

Who would want these papers? Little tabloids with pictures of people smiling and handing checks to each other, kids lined up in rows behind a soccer ball or, our most common photo, the twisted wreckage of a car crash. There was nothing new on our front pages. Change the names and last year's stories could be inserted for this year's. Donation, sports playoff, crash. I wanted to do more, to tell this community its stories the way Jontha had done in Saint Paul.

"No overtime," Frank said, as if he needed to be the one to officially close our conversation.

That's not a no to an observational story, I told myself.

I had to get out of the newsroom, so I went early to the fire department.

As soon as I crested the stairs, Blue grinned.

He was reclining in the Barcalounger.

"Come over here," he said. "I've got something for you to write in your skinny little notepad."

His smile told me it wasn't a hot tip about the fire board.

"What do you want me to write?"

"My phone number."

I took him in as I walked over. He radiated a calm confidence, his hair the only betrayal of something wild inside. That and a tattletale spring on the bottom of his chair's footrest. It amplified the nervous jiggle of his foot.

I leaned down and wrapped my hand around that foot, warm in a white tube sock. "Why do you want me to write down your phone number?"

"Because we might not get to everything I want to talk about before my shift ends."

I smiled.

He said, "I cook more than chili, you know."

"I imagine you do."

He gave me his number, then made me read it back to him. He gave me his address too. I was aware of the time clock clicking, the microwave chirping. The hairs on my arms standing straight up.

Then the fire alarm convulsed, and Blue leapt into his boots. In seconds, he was flying down the pole, a spiral of determined energy.

I sped along behind the day-glow green fire engine to a restaurant downtown. Nothing. False alarm. Through my car window, I watched Blue pace back and forth in front of the low fieldstone building.

It was getting close to my lunch break. I didn't go back to the office. Instead, I drove back to the fire station. Blue was already leaving in his car. I followed, far back and unobserved.

I guess I thought I would stop, wait a little bit, and call him from a pay phone. But he didn't drive home. He turned out to the game lands and parked in the gravel lot. I pulled my car to the side of the road. I started to call out to him but caught myself. That would seem strange.

I got out and stood by a pair of birch trees at the edge of the lot. Through a break in the trees in front of me, I could see him running. He looped around one, two, three times, arms pumping, hair a thousand exclamation points in the wind. His feet made a slapping noise on the mud service road when he passed close to where I stood.

If he saw me, it didn't register on his face.

I knew what I was doing was creepy, but I could not look away. My hands grasping behind me found the trunk of a birch tree. The papery bark gave way as I dug my nails into it.

I'd never seen a man run so fast outside of a track meet.

As Blue passed again, I scrutinized his straight spine, his sharp-angled shoulders. Why was he running?

I never figured that out. After the fourth loop, Blue stopped, checked his watch, and walked back to his car. I could make him out in the parking lot, sitting sideways on the driver's seat with the door open. He took off his shoes, then he pulled something that looked like a wine skin off the dash and used it to squirt water onto his feet. The motions of his hands were so smooth, it seemed like something he had done many times before.

I sat in my car, at the game lands again at sunset, hiding in the little grove of trees just off the well-worn path. The heart-shaped leaves moved in the wind. I knew I was dreaming because the leaves didn't rustle, they whispered his name.

I wasn't sure what I was doing. I just knew that something about Blue didn't add up. I wanted to figure him out before . . .

"Before what?" I asked my dream self. What did I want? Sex? Check. Companionship? Check. A reality check on this strange town? Why did I think he could offer that?

Then he was there. I saw his feet first. The clay responded with a clap. That was the only sound.

I caught my breath and reached for the birch tree. It felt silky on my fingertips. And then he was behind me. I could smell him, smoke and sharp sweat.

He wrapped his arms tight around me. "What the hell are you doing, Hallie?"

I said, "This isn't funny."

"No, it's not," he seethed into my ear. "You're spying on me. Why?"

The real answer was that ever since I saw him run, I'd been thinking about nothing but him. The real answer was that he was waking up something in me that threatened to rip me apart.

I scratched for words.

"You don't add up."

"Neither do you. Big city reporter in the middle of nowhere, spying on a firefighter running in the woods. Why are you here?"

"I'll tell you if you let me go."

He tightened his grip. "You don't want me to."

It was true.

"What do you want?" he whispered.

I was aware that it could take a lifetime to answer that question.

He circled around. "You don't like country bumpkins, but you like me."

"You make me feel . . ." How to end that sentence? Raw? Alive?

"I make you feel like a grown-up woman. And that's scary to you because you're not writing every word in your notepad."

That's when I woke up.

The clock said two a.m., but I had to call Amber. "I think I'm going bush. I had a dream about one of the local firefighters."

"He's not the fire chief, is he?"

"No."

"Then I don't see any conflict of interest. Is he hot?"

"He's got glistening black hair. Gorgeous eyes. And that firefighter body."

"Sounds hot to me."

"Here's the thing: He's thirty."

"That's ancient."

"I know."

Amber said, "We'll talk about it when I visit. You can't get attached to some elderly man. Keep it casual, okay? Just sex."

Chapter 14

It was another hot night. Frank turned down the AC when he left for the day to save electricity, so it was cooler to go outside for my break than to stay in the office. Sandra was sitting at the picnic table by the parking lot.

"There's room for two."

She had a checkered dish towel spread on the table and I smiled when I looked at the food she had on it: two rice cakes, a pile of carrot sticks and celery, and a Tupperware container of hummus.

It turned out Sandra was a vegetarian, too. I suppose it was because of that, and because she had been so kind that night after the drownings, that I liked her.

"You're the only other vegetarian I've met here," I said.

Sandra said she gave up meat after her father-in-law died unexpectedly of a heart attack.

I asked if her son had always been a vegetarian.

"No, but when Matthew started developing attention problems and getting in trouble, I took a hard look at what might be causing it: the noisy environment at school, sugar, all the weird chemicals they shoot into cattle and put in their feed."

She said when she switched her son to a vegetarian diet with very little sugar and took him out of the public school, his behavior improved.

I was impressed. "That's really something, that even on a stuffer's pay, you manage to send him to private school."

Sandra laughed. "If you doubled my income I couldn't pay for private school. I homeschool him."

"You don't seem like the typical right-wing wacko who keeps their kids out of school." I think that offended her, so I switched into interviewer mode. "How old's your son?"

She said he was ten. "When we got the attention deficit diagnosis last year, his teacher told me to put him on Ritalin."

"Did your doctor say he needed it?"

"The doctor said he needed a controlled environment. They don't have that in the schools here. Even at the elementary level it's an absolute zoo. Half of the teachers don't know how to teach, and the other half don't give a damn. He came home once with a black eye, and when I called the teacher, she said she hadn't noticed."

Sandra jabbed a celery stick into her hummus. "I feel guilty that I didn't look into why he hated school. He's a good kid. He was always a quick learner, but he was coming home with bad grades. One day he refused to go to the bus stop. He was crying and I asked him what the problem was, and he said no one learns anything at school. This is what he said: 'The teacher yells and then we go home.'"

"So, what did you do?"

Her reply came like a confession: "I made him put on his coat. I marched him to the car and drove him in. By the time we got there he was twenty minutes late. I walked down the hall with him. Through his classroom door, I could hear the teacher. She was mimicking a kid, 'I don't understand. I don't understand.' I don't know if she thought she was being funny or what, but I remember her tone was so withering. I was there with my hand on the doorknob and Matthew looked up at me. He said, 'See, Mom?'"

"And?"

"We went to the principal's office and I withdrew him. When she asked why, I didn't have the guts to say."

I gave a Mona Lisa smile because I didn't know if Sandra had done the right thing. I asked her what she thought would happen if she had explained her reasons.

"Nothing. That's what gets me about this town: Nothing changes. You complain, you get labeled a complainer. I didn't want my kid getting labeled. And I'll see that damn teacher in the grocery store, at the post office. She's the superintendent's sister. She's not going anywhere."

Sandra gave a weary nod. "My brother-in-law says over at Trojan they've got a saying, 'See nothing, say nothing.'" She shifted on the bench. "Did you ever call Luke about that fire follow-up?"

I did not want to explain how I already knew that I would get nothing I could use from her brother-in-law. Fires and car crashes in which somebody dies are devastating to the family and friends of the victim, but that kind of loss, no matter how earth-shattering it feels, isn't news.

I suppose Sandra must have sketched in that I didn't think the tip was important. She asked, "Aren't you supposed to do the education beat? How come there are hardly any stories about the schools?"

"That's a sore point. Technically my beat is cops, courts, and schools. But since everything with police and fire happens in the evening, I work from two to eleven."

"Why don't you change your schedule?"

"I tried. I told Frank I wanted to come in early to get out to the schools. Do you know what our illustrious leader said? 'They send out press releases.'"

When I did the firehouse beat check, Blue handed me a bowl of chili that he guaranteed was one hundred percent vegetarian. I said, "Some pinot would turn this into a nice dinner."

He paused. "We can't drink on the job."

"What about after your shift?" I asked.

Blue locked eyes with me. "There's a bottle of something in the cupboard. It's not cooking sherry."

I raced back to the firehouse on my dinner break.

Blue met me behind the building with a stack of Styrofoam cups and a battery-operated candle. "These are really much safer," he said, showing me how the little flame thing flickered once it warmed up.

"I know you just made an opening for a double-entendre about warming up, but I'm defective. I can't flirt."

He grabbed my belt loops. "There's nothing defective about you," he said, eyes searching my face. "Just tell me you're sincere."

"You're a good man, Blue. I like firefighters."

"Do you like firefighters or do you like me?" He lowered his eyes, as if he didn't want the answer he was expecting.

I said, "I like you."

"Why?"

"The first time I ever saw you, I watched you walk down to the river at that fatal house fire. There was an intensity about you, as if you didn't accept fate: a dead man, an obvious cause."

"That was an arson."

"He was smoking in bed."

Blue shook his head, as if he'd been making this case in his mind for days. "Nobody who works at Trojan smokes. The company makes you pay double on your health insurance if you smoke. And the cigarettes in his ashtray? Menthol. White people don't smoke menthol. At least not in Bryce County. There's not a single store in town that sells them."

"That doesn't make it arson."

"I've been seeing a lot of menthol cigarettes at fire scenes. Tell me: When a hooker smokes, wouldn't she ordinarily get lipstick on her cigarette?"

"I think I've got to get back to work," I said, pulling out my notepad.

Blue shook his head. "You can't put this in the paper, not yet."

"Rain check on whatever was going to come next?" I asked. "Next time we meet, no talking, okay?"

"Meet me after you get off work."

I told him I couldn't. How I wished I hadn't RSVPed yes to Sugar's invitation.

⚊⚊⚊

A source, I reminded myself as I knocked on the door to Sugar's apartment. *She is an extremely valuable source.*

A faint smell of trash wafted out when Sugar opened the door. She was wearing a kaftan printed with pink butterflies.

I had worried in the grocery store that a four-dollar Chablis was not good enough for a hostess gift, but Sugar was clearly pleased as she set it on the counter in the kitchenette next to a bottle of Mountain Dew and a package of Nutter Butters.

Sugar grabbed a bag of Cheetos and returned to the love seat.

"Sit down," she said, pulling a basket of laundry off the seat next to her.

"What a cozy place."

"Home sweet home," Sugar said with no irony whatsoever. "You can throw your coat on the bed."

The bed was just beyond a four-foot-high partition of glass brick.

"Don't you love it?" she called as I took in the bedroom.

On the three sides that had walls, Sugar had taped the police academy portraits of the entire force.

"Quite a collection you've got here."

"My boys? I make them give me a photo when they do their new-hire paperwork. Look at Ricky. He was nineteen when we hired him."

I looked at the photo, smudged with lipstick. Ricky's head looked small in the police uniform hat.

"Did he go to the police academy right after high school?"

"Naw, he was waived in. His uncle knows the chief. We sent him for weekend firearms training. But I didn't invite you over to talk about work."

Damn.

I peered around the glass bricks. Sugar had pulled out a stack of *Seventeen* magazines and a manicure set.

"I want you to paint my toenails."

This was not in the job description. "Why don't we wait until some of your other friends get here?" I said and headed to the drinks.

"It's just you and me."

In the kitchenette, I saw a small stack of invitations, just like the one I had received, pushed into a corner of the counter.

I poured a Solo cup of Chablis.

"Put some Mountain Dew in it," Sugar called. "That'll make it a summer hummer."

"If I recall, a summer hummer requires vodka."

Sugar pulled herself out of the loveseat and slid open the door of her entertainment center. Inside there were at least a dozen bottles of liquor.

"I've got lemon, I've got raspberry and I've got plain. And peach schnapps. We could do fuzzy navels if you want."

"I think I'll just have the Chablis. I've got to drive home."

"No you don't. Let's have a slumber party!"

Sugar waited a minute for me to say okay, and when I did not, she asked, "What do you sleep in?" changing the subject, I suppose, to deflect her disappointment.

The question seemed intrusive. "Pajamas. Why?"

"Ricky thought you was more the teddy type."

"Why in the world was Ricky speculating about that?"

Sugar shrugged. "You're new. It would be easy to fix you up with one of the cops. Then we could double date."

"I don't think that would be very professional."

"Why not?"

"Well, think about it. I cover cops. If things worked out and I got romantically involved with one, people would think I could not be objective."

"Allison runnoft with the prosecutor. Nobody said she was not objective."

I needed a break. I stepped out onto the patio and took in the view: a dumpster.

I tried to imagine why someone would take this apartment with a patio that would only smell worse as the summer heated up. My natural impulse was to recoil. But Sugar was where all official information from the cops came from. And if I played my cards right, she could tell me the unofficial stories, too.

Empathize, I told myself. What would it be like to be her? To grow up in a town like this, stuck in place by a poor education or an inflated sense of family obligation?

When I went back inside, Sugar put on dance music. "What were you like in high school?" she asked.

I said I was in the drama club. "What about you?"

"I wasn't in the drama club. No siree. Those girls didn't like me 'cuz I was fat."

"That's cruel."

"They could act, though, that's for sure. They'd come around when voting for prom queen opened up. 'Oh, Sugar, I just love what you're doin' with your hair.' 'Sugar, I've been meaning to ask you over sometime.' But manicure parties? Pedicure parties? The invites never came."

Sugar was tearing up. I looked around for Kleenex. The box next to her manicure set was empty, but there was a roll of toilet paper on the counter. I rolled some off.

When Sugar took the tissue from me, I could see her nails were bitten down to the quick.

"Sugar," I said, wanting to change the subject, "I sometimes hear things on the scanner, but then there's not an incident report or anything on the shift log."

Sugar shrugged. "Not everything's worth writing up."

"I look stupid to my boss if I don't know what's going on."

Sugar gave a drunk smile. "If you knew everything, we'd have to kill you."

It was 11:30 when I left Sugar's apartment. I called Blue from a pay phone outside the complex's laundry room.

"I just wanted to see if you were still up."

I could hear the sleep in Blue's voice when he asked, "Do you want to talk?"

"No. Can I come over?"

In the five minutes it took me to get to his place, Blue had dressed, set a bottle of wine on ice and put on music.

I said, "You didn't need to go to any trouble," and took off my shirt.

"You are definitely not a Green Meadow girl."

I spread my fingers against his lips. "No talking."

He pushed my hand aside and kissed me, then said, "I like your heat."

He was so . . . I don't really have a word for it. Present? Like there was no rush. He asked if I would be more comfortable in his bed, and when I nodded, he asked, "Is this what you want?" and waited for my answer, a steady bass note under the fire.

The sheets were still warm from where he had been sleeping. He pushed my hair back from my face. "Are you sure?" he asked.

"Yes, yes, come on already." That's what the voice in my head was screaming. He was there with me in the moment. I tried not to notice the silk rose on the nightstand.

After, he turned on his side to face me. "You are so incredibly beautiful," he said.

"You don't need to do that."

"What?"

"Talk to me like that. There's no need for compliments. It was a mutually satisfying experience."

Blue looked confused. "What do you like to do at this point?"

"I like the quiet. It's the only time my brain is not buzzing with words."

Blue squeezed my hand.

"Really, I just want to lie here, if that's okay."

At midnight he got up and asked if I needed a toothbrush.

I grabbed my clothes from the floor. "It's not like that. I'm not sleeping over."

He looked puzzled. "Can I at least walk you to your car?" he asked.

He told me he had to go to Indianapolis to meet with someone at an insurance company. "I won't be near a phone, but know I will be thinking about you every minute of that drive."

Just sex, I reminded myself.

Chapter 15

So that I would have spending money when Amber arrived, I went in first thing that Friday morning to get a reimbursement from petty cash. When I asked Kim for it, she asked, "Are you a cherry chip or chocolate girl?"

It was sweet of her to want to bake me a cake, but I told her not to bother since I would not be in on my birthday.

"That's the thing," Kim said, giving the straight-lipped smile that I had come to recognize meant bad news. "I'm going to need you to work today, and Frank's changed next week's schedule."

She passed me the sheet. Charles was crossed off for Friday and Saturday. My name was written in below.

"No way," I yelled.

Kim whispered, "Frank made the changes. It's okay, though, you can bring your girlfriend to the newsroom, I don't mind."

"I mind. I get no vacation days for six months. I'm already owed two days of comp time, which, by the way, is illegal. I read that poster in the break room."

Kim said, "This is a newspaper. We work when there's news."

"You are a doormat, Kim. The *Daily-Observer* has gotten a free year of work out of you and you're never going to take a minute of that comp time."

"I exaggerated."

"I've earned two comp days. Today is my birthday. I'm taking it off."

Frank came in through the swinging doors at the back of the newsroom.

"I can hear you all the way in the publisher's office. What's your problem?"

"Kim promised I could take a comp day and now you've gone with your imperious cross-outs and switched it so I have to work on my birthday and my regular day off while you boys get another long weekend."

Frank pulled off his glasses and squinted at me, then he asked Kim to go back to his office. He meant his other office, the publisher's office. He had two desks, two phones, and the only two chairs in the building that were actually comfortable. He was not getting my two days off.

I slammed myself down in my stupid molded plastic chair and pounded out a list of all the reasons why I should be given the time off I was promised.

Kim didn't want to read my list when she came back. She wanted to go up to my apartment.

"No, it's a mess up there."

Blinking behind her Diane von Furstenberg glasses, Kim's face reminded me of the fish in the koi pond at Sir Splash-A-Lot's, sucking in air, hoping for somebody to throw a breadcrumb.

"Listen, I'm sorry. I know this was important to you, and I'll make it up to you. Your friend who's coming from Minneapolis, you can have her in the newsroom, and you can take a two-hour dinner. Go to any restaurant that you like. I'll pay for it from petty cash."

"You can't promise that. If there's a five-car pile-up, I will have to cover it."

Kim said, "Frank decided he wanted to go out on Charles's boat for the Rhubarb Regatta."

"You're the boss. Order Charles to loan Frank his boat."

"You're not going to budge, are you?"

"I was happy to work every day of Memorial Day weekend, but the boys can't expect to get every weekend they want off."

"The boating season just lasts through September."

"So you're going to schedule me to work on Labor Day, too? How ironic."

"What is this about?"

"It's about you not keeping your promises."

Kim's voice went high. "Don't do this to me. They have seniority. Frank's the managing editor and publisher. Charles has worked here since before God was born."

"And it's always going to be that way. The boys will get every weekend they want if we don't stand up to them."

"We? You are alone on this."

Kim's orange hair reminded me again of koi, how they never look real. That must be from eating so much white bread.

She said, "You can win the battle but lose the war, girl."

—

Fury fueled my movements as I stomped upstairs.

The phone was ringing. Amber.

"Don't come," I said, "they're making me work on my birthday."

When I told Amber what Frank had done, she was furious, too.

"Quit," she said. "You told me yourself the paper is a piece of shit."

I looked at the teamwork poster. "It is a piece of shit, but it's *my* piece of shit. I made over a hundred applications. This is the only place that interviewed me."

"Those people don't deserve you. Come home."

I looked around the apartment. It didn't feel like home, but I had put a lot of time into cleaning and arranging things so I could be comfortable for the year I would be here. "There are no jobs for me. I applied to every news outlet in the Twin Cities."

"They need another server at my restaurant."

I should have thought before I said what I said next: "I can't wait tables. I went to college for four years—" The words just hung there, stupid.

Amber said. "I went to college for four years, too. I was right there when you took first place in every competition. Do you think you're better than me?"

I have a real problem with lying. I can't do it. But I knew if I answered Amber's question, I would lose the closest thing I had to a sister.

I said, "I still have ambition."

"Ambition?" Amber mocked, "What's the big story you have to cover? Rhubarb Days?"

I said, "It's a start," but Amber was still mad about the server thing.

"My tips bought you groceries when you were broke. And my dad bailed you out on rent."

"You have that safety. You can be Daddy's little girl when you need help."

She wasn't listening. "You think you're better than everyone," Amber yelled. "You think you're better than me."

She wanted me to deny it, to say I was not better than her. But like I said, I can't lie. That's why my best friend in the world said she would never speak to me again.

I was mad at everything. Mad at Amber, mad at Frank. Mad most, I think, at myself. I vacuumed the apartment, lifted every piece of furniture and dusted behind it. I hammered a nail in the drywall above the phone and hung a Casselberry-DuPree poster.

When I stopped pounding, the phone was ringing.

Amber?

No, just Kim.

"We need to talk."

"I'm right upstairs," I said into the phone.

Her shoes clanged on the stairs as she trudged up. "Those are mighty steep," she huffed when she arrived.

"I don't think they were meant for everyday use," I said flatly. "They look like a fire escape to me."

"Don't tell that friend of yours at the fire department," Kim teased. "We had the front stairs removed in a remodel a few years ago."

How did Kim know about Blue? Green Meadow suddenly felt smaller, and not in a good way.

I said, "I guess it wouldn't violate fire codes if nobody was sleeping here."

"Right. About that: Frank wants you to move out."

I felt a jolt of disbelief. "We settled this when I agreed to crash on your air mattress when Jed came up from corporate."

Apparently my alarm was not registering, because Kim only shrugged. "Frank told me just now that you have to go."

I sucked my lower lip into my mouth so as not to explode. Probably Frank had already written in my personnel file, "Has problems with explosive anger."

I screwed up my face in a sardonic grimace. "Am I playing my music too loud? That can't be it. I don't leave work until midnight."

Kim shifted.

"What's going on?" I asked, trying to sound casual.

"Frank may need the apartment."

Keep your voice even, I told myself. "You know what I'm paid. I can't afford rent on top of my student loans. We had a deal."

"Frank doesn't see it that way. He says everyone else has managed on that salary and you can, too." She sounded more like Frank than herself.

"I must have misread you," I spat. "I thought we were friends."

Kim crumpled. I think what she wanted most in this world was a friend. God knows the troglodyte she was married to couldn't carry a conversation in a bucket. "We are friends," she said and searched my face for agreement. "Can you just do this as a favor for me and not ask why?"

I liked Kim. She was the only person in editorial who did not make me want to gag. Why was she doing this?

"Please don't ask why," she repeated.

"No," I said. "You don't ask someone to pay three or four hundred dollars a month rent that wasn't in their budget as a personal favor. We have a contract."

"An oral contract."

I let a lot of time pass.

"Hallie, this isn't easy for me."

"I moved everything I own to the middle of nowhere for a job that barely pays. The apartment is the only thing that makes it doable! And you're talking about what's easy for *you?*"

Kim smoothed her skirt and made a crinkly smile, a smile that in the past I had stupidly found trustworthy. "Let's maybe pick this apart, because I think we can work something out."

I said, "Why in the world would I believe you would stick to some new agreement?"

"We could put it in writing?"

I laughed a one-syllable "huh" that was both a question and an answer.

That made her mad. "Frank said you need to be out by the end of the month."

When the tears started rolling down my face Kim couldn't hold her rigid stance. "It's okay," she said, digging a packet of Kleenex out of her purse. "We'll find you a place."

"You lied," I sobbed, "from the very first phone call, you seemed so sincere and so committed to doing good journalism."

"I am sincere. I am committed."

"You hired me at a substandard wage. Housing was part of the deal. You're effectively cutting my pay by a third. I can't countenance that. I quit."

Apparently Kim hadn't thought of that possibility.

"You can't quit. You have to give two weeks' notice. Allison up and quit; left without a word. Left us high and dry with no one to cover courts or police."

"I'll leave you high and dry, too. I'll put an ad in E&P saying exactly what you did. You'll never get another résumé."

I got a big box out of the closet and began throwing things into it.

Kim followed me around as I picked up anything that was loose. A pillow, notebooks, dirty laundry, they all landed in a heap in the box.

"That dish towel stays with the apartment," she snapped.

I fixed her with a stare.

Kim just started laughing at me. It seemed like she couldn't control it. Between snorts, she said, "You're not quitting. You'll find a place to live here. Come on, admit it. You love this paper."

"What did I do to deserve this?"

"This is not about you," Kim said. "You've got to know that, Hallie. We're really glad you're here."

"We? Is that you and your tapeworm, or are you speaking for Frank, too?"

"Frank likes your work. I think you two have clashing personal styles. But this isn't about that."

"What is it, then?"

She said, "There's a problem with his house, so Frank may need to move in here. He's been renting with the understanding that his house was going to come up for auction. But something was wrong with the paperwork, so it's not going to be auctioned after all. Frank's wife is threatening to leave, she's so mad."

Kim was moving into dirt-dishing mode. "I told Frank I wouldn't tell anyone—"

"And you told me the apartment was part of my pay. It seems like you've got problems with follow-through."

Kim moved me away from the vent. "What do you want?" she whispered.

I had been crystal clear that I wanted my apartment as agreed. I had to think fast. What could I get from Kim that would get me out of Green Meadow with a killer portfolio?

"The Silverton Award," I snapped. "I will tell you what my best story is, and I want you to nominate it for the Silverton."

"You've got a lot of brass. They only give one of those for the whole state. We've got a whole newsroom—"

"We've got Charles, yourself and me. Charles's stories are shit."

"I don't know if I'd say that."

"Did you nominate anything he wrote last year?"

"No."

"Or the year before?"

"No."

"I rest my case. He's not going to do anything new or innovative. You might, but because of your reneging on the apartment—"

"It wasn't my call."

I held up my hands. "You gave your word. This is going to be very expensive for me. You will not put yourself out as a nominee. You will nominate me for this year's prize."

"The deadline is at the beginning of September. You will hardly have been here six months."

I said, "I will tell you the story, and you will nominate it. I want you to put that in writing."

Kim looked at me like I was crazy. But, she pulled a reporter pad out of her purse and wrote what I said, even the words "I will nominate Hallie and not Charles, nor myself, for the Silverton prize."

She signed it "Kim." I made her write her last name too.

"You're strange," she said.

"You chose strange because you liked my work. Live up to your promises," I said, like I was kicking her.

Chapter 16

I was angry, but I still had to do the beat checks, still had to go through the motions.

Ricky was reading a magazine in the dispatch room when I got to the cop shop.

"Sugar says you and her had a great time last night. She says you really know how to cut a rug."

It struck me as funny that she had said that because I had not danced. Sugar had put on Milli Vanilli and insisted my Doc Martens were like the shoes the duo wore. "Girl, you know it's true," she'd crooned. "Come on, show me your moves!" When I demurred, she did a half-hearted moonwalk, then went into the kitchenette for more Pizza Rolls.

Ricky winked. "Sugar said you probably had to sleep off a hangover. She's pretty fucked up herself."

"S'that her?" Sugar's scratchy voice called from the bathroom. "Send her in."

"I think she wants you to hold her hair," Ricky whispered.

"Sugar, I'm running late," I called. "Is there any news?"

The toilet flushed. Sugar came out, zipping her pants. "We had some fun, didn't we?" She wiped her mouth on her uniform sleeve. "I finished the bottle this morning."

I hoped she meant the wine and not the schnapps.

There was an incomplete report on a single-car rollover; just property damage. Ricky said it would be done soon, but I told him not to rush on my account. "I've got to get going. I have to go look for an apartment."

Sugar said, "I thought they gave you a free apartment."

"I thought so, too," I said, trying not to let my bitterness show.

Ricky whistled. "That's a big bite in the budget."

I asked what the going rate was for a decent one-bedroom.

Ricky said he knew a recent divorcée who was looking to rent out a room in her house for $200, but a place of my own would be $300, plus utilities, and probably more like $400 if I wanted a security building.

"But no crime ever happens here," Sugar chortled, "so's you might as well not pay extra for a lock." Then Sugar got a gleam in her eye. "You could move in with me. You've seen my place. The love seat folds out into a bed. You can have it for a hundred."

"That's sweet," I managed, "but I need a place of my own."

Sugar winked. "You can have the bed when you're 'entertaining.'"

I cringed. "No—"

"I'll throw in utilities if you promise not to use too much water."

I said, "I can't move in with you." I think it sounded the same way it did in my head, because Ricky's eyebrows shot up.

Sugar looked like she'd been stabbed. "Fine," she said. "If my place ain't good enough, just say so."

She bolted for the bathroom. Ricky followed her, but not without first saying, "See what you done?"

I had blown it. Sugar, despite my feelings about her, was probably my most important source in Green Meadow. She was the gatekeeper for everything the police did. And because she had taken a personal interest in me, she was willing to explain background stuff so I didn't have to look stupid always asking Charles or Kim.

I rushed to the bathroom door. "Sugar," I pleaded, "I'm sorry."

I could hear her sobbing and blowing her nose. I could hear the words "snoofy" and "stuck up."

"Sugar, it just wouldn't work."

She kicked the door open. "Why couldn't it work?" she demanded.

I flipped over an empty metal trashcan and sat on it. I did it so I would be lower than her, so that she would see me as a supplicant. "Even though you've been nicer to me than almost anybody in Green Meadow . . ."

I trailed off. I didn't know where I was going with that line.

I know what was called for was some kind of excuse, that I was allergic to something or could not share a bathroom. But . . . that would be lying. So, I told her the truth.

"Have you heard about the line between church and state?"

"That's why the goddamn atheists sued our manger scene," Ricky said, stepping uncomfortably close to me.

"Don't waste no breath on them," Sugar said. "They're all going to hell."

I started over. "I work in the Fourth Estate."

Ricky and Sugar stared at me blankly.

Remember your audience, I reminded myself. "Journalism is the Fourth Estate. There are three separate branches of government that are all supposed to keep each other in check, but the saying is that journalism is the Fourth Estate. We're not part of government, but government works because we're the watchdog on all three branches."

Sugar rolled her eyes.

Ricky said, "That's not true. Government don't need newspapers. The paper in Jasper County closed last year and nothing happened. Sky ain't falled."

"I don't know about Jasper County, but I know here, and the kind of journalism *I* do means I can't get too close to public officials."

Sugar wrapped her arms around herself, like there was no one in the world to comfort her. "You mean we can't be—" she sobbed. "I thought you was my new best friend," she wailed and pulled the bathroom door closed. The force nearly knocked me off the upturned trashcan, but I wobbled backward to my feet.

"She's a *dispatcher*," Ricky spat. "She makes minimum."

I had done everything I could to make Sugar think we were friends. But there was no way I could keep that up 24/7. At that moment I understood why none of the cops reciprocated with her. Even with the sexual equivalent of free utilities, it would be a bad deal.

Still, I needed her.

"I'd get fired if Frank found out," I called through the bathroom door.

"Not so." Sugar came back out. "The girl before Allison lived with me. She was my best friend."

"How come you never mention her?"

"She don't call no more."

Ricky said, "The bitch," and Sugar nodded like she was keeping time to music.

I reached for Sugar's hand. I said, "There's a lot you haven't told me." I asked her if it hurt to have her best friend leave and never call and then another friend run off with the prosecutor.

"Why don't nobody love me?" Sugar sobbed.

Ugh. "That's not true, is it, Ricky?"

He gave me a dirty look, but he said, "Sugar, this force depends on you."

"There are different kinds of love," I said, "you've got to look around and see what you've got. If I tell you moving in would be an ethical breach, aren't we good enough friends that you can believe me?"

Sugar stared straight ahead.

I sang, "Girl, you know it's true," just like Sugar had in her apartment.

She cracked a smile. "I love you, too."

Ricky said, "Girls make no sense," but he seemed as relieved as I was.

I asked Kim to go out for a beer with me. She agreed, but she was pretty frosty when we got to the A-OK Corral.

I said, "The last time we were here you really opened up to me."

"Some friend you've turned out to be."

"Hold on a second. You lure me to Indiana with a promise of a free apartment, then take it back?"

Kim didn't answer. Instead, she said, "You have no idea how hard it is for a woman with a young child to be taken seriously in this company. I had to fight to be named assistant editor over Charles."

"Charles can't write."

"No, he can't. He can schmooze, though, and Frank and Jed like him. I had to write all the obits for a year to get this job. That was the deal. They fired our half-time obit lady, and in order for me to become assistant editor ahead of Charles, on top of everything else on the county beat, I had to write every obituary for a year. And now that I've got the number-two spot in the newsroom, Frank and Charles are so buddy-buddy that every time I want to do something, Frank says to talk to Charles first. I've got no authority, I get no respect, but I got them to hire you because you can write. And what do you do? You whine that you have to get your birthday off in your first year. This is a newspaper! What did you expect?"

"I expected to be treated with respect, just like you want to be. I expected that if I was offered an apartment to live in, it was mine to live in all the time. I expected that when you shook hands on the deal, you'd honor it."

"I honored it to the extent Frank would let me."

"If he had the ability to undo it, why did you make the offer in the first place?"

"I really wanted you here." She hesitated. "I thought I could learn from you."

That was something I could work with. I tried to soften too. I said, "I've already learned so much from you," even though I wasn't sure I could back that up. "It's just—I have bills. I have a certain amount of money that I need each month, and you've changed that equation by taking away the apartment."

"Frank took the apartment. I argued for you keeping it. I really did."

I doubted that she put up much of a fight, but there was no use getting into it. I would never trust Kim again, but I was still working with her. And she clearly wanted to make up.

I said, "You've got to support me in the newsroom, okay?"

She grabbed my hand. "I will make sure your rent is something you can afford. I promise."

I did not see how she could make a promise like that unless she could give me a raise, but I kept my mouth shut. A boss who owes you is better than a boss who's mad at you.

Sunday morning, I packed my things in Xerox paper boxes I had collected from the ad department's copy room. Finding a place to take them was the hard part. The cheap apartments had all been snatched up in May by Sir Splash-A-Lot's summer workers. Every listing in the Weekender classifieds was out of my price range.

I sat facing my boxes and tried to make a plan. I had a piece of typing paper that I folded into thirds. In the first column, I wrote out all my expenses—student loans, food, gas, and the big unknown—rent.

The middle column was for discretionary spending. There was the trip I was going to take back to the Twin Cities when I'd finally earned some vacation days. With Amber not speaking to me, it was easy to cross that out.

Less cereal, more oatmeal. No oranges out of season. I tried to imagine what Professor Wassle would tell me, since I couldn't afford to call him.

He'd say to stay at the *Daily-Observer* because I needed a year somewhere.

He'd also tell me to think of what came next. A bigger paper, but probably still in Indiana. With a little luck I could go from the *Daily Zero* to the *Gary*

Post-Tribune. But I'd rather go to one of the Chicago dailies. That would be a real step toward the *New York Times*. And to skip ahead to a Chicago daily, I needed a solid record of breaking major stories and contextualizing crime and education stories to show new trends. I needed to be more than a spot news reporter. To do that, I needed an ally.

I called Kim and invited her up. "It's time for a newswomen's empowerment meeting."

Kim looked confused as I seated her at the head of the dining room table. "Do you see that teamwork poster?" I asked. "Do you notice that only the coxswain can see where the boat is going? If the *Daily-Observer* is going to publish stories worthy of a Silverton, we've got to both know where we are going."

"Shouldn't we wait until Frank and Charles can be here, too?"

"You've told me more than once that Frank's job is too big. If he's going to keep us afloat with ad revenue, to extend the metaphor, we have to recognize that he isn't going to have the mental energy for major innovations in editorial. You're not number two. You're the unofficial number one."

"And Charles?"

"Charles is set in his ways. Let's keep this to a circle of innovators. The first thing I need to know is where you see yourself one year from now."

Kim looked flummoxed. "I don't know. Misty will be going into third grade."

"I know where I want to be: I want to be picking up my Silverton. And while I'm up on the stage, I'd like to say, 'I could not have done this without the help of Kim Joseph.' I'd like to publicly thank the *Daily-Observer* for taking risks with new approaches to crime and education reporting, and I'd like to introduce you as the editor, not the assistant editor."

"Frank may not spend much time in the newsroom, but he'll still be editor."

"I don't think so. From the chain's perspective, what is important?"

"Ad revenue and circulation."

"And what makes people who have to watch their spending choose to subscribe?"

"Seeing their kids' names in the paper. Having the lunch menus. Grocery coupons."

It was a stretch, but I said, "You're totally right: relevance. We've got to make this paper more relevant. Think about our last few issues. What was on the cover?"

"They all run together, but in the Weekender, car crashes. Weekdays it's usually a big donation to Little League or what have you."

"Who do you think reads those stories?"

"People who knew the crash victims."

"And?"

"People who lived nearby."

"What about the donation stories?"

"I guess the people who gave and the people who received."

"If you were busy, would you read those stories?"

"Probably not."

"What do you read? When you're at the hair salon or waiting in the doctor's office, what do you pick up?"

"I like the parenting magazines. And *Ladies Home Journal*."

"Why?"

"They always have useful information. I can usually find tips on cooking on a budget, or things to do with Misty."

"That's what we have to do. We have to change the way we cover education and crime to make the stories useful. Instead of just writing about people who got hurt, we have to write about how not to get hurt. We've got to tell people how to navigate these schools if they are as bad as everybody tells me they are."

"They are."

I asked, "Who do you think is served by the way we report now?"

"Well, the city fathers. Any time the council decides to do something, we cover it. And I suppose it helps the police chief and the fire chief that people know what their departments are doing. And the presidents of the Rotary club and the Kiwanis."

"Right. So there are a whole lot of other people—the town mothers, if you will—who aren't on your list. Regular people need information that they're not getting."

"I'm not sure I follow you. What kind of information?"

"I don't know specifically. But if we contextualize, talk about crime trends instead of just individual crimes, and put news in the context of social issues, I think more people will want to read us."

I liked how Kim was nodding. I went on, "You've told me that Frank doesn't like change. But you know who does like innovation? Jed. And if Jed likes a fresh approach, Frank will come around." I finished, "It would be a good example to Misty if we won a Silverton, wouldn't it, Kim?"

"Sure."

"Let's start with the town mothers. Literally. What do they need to know?"

"They need to know who's qualified and who's not at the school," she said excitedly. "Misty's kindergarten teacher was fine, but first grade? Misty couldn't learn from that woman. I don't know where she went to college, but it wasn't Hamilton."

"Have we ever run a story like that, looking at who's qualified, or what parents can do if their kid gets a dud?"

"No. But I don't think Frank would like it."

"You really think Frank doesn't want stories about incompetent teachers?"

"I think it will have to be slipped into the conversation in a way that he doesn't think anybody is being criticized."

"We're going to get some resistance. But if we stand together, we can move this paper forward."

Kim balled her hand into a fist. "I'm really glad we hired you," she said. "You've got real spark. You could be an editor here someday."

Hell no, I thought, but I said, "If we team up, each of us can help make the other more successful now that we know where we want to go."

She started to read the teamwork poster caption, but I stopped her. I said, "We need our own motto: For the town mothers!"

"You know," Kim said, quieter, "I was wrong about the Silverton. You're the only one in the newsroom who's got vision. If anyone can get a Silverton, it's you."

Chapter 17

I did beat checks every day at the fire department, police station, and courthouse. With the schools, though, there was only the monthly school board meeting. During the public comment section, two parents complained that Green Meadow schools went longer into the month of June than any area school system. Then Superintendent Quidley asked for special authorization to hire a half-time PE instructor who only had provisional certification.

After the meeting, I approached the superintendent and explained my two-to-eleven shift predicament. I asked how I could get to know the schools better.

"My wife and I were just talking about how there should be more coverage of the after-school art program she does with the special ed kids. The last girl was out almost every week."

"That sounds fascinating," I said, trying to mean it. I could not imagine more than a single feature on the program, but unlike the school board meeting, there would be actual students at After School Arts.

The next day, I met the superintendent's wife at a folding table behind the middle school.

"I worked in public relations in Indianapolis," she exclaimed, "so really, I'm a journalist, too." She spread her arms like she was going to hug me. There was an awkward moment, and I extended my hand.

She took it in both of hers as if it were hers now, as if she had won it.

Mrs. Quidley wore a lot of makeup and had long platinum blonde hair. Every sentence she uttered was tinged with excitement. She kept looking at my notebook and saying, "Write that down!" What I managed to get out of her was that her arts enrichment program gave special ed students an extra art class after school once a week: "They learn to express themselves and experience the benefits of art therapy."

"So, were you trained in art or behavioral therapy?"

Her face went cold. "I told you, I was in PR in Indianapolis."

This wasn't going well, but I stuck around for the craft project anyway.

"I made this one myself," Mrs. Quidley said, holding up an example for the students. It was construction paper Mickey Mouse ears glued to a paper plate. It wasn't enough of a likeness to merit a copyright infringement suit, but the kids could tell what it was supposed to be. They cut out their own black circles and glued them onto their own paper plates.

It was hard to see any therapeutic value, even harder to argue there was any self-expression. The slower kids were told exactly where to draw the eyes and glue the ears. One of the kids she snapped at looked to me for a witness. His face suggested the indignities were more extreme when there was no reporter present.

I had to leave before the project was through, so I didn't get a chance to interview the kid. Maybe their bus driver would talk to me later and tell me whether the students' behavior changed after Mrs. Quidley's art class.

Whatever the big story was, it would have to come later. I only had enough for an eight-inch run-down of the program. Kim told me she liked the story, but a few hours later, Frank said he didn't like the line "not trained in art or behavioral therapy." He killed the whole story and just ran the photo with an extended caption.

"You say you want to write about the schools, but when you get time to do some of your Pulitzer participant observation, it's just crap."

He said 'Pulitzer' like it was a pejorative. I wanted to yell back. But I could see Kim standing behind Frank making a gesture with her hands like she was smoothing a tablecloth.

Trying to keep my voice even, I explained to Frank that it was important to parents who had children in the school that Mrs. Quidley was not qualified to conduct art therapy or teach special ed.

"Everybody in town knows she's the superintendent's wife. There's no need to point out what her training is or is not." He stalked back to the publisher's office.

Kim met my eyes. "Just so you know, I, for one, agree with you. That's exactly the kind of information the town mothers need." She put her arm around my shoulders. "I'll work on him. I'll explain how it's in the best interest of advertising and circulation to serve the widest possible audience."

I wasn't sure I could keep my cool if I saw Frank the next day, so I told Kim I was going to the middle school. I thought I'd walk the halls, maybe do a day-in-the-life story.

It turned out to be a bad idea. Not one of the middle school teachers would let me visit in their classrooms—not even Mrs. Nevil, who was doing a special journalism project with her English class.

"Just get the information from the press release. Mrs. Quidley will send it." she said.

All I could infer from her tone was that Mrs. Quidley was not pleased with the coverage of her special ed arts program.

I asked, "Have I offended someone?"

Nevil said, "I am not qualified to comment on that," with the ham-handed sarcasm used only by middle school teachers.

Down at the cop shop, I complained to Sugar about Quidley freezing me out.

She extended the oversize plastic travel cup that was her constant companion. "Have some Mountain Dew. Always makes me feel better."

Just then, Ricky swung in. Darnell followed with his German shepherd. The dog sniffed my crotch, then sat down and offered a paw.

"He likes you," Sugar cooed. "He wants to shake."

Darnell plopped down on the couch beside the dispatch console, propped his feet on a stack of files, and patted the seat for his dog to jump up.

Sugar put down her bladder buster and asked them, "We got anybody undercover in the schools?"

Darnell laughed. "Undercover! We've got to find out once and for all what's in that mystery meat they serve in the cafeteria."

"Mystery meat," Sugar snorted "you combine that with tater tots and you've got all four food groups."

Darnell corrected her. "No, you don't. You got no meat."

That cracked Sugar up. She laughed so hard her whole body shook and Mountain Dew came streaming out of her nose. Cujo jumped up and started licking her. Ricky pulled a roll of blue shop towels out of the janitor closet and wiped the front of her uniform.

I guess they saw the expression on my face. Everybody froze.

"Doesn't that bother you?" I asked Sugar.

"Ricky drying my décolletage? No. It gets me hot."

"We've known each other since kindergarten," Ricky said.

"No, before that," Sugar said. "Vacation Bible school. You still wore diapers at age four."

She pronounced 'four' like it had two syllables.

"You were always climbing up on the changing table to help get them off," Ricky shot back.

Darnell said, "Some things never change."

"You were there, too?" I asked him.

Darnell said no, he was a couple years older than them, but he met Sugar and Ricky when he repeated first grade.

Ricky turned to Darnell. "You can get Hallie in the school. Take her with you when you do DARE tomorrow."

Technically, I knew I would be trespassing if I had been told not to come, but no one in Green Meadow would know that. The cops walked on water as far as this town was concerned.

Blue was back from his trip to Indianapolis, so I went to see if he was still on his shift at the firehouse. Our ruse was that Blue was going to show me an antique trampoline for a feature on innovations in firefighting.

"Use of tramps has been banned since the mid-sixties," he said, louder than necessary. "But the fire chief is a history buff. He can't bear to part with the old equipment."

He ushered me into a storage room behind the main truck bay. He quickly made a nest out of coiled hoses. Then he spread over it one of those gray wool blankets they put on shock victims.

I'd had trysts in odd locations before, but this felt different than a sudden mutual urge in a subway station. I didn't know what to say as he gestured to the cushiony place he had made for us. So I said, "Just hold me."

"Oh, you're one of those."

"One of those whats?"

"Hot chicks who don't actually want to have sex."

"I am not a chick."

Blue's lips curled into a sly grin. "You're cute when you're mad."

"You're cute when you're naked."

"Not cute. Manly. Irresistible."

"Prove it. Take your shirt off," I said, leaning into the side of the trampoline.

"You just want to see if I've got suspenders on."

"Do you?"

"I could run and get them if you want to do more than cuddle."

I toyed with the possibilities. "Do you like to slide down that pole?"

"We all do. It's faster than the stairs."

"I could be waiting for you by the engine."

"They'd all watch."

I said, "Kinky, but go on."

"You want that kind of thing? Talk to Ricky over at the police station. The guys over there are just plain sick."

"There go your romantic eyes."

Blue's voice went flat. "Thinking about the cops totally kills the mood. You want a foot rub or something?"

"We're not going to—"

"No. Not now." I rolled my neck from side to side, the moment having passed.

Chapter 18

Darnell screeched up in a new Camaro. It was fire-engine red with wide tires, like something from the Indy 500. His dog was in the back seat, nose pressed against the window.

"Drive you to school, girly?" Darnell slurred.

I reminded myself that going with him to watch the DARE presentation was the only way I was going to get inside a classroom.

"How'd you get this car?" I asked.

"Forfeiture. Hop in."

I got in. "What do you mean, forfeiture?"

"When a suspect is charged with a drug crime, we can take any assets used in the criminal enterprise," he said and hit the gas.

"Just take them?" I asked.

"If they're found innocent, we have to give them back. But once they're convicted? Police property! Mostly we auction stuff. It pays a couple salaries. But this ride was too sweet to part with. Besides, it gets the kids' attention."

I had another question, but Darnell touched the automatic window controls and air came rushing in, blowing his paperwork into my lap.

"Aren't you supposed to use a clipboard?"

"There are a lot of things I'm s'posed to do."

Darnell couldn't have been more than twenty-four, but in the mirror on the visor, I could see dark circles under his eyes. The shirt of his uniform was creased. Even his hair had a dingy, rumpled look.

"What did you do last night?" I asked, trying to sound conversational.

"Last night? This morning? It's all a big blur," he said. "What's it like for you when you drink?"

"What do you mean?"

"If I don't throw up, it takes two or three days to get it out of my system."

"You should take vitamin B. And drink lots of water."

"That's what they say to do if you smoke too much pot." Darnell put his hand on my knee and locked eyes. "Do you get high?"

I said, "Watch the road, please," and removed his hand.

"Sugar says you're a thespian."

I chuckled. "A thespian? Really?"

"You ain't answering my question, darlin'. Do you like to party?"

I cleared my throat. "I believe you're an officer of the law."

"Oh come on. You're a friend of Sugar's, you're a friend of mine."

"If the statute of limitations is seven years, yes, it is possible that seven years ago I might have been at a party where there was marijuana."

Darnell shook his head. "Anybody ever tell you you're strange?"

"From you, Darnell, that's a compliment."

Cujo stuck his head over my headrest and began licking my ear.

"Leave some for me," Darnell scolded him.

At the middle school, the kids chattering in the hall reminded me of a flock of grackles, spreading out to fill available space then contracting to turn into doorways or ascend stairs.

Mr. Everson's room was painted green. A patina of grime reached four feet up the walls.

Darnell sat on Mr. Everson's desk and told his German shepherd to lie down. He grabbed the edge of the desk, locked his arms straight, and rocked like a chimpanzee.

"Kids, this is your brain," Darnell said. He looked around frantically. "Shit, where's my props?"

Mr. Everson said, "We don't have the fry pan or the burner you wanted set up."

Darnell composed himself. "Imagine a egg, kids." He held his hands up, like a movie director framing a shot. "Can you see that?"

A kid in the back asked, "Robin egg or duck egg?"

"Elephant egg!" another boy shouted.

The whole class erupted in laughter. Darnell's eyes narrowed.

"Kids, I'm here to give you information that may *save your life* one day. Imagine a egg, okay? A ordinary chicken egg."

"Grade A?" the kid in back asked.

"No, grade B, like you," Darnell shot back.

A girl muttered, "More like a grade F minus," and that set the class off again.

Mr. Everson slapped his hand on the desk. "That's enough."

Darnell's face flushed a deep red. The dog started growling. "You better watch yourselfs," Darnell barked. "This here is Cujo. He's a trained attack dog. We ever catch one of you with drugs, well, I just hope I remember to say, 'Down, boy.'"

The kids didn't make another peep.

Mr. Everson looked at his watch. "Okay, then, let's thank Officer Kellan for this excellent presentation." He clapped loudly and the students followed suit.

That was it. There was no scientific information on the effects of drug use. No explanation of the criminal penalties. I'd seen the DARE teaching protocol. Darnell's threat was not in the script.

The kids looked really scared though.

I got out my pad and started talking to a girl in the front row.

"Did you get any new information on drugs today?" I asked.

The girl raised her hand to her mouth and bit a fingernail. "Not really—"

I felt a heavy hand on my shoulder. Mr. Everson said, "Don't interview the children."

I said, "That's going to make it hard to write a story." He didn't budge. "How about I interview you, then?"

"If you must."

"What did you think of today's DARE program?"

"DARE has been phenomenally effective at keeping kids off drugs," he said, exactly the words in Mrs. Quidley's press release. "The children get the medical information they need to make the right decisions for their future. DARE keeps our children safe."

"Is there usually some sort of visual component with an egg? Did something go wrong?"

"No comment."

—

On the ride back, I asked Darnell if there was a serious drug problem in Bryce County.

"Drugs ain't a problem here," he laughed and rubbed the dashboard. "Not a problem at all."

"Was the Whitmore boy involved with drugs?"

Darnell blinked. "Who?"

"Peter Whitmore, the boy who drowned. You knew him from the high school."

"Naw," Darnell said and turned on the radio, too loud to hold a conversation.

Since I didn't get any good interviews, my DARE story was not very good. I did get some great photos though. Frank liked one of Cujo getting a drink from a water fountain.

Frank said, "It shows he's a big part of the drug enforcement team. It tells the whole story."

I didn't weigh in on that, but if I had to rate the members of the DARE team, I'd say Cujo held those kids' attention in a way Darnell could not.

A couple of parents called the next day to complain about the photo. They said a dog should not be allowed to drink from the same fountain their children use. Frank took those calls. I heard him say, "We don't pose photos. The photographer just happened to get a picture of something that was already happening."

While he was on the line, I took another call about the picture, but it wasn't a complaint.

"Is this Hallie Linden?"

When I confirmed that I had, indeed, taken the photo, the man on the other end said, "That's no police dog. Cujo shouldn't be around children."

When I asked the man who he was, he hung up.

Later that day, the police chief called me in for "a talk."

I was nervous but also excited. For some reason, I was finally getting access to Conrad Kellan. I didn't know what he wanted to talk about, but I knew I needed him to like me.

When I sat down opposite the police chief's desk, I noticed the shelf behind his chair held three photos in black frames; the young women looked nearly identical in their high school graduation robes.

"You're a family man," I said, letting it trail off so that he could find whatever question in that statement he wanted to answer.

The chief followed my eyes. "Those are my girls," Conrad Kellan said. "And you've met my boy."

Of course: Same hairline. Pushy. Presumptuous. Darnell was Conrad Kellan's son.

I said, "He's a chip off the ol' block," trying to make it sound friendly.

"It took some tryin' to get a boy," the chief said, blowing a line of smoke at me. "I'm glad you like him. He's got a ways to go before he's ready to take this seat the way I took it from my pap. But everything you can do to help build respect for our force helps. Miss Linden, I really enjoyed your story about his work in the DARE program."

"Your father was the chief of police, too? How is it that your family has been so successful in law enforcement?"

"Pappy said Teddy Roosevelt only had the half of it. Speak softly and carry a big stick, yes, but *use it* once. When correction is applied swiftly and with undeniable force, subsequent offenses go way down."

"Isn't that skipping the judicial branch?"

"The judge was Pappy's cousin. They agreed on most everything."

"Why did you call me in here?" I asked.

"I just see that you've helped us out with the story on the DARE program and I appreciate that. I wanted to see if maybe I could help you out. What kind of car do you drive?"

"A Chevette."

"A Chevette?" The chief threw his head back and laughed. "You're living in the state that hosts the Indy 500! Wouldn't you like a nicer car?"

"Cars are all pretty much the same to me. Mine gets good gas mileage."

"But wouldn't you like something sportier? Maybe a Camaro like Darnell drives. Or do you like Frank's TR-7?"

A lot of people in town seemed to be really into cars. Darnell in the Camaro I understood; he had gotten that from a drug seizure. It probably significantly sweetened the job for him. But there were Green Meadow bank tellers and Trojan security guards driving Mercedes.

"My Chevette is paid for, so I like it just fine."

"That's the thing," the chief dropped his voice. "At a police auction, one rarely pays the full Blue Book value."

I didn't want to tell the chief how low my salary was, nor that I would soon have to squeeze rent out of it.

"I couldn't accept any personal favors," I said, "if that's what you were offering."

The chief threw up his hands, as if I had misunderstood him. "Favor shines on those who are in the right place at the right time. That's all I wanted to let you know. Don't you news types take tips? I was going to give you a tip on when an automobile you might want would be coming up for auction. But if you're happy with what you're driving, suit yourself."

Here I had been excited that I had finally gotten some face time with the police chief, but the whole discussion felt like a sales pitch. I wanted to walk out, but I needed to stay on positive terms with the chief.

I said, "You seem to be offering something I don't want and can't really accept because of my professional ethics. But it's the thought that counts, so thank you." I leaned forward. "There is a favor I can ask for, though. Sometimes police reports are coming in months late and my editor thinks I missed them. For some reason, Sugar doesn't always give them to me at the time of the accident or the arrest—"

The chief cut me off, "Miss Linden, we have procedures," all the chummy warmth gone from his voice. "You can go now."

Chapter 19

Iwasn't going to get any stories at the middle school with the teachers freezing me out, so I decided to try the high school to do a follow-up on the two drownings.

Kim wasn't in when I got to the newsroom at eight; Frank, unfortunately, was.

Do what it takes to get a Silverton and get out of here, I told myself. So, I gave Frank my version of the brown-nosing smile: nose wrinkled, mouth pulled up on the sides. I said, "I was thinking about going over to the high school to see if the kids are still talking about the drownings. I'll find out from the principal how many students participated in the grief counseling."

Frank said, "This is a rural district. Kids may get grief counseling where you're from, but we don't coddle kids like that here."

At least for now, we are on the same team, I said in my head. I tried to tease out what Frank was saying, separate it from all his negativity. He wasn't saying not to go to the high school. He wasn't saying he thought it was a bad story idea. He was just saying things are different in Green Meadow. Maybe phrases like 'grief process' and 'getting closure' were not used here, but I knew from my anthropology classes that mourning is universal. Maybe farm kids are inured to death from seeing their pigs and chickens on the dinner table, but there's no way they would not be affected by two classmates drowning.

"How do you think the students will memorialize them?" I asked, trying to sound upbeat.

Frank said, "They'll dedicate the yearbook to them if it hasn't already gone to the printer. If it has, they'll mention them in the prayer at graduation."

"They won't do both?"

Frank snorted. "Those kids were truants. Dying like that is probably the only way either one of their names was ever going to be spoken at a graduation ceremony." He laughed at his own joke and I had to remind myself that he hadn't been there, hadn't seen the mothers.

I tried to shrug their wailing voices out of my mind as I headed out to the high school.

It was a sandstone building, probably rock from the now-closed quarry that Kim had pointed out on the town tour. The cornerstone said the school was built by the WPA in 1936.

Inside, I saw there had not been many renovations, but it was clean and well-maintained. At the front office, when I explained what I wanted, a secretary walked me back to the principal's office.

I could tell the principal was still torn up himself.

"It makes no sense, why they walked across the old bridge like that."

"Were they habitual truants?"

He shook his head and looked down at a framed picture on his desk. After a minute, he turned the picture around for me to see. It was a photo of him grinning, holding a fish.

"They just wanted what every man wants at this time of year," he said. "To match wits with nature. I don't know how it is where you're from, but the boys here need a challenge. You know, not every one of them makes the football team."

I asked if there had been counseling to help the students in their grieving process.

"Mrs. Quidley did offer to meet with anyone who was upset. But I don't think any went."

"So the two boys weren't popular—"

"No, I think that was more about Mrs. Quidley. Oh, Lord. Please don't say in the paper that I said that. You know who her husband is."

Just to reassure him, I scribbled through the quote in my notepad.

The principal started over. "They skipped school to fish. I had to call the truant officer about them a few times. But Peter and Mason were nice kids from nice families."

"Did either of them have a girlfriend?"

"I wouldn't know that. When they had to come down to the office, we mostly talked about fishing." He apologized again. "I'm afraid I'm not going to be much help for your story."

I said, "I want to do them justice, their memory."

The principal nodded. I think he liked the story idea. He swiveled around and picked up a desk stand microphone, not unlike the one Sugar used. He switched it on and said, "Mark Newman, James Thompson, Terrence Dunn, please report to the principal's office."

Presently three lanky teens appeared at the office door. The principal introduced me and set us up in a conference room.

We had the conversation that could be expected. The drowned boys, Mason and Peter, were the nicest kids you'd ever meet, one said. "Mason knew the best fishing spots. He really studied that river."

"So, he would have known that crossing was dangerous?"

"We all know. There's big signs."

The second boy, James, jumped in. "They were nice kids. Whatever you write, you've got to say that."

One of them teared up describing the fishing flies Mason tied, as if that was an art form. He said the older boy had taken Peter under his wing when Peter's parents split up last winter. I was trying to be friendly and positive, but all I was getting was the kind of response kids would have to any death. The quotes were unusable, just vague positivity about their lost classmates. Yet I felt certain that there was a story. Rational people don't ignore warning signs. And everything these kids were telling me suggested their drowned friends had been rational people. So why did Mason and Peter walk on that bridge?

I didn't have enough for the kind of story I wanted to write. The drowned boys sounded nice. They were average students. Their friends thought the problems they had in school were all a direct result of skipping class to fish.

The bell rang. James and Mark jumped up. "Sorry, we've got a test."

Terrence stayed behind and I seized the opportunity to try for information that might not be so forthcoming in a group interview.

"Was there anything unusual about either of the boys?" I asked. "I need details so readers who did not know them will understand who they were."

Terrence said Peter had been in a car accident around Memorial Day. "Maybe that did something to his balance," Terrence speculated. "I mean, other people have waded across on the old bridge and not fell in."

"Do you think they might have been drinking?" I asked. "You can answer off the record if you want."

"No. Definitely not. Not Peter, anyway. He drank a lot when his folks split up, but after that crash he swore off it."

"He just quit cold turkey?"

"The other driver was killed, ma'am."

"And you're saying Peter Whitmore was drunk when the car accident happened?"

"I'm not saying anything, but everybody knows it."

He leaned in. The way he had one shoulder up and his head tilted down told me he was about to deliver something he thought was important. I hoped it was the explanation I'd felt lurking beneath the surface of the conversation.

"You know that river is haunted," he whispered.

Ugh. This was even worse than the generic emotion from Mark and James. But I had to be present with my interviewee, to try to see the world from his perspective.

"What do you mean, the river is haunted?" I asked.

"Do you know that song about the *Edmond Fitzgerald*, the ship that sank in Lake Superior? It's like that. A lot of people have died in the stretch of river that cuts through Bryce County. And I—" He put his hand over his mouth, as if that would stop the words.

"What?"

I listened as the clock ticked. If you keep your face neutral enough, people will usually answer.

"I skipped, too," he finally said. "I was fishing that day, not too far from the spot where they drowned, and—" Another pause. Another hand to his mouth.

I waited.

"I snagged a jar. Not the twist-top kind. An old-fashioned one with a hinge top that comes down, and there's a rubber ring to make it airtight."

I didn't see that the jar had anything to do with my story, but it seemed very important to Terrence, so I had to ask about it before moving on to the questions rushing in my head. "Why do you mention the jar?"

"It was filled with teeth. Human teeth."

I jumped to the conclusion that it was probably from a woman somewhere along the river who had a special jar for when a child lost a tooth. But I could see in Terrence's view, some monster was drowning people for their teeth.

I asked Terrence if he thought Peter and Mason had regarded the river as haunted. He said he didn't know, so that weird detail was useless for my story.

"Were you there when they drowned?"

"I saw them fishing. Guys are kind of territorial. Since I didn't come with them, I had to find a different spot. There was an old guy fishing at the good spot below the new bridge, so I hiked upriver. I went up the bluff above Old Main Street. It's beautiful up there. You can see for miles. Don't laugh, and don't put this in the paper: I spun around like that nun in *The Sound of Music*. And then I stood there, just taking it in. And I see a cop car back behind the Arco station."

Terrence said, "I was worried it might be the truant officer, Darnell Kellan. I yelled 'Cop!' as loud as I could. I know Mason and Peter heard me because they grabbed their rods. I saw Peter hop that fence to walk across the old bridge. I ran as fast as I could down the far side of the bluff. If it was Darnell, I figured he wouldn't try the bluff—he was probably after Mason and Peter. I mean, they skipped all the time. Since I had to lay low until the coast was clear, I thought I might as well drop in a line. That's when I snagged the jar."

"Did you hear Mason yell for help? Did you hear him calling to the old fisherman?"

"No, the only thing I heard was the sirens, later."

"Did you watch the search?"

"No, ma'am."

"Why not?"

"I thought they was getting arrested. Darnell, the truant officer, can be pretty mean. I figured he was going to make an example out of them, it being so close to the end of the school year. I didn't want to get arrested myself."

Back at the paper I inventoried my notes. The three classmates of the drowned boys had described them as "nice" and "average." I had the principal saying they were from nice families. And one superstitious kid telling me off the record that one of the victims had been in a fatal DUI. If there was a kernel of a story in my notepad, that was it.

I called Sugar at home. "Do you remember a teenager, Peter Whitmore, being in a fatal DUI around Memorial Day?"

She said, "That's one of them boys that drowned."

"Right. I'm writing a story about how the kids at the high school are handling the loss."

"That's a news story?" Sugar asked. "My daddy got smashed flat by a Trojan test truck. No reporter come to ask me how I felt." Her voice sounded raw.

"It never heals, does it?"

Sugar apologized for changing the subject to herself. "I wish I could help you. I did give you the report on the fatal."

"Do you remember what the kid was charged with?"

"He wasn't charged. Darnell said he would take care of it himself. He does DARE and he's the truant officer. I think he wrote in the report that the driver who died was at fault. He said leave it to him as far as the Whitmore kid."

Peter Whitmore was the teen driver from that fatality on my first three-day weekend. I clearly remembered he was drunk at the accident scene. The charge should have been felony operating while under the influence or vehicular homicide.

"Does that happen a lot?" I asked. "If Darnell knows a kid from his work at the school, is it common for him to not make an arrest?"

"Sometimes, I guess. I'm sure the kid blew over the legal limit, but they've lowered the standard so much, who's to say if he was really drunk?"

Chapter 20

The Whitmore home looked like something out of one of those decorating magazines. The hedges were clipped to crisp angles. The porch had a rocking chair and a bench with a blue and white striped cushion. The sweat rolling down a pitcher of lemonade atop a low table was the only thing that looked like it might not have been planned.

Mrs. Whitmore came out when she heard me on the steps. She moved slowly, barely lifting her feet when she walked. Her face was drawn, and on her drab floral dress she wore an oversize button with Peter's photo.

"Thanks for the story," she said.

I was surprised that she liked it. I had been on autopilot when I wrote about the drownings. Except for my lead, it was a boilerplate accident story.

I said, "I know that was a horrible day for you."

I could tell from her eyes that she was already back in it. "They tried. They really tried. That firefighter, the tall one, he kept doing CPR. He wanted to save my baby."

That would have been Blue. I could picture him pumping the boy's chest long after all but the mothers in the crowd had given up hope.

I said, "Everybody wanted them to live," and Mrs. Whitmore reached for my hand. I don't think you're supposed to hold hands with sources, reportorial distance and all, but when she squeezed, I squeezed back.

"It was the worst day of my career, watching the rescue attempt and seeing how hard it hit you. How are you doing?" I asked, pretty much sure I already knew the answer.

She looked at me as if trying to decide how deep to go. Finally, she confided, "He's in my dreams every night."

I nodded. "They say it's harder losing a child than a spouse."

"When my husband left just before Christmas, it felt like the floor had fallen out from under me. I had no idea how much worse things could get."

When the quotes I got at the school had been so bland, I wracked my brain for something that would move the story from a death aftermath to something larger, something that might be worth submitting for a Silverton.

What was the bigger issue playing out in Peter's death? He was in the fatal drunk driving accident and then leapt the bridge fence a short time later. It seemed like he had changed a lot since his parents split up.

That could be a prize contender—Peter, the poster child for how divorce can affect kids.

I had a lot of questions about the trouble at home. But if I was going to get Mrs. Whitmore to open up on that, I was going to have to be patient.

People who have never done it think it's hard to interview a recently bereaved person. Sure, they cry. Sometimes they get mad at your questions. But most interviewers give the kind of listening bereaved people need only for a short period of time. The loved ones are in it 24/7, a lot of them thinking about what went wrong, reliving an accident again and again. They know it's weird to be that obsessed. But if you're just there with them, acknowledge that it is their whole life now, they appreciate the company.

Another weird thing is that they can modulate. You just ask about something mundane and they snap back to the present. They function, if only for a minute or two.

I said, "That lemonade sure looks nice."

When Mrs. Whitmore went in to get ice, I sat on the bench and positioned my notebooks so that she would take the rocker. I wanted her to be comfortable. We might be there a long time.

She poured two glasses. I tried to think of pleasantries. "What a beautiful porch."

"I clean when I can't stop thinking about it," she said.

"The drownings?"

"All of it."

"I talked to the principal and some of Peter's friends at school. I'm going to write an aftermath story, about the hole Peter left."

She drew a sharp breath.

I reached for her hand this time. "I can't begin to fathom the pain you are in. But I'm going to ask you to stick with me, even though it might add to that pain. I want to write about the difference in Peter before and after your divorce, how the pain *he* was in might have contributed to his death."

She took a while to think about it. "What do you want to know?"

"I didn't have the privilege of knowing Peter. But everything I've heard from the principal and his friends at school is that he was a smart boy. Have you had any thoughts on why he did it?"

"Tried to wade across on the old bridge? I've thought about it a thousand times. We had our problems, but you've got to believe we taught him common sense."

She stared into the distance and rocked furiously.

"Did he change, Mrs. Whitmore? Did your divorce change Peter?"

"How could it not change him? A boy lives sixteen years. He learns to pitch, ride a bike, hunt, and fish from one man. One man teaches him how to clean a rifle, teaches him how to shave, gives him advice when he wants to ask a girl out. Then it's, 'Oh, sorry, turns out I don't love your mother.' Sixteen years, he's there for every lost tooth and sprained ankle, and then one week, all Peter hears from his dad is a postcard from Virginia Beach where he's gone on vacation with his girlfriend."

"So Peter took it hard when his dad left?"

"No. When Raymond left, Peter didn't say a word. I was pretty caught up in my own feelings, forgive me that. The only time I really got an inkling of how bad Peter was taking it was in the spring when he went out to look for the tackle box."

"What happened?"

"I heard this pounding out in the garage. So I went in through the side and he's punching the garage door. I look over on the workbench and there's the tackle box. It's open, and most of the stuff's missing. There's just a few bobbers and some plastic worms. I guess his dad had taken all the best lures when he divided out his half."

"Were they expensive?"

"That's what I said! I said, 'Money's tight, but we can buy you whatever you need.' Peter kept pounding the door. When I tried to stop him, he said, 'Dad took all the good lures.' It had hit him finally: That part of his life was over."

"And he wasn't ready for it to be over?"

"You're not very old, but you probably know that when a man and a woman are in a relationship, you hold back a little. You don't give yourself completely. Just in case it doesn't work out, you've got to have some little part of yourself that you can return to. Kids aren't like that. Even though they see dads moving out down the street, they never think *their* dad could go."

She stopped, seemed to question if she should say more, then plowed on. "When I found out my husband was cheating, I didn't tell Peter because I wanted to work it out."

"Stand by your man?" That was the wrong thing to say. I knew it as soon as the words were out of my mouth.

"You don't have kids, do you?" She didn't wait for me to answer. "Kids make that decision easy. It wasn't about what I wanted. It was about what would keep this nice home for my only child until he graduated. It was about food and the water bill and electricity."

"Were you a stay-at-home mom?"

"I gave my family my full-time attention. And now they're both gone." Her rocking slowed. She was drifting into an emotional place, self-pity, probably.

I said, "Let's focus on Peter. Describe for me what he was like before your husband left."

"He was a real outdoorsman," she said. "I think Peter's proudest day was the first time he bagged a deer. It was a buck with a nice set of antlers. When Peter came home, he didn't tell me what he had in the truck, but he was leaping out of his skin, he was so excited to show me. Do you want to see a picture?"

I said, "Sure," and she went back into the house and returned with an eight-by-ten photo in a gleaming gold frame. There was Peter, looking nothing like the dead boy pulled from the water. His cheeks were rosy; his smile stretched the downy beginning of a moustache.

I tried not to look at the dead deer.

"We ate venison for breakfast, lunch, and dinner that week. I've probably still got a few of those steaks in the freezer."

I wanted to keep her on task. "So, he was outdoorsy. What else?"

"He was smart. People-smart. He could read people pretty well."

"But he skipped school."

"Just to hunt. He got decent grades. Do you want to see?"

She disappeared into the house again. I had some qualms about what was coming next. I was going to have to ask about Peter's drinking, and about the accident. There was a good chance he was not going to come off in my story as the good kid Mrs. Whitmore was presenting. But I noticed that when she came out with a large shoebox, her feet weren't stuck in the sad shuffle I had noticed when I first met her. Talking to me, I think, was helping her make sense of what happened. Or at least put it in perspective.

Mrs. Whitmore hesitated.

"He was a sentimental packrat. I guess boys don't scrap. He kept everything in shoeboxes under his bed."

It was actually a boot box, but I caught myself before I corrected her. I said, "Lyalts?"

"His latest acquisition. He got them last month. Expensive boots."

She sat back in the rocker with the big box on her lap. Everything about her was a contrast to the angry rocking just a few minutes earlier. It was as if she was balanced between the irrational raw stage of grief and the acceptance of reality that comes next. The box was somehow part of that step.

She shook her head. "I can't open it. We were a family that respected each other's privacy."

Slowly, I leaned over and put my hands on the sides of the box.

"People need to know," I said, "the details are what will make it real enough for other parents to think the same thing might happen to their kid."

Her tears started silently then turned to great hiccupping sobs.

"Can I see what's in here?"

She nodded. "Be careful. That's all that's left of my baby."

Gently, I took the box and lifted the lid. Inside was a stack of photos, a postcard, Peter's fall semester grade report, and a spiral-bound notebook.

I picked up the grades.

Mrs. Whitmore said, "He got an A in shop, an A in phys ed, and an A in health. Most of the rest are Bs."

I looked at the notation for attendance. "He only had three absences fall semester."

"That was at the start of hunting season."

"So he wasn't a truant?"

"No."

I didn't know how to ease into my next question, but she seemed to have pulled herself together. "Did Peter have a drinking problem?"

"I wouldn't call it a problem. It's a rite of passage. You know, first deer, first beer."

"But he was in that fatal crash."

"That shook him up. That's for sure."

"Tell me about that day."

"The Saturday before Memorial Day. I was worried sick about him because he hadn't come home the night before. I know kids act out, and I knew he was drinking. But when the police cruiser pulled up, I feared the worst. Officer Kellan came to the door first. He said, 'Pete's been in an accident. He's okay, but he's a little shaken up.' He said it would be best to let him rest."

"What was Peter like when he came in?"

"He didn't say anything. In fact, he didn't tell me for a couple days that the other driver had been killed. When I called the police station after he finally did tell me, Sugar said it had been taken care of."

"What did you take that to mean?"

"I wanted to know if there were going to be charges against my son. I'd asked Peter if he was drunk and he wouldn't say."

"Do you think he was?"

"He had gone to a kegger. But I'd like to think he wasn't drunk when he got behind the wheel. I mean, he was a good boy. We taught him common sense."

"What about drugs, Mrs. Whitmore? Do you think it was possible that Peter got mixed up with kids who were doing drugs?"

There was a very long silence. "You're not from here," she finally said. "Kids here don't use drugs."

I looked down into the box. The top photo on the pile showed a group of happy kids in front of a tent. I opened the notebook. The first page had a date at the top. Every line was filled with a loping cursive. My heartbeat quickened. I wanted to be alone with that notebook.

"Can I borrow this box, Mrs. Whitmore? I think our photographer could use these mementos to make a nice photo illustration."

She bit her lip and tapped her fingers together quickly. Her eyes welling up, she whispered, "Promise to take good care of it?"

I remembered what she'd said about this being all that was left of her son. I pressed my lips together and nodded.

"Don't you want the photo with the buck, too?"

"Of course."

Chapter 21

It was two o'clock when I carried the box into the newsroom.

"So you liked the A-OK Corral?" Kim teased.

I gave her a quizzical look.

"You bought boots. You're trying to look more like a local, right? I like that, 'Putting down roots.'"

I said, "The boot box is for a story on one of the kids who drowned."

The giggle left Kim's voice. "One of them was wearing boots when he drowned, wasn't he?"

"Peter Whitmore was. But the physics, what held him under, there's not a lot to be learned from that. I'm trying to figure out if there's some bigger lesson. Remember, like we talked about? News you can use? I'm thinking the angle is what turns a good kid bad. His dad walked out just before Christmas."

Kim said, "Kids die in a small town. Farm accidents, hunting accidents. You'll get used to it after a few years here."

"I don't think this one was unforeseeable. He changed after his dad left. He started skipping school, he started drinking, and he was in a fatal drunk driving accident."

Kim didn't remember the fatal.

"It was the Saturday before Memorial Day. You rolled it into an accident roundup story."

"They all run together in my mind."

"The boy's mom said he didn't act out after his dad left, but she knew he was drinking."

I could see Kim was starting to grasp my vision of the story. She said, "Divorce is real hard for kids," in a way that suggested it was something she had thought about a great deal. "But how do you write about that without it just being a public airing of one family's dirty laundry?"

I told Kim about a precision journalism story in the *Pioneer-Press* that compared children's test scores before and after a divorce.

She said, "It would take years to get that kind of access in a school."

"I know. The principal at the high school likes me, but no educator is going to go on the record about the things parents do that send their kids off the deep end."

Kim motioned to Frank, who was on his phone at the back of the newsroom. "I'll try to soften the ground with him. He's going to say it's not anybody's business, it's personal."

"'The personal is political.'"

Kim considered for a minute. "It is, isn't it?"

She asked how I was sourcing the story. "Any good quotes at the school?"

"All the principal said was that the boys liked to fish, and they were nice kids. I talked to three of their friends. One witnessed the first boy jumping the fence, but not him falling in."

Kim frowned. "It sounds kind of speculative."

"No," I tapped the box, "not speculative at all. I've got Peter's journal."

Kim whistled. "How did you get that?"

"I just asked to borrow it."

I felt like doing a victory dance. I couldn't think of a better story to submit for a Silverton. *I had the kid's diary!* I set a couple of the snapshots from the box on my desk and got out the journal.

The *Daily-Observer* had three copy machines, the coin-op one in the front by the reception desk for people who came in off the street wanting something from a past issue, the newsroom's old Xerox, and the big machine in the ad department's copy room.

Call me paranoid, but I feared Mrs. Whitmore might demand the box back at any time. So, before I started writing, I set up on the newsroom Xerox to copy every page from the diary. It was a hundred-page notebook, and Peter had filled each sheet on both sides.

The sound of the Xerox machine took me back to those days when I had to make dozens of copies of my résumé. You press the button, and the camera makes a slow pass under the document. There's no way to speed up the process. You position the document, press, and wait.

I was standing at the Xerox, relaxing into its rhythm, when Kim came over and lifted a page out of the tray.

When I explained that Mrs. Whitmore had only loaned me Peter's diary, Kim said, "You can't copy that whole thing. Our fiscal year ends at the end of June. The newsroom is already over budget."

"This would cost less than twenty dollars at Kinko's."

"I can't get the weather radio fixed until next month. Every expense that can be delayed has to wait until July. And you can't say this is a necessary expense. Why are you even copying it?"

"I told Mrs. Whitmore I would return it tomorrow. I won't have time to read it before then."

"You're not going to use it for more than one story. You don't need every word."

I had to remind myself that Kim had not had the benefit of working in a newsroom with a Pulitzer winner. She wasn't accustomed to mining information, being able to give stories the follow-up they deserved. I decided not to make a speech. Instead, I said, "We agreed to back each other up in the newsroom."

Kim said, "Okay. I don't understand why you need it. But could you at least do it on the ad department's copier? They'll all be gone at five."

Kim wasn't asking for much. And she was my boss.

She picked up another sheet from the stack of copies. "Penmanship wasn't his best subject."

I showed her one of the first pages. "The early stuff is easier to read. But as you flip through, his handwriting changes."

She shrugged. "Probably drunk."

⟁

I squeezed in the obligatory interview with the father. Didn't get much, but he, like his ex-wife, was on board with the story idea.

"Peter was a good boy. Something changed," was the best quote I got from him.

It was a little after four when I got back to the newsroom.

Kim said she had "buttered up" Frank for me and he was willing to put the story on the front page.

"Can you have it done by five?"

I had assumed I would have most of the evening to craft the story. An hour wasn't a lot of time, but if this was going to be a Silverton contender, it needed to go on page one.

So I flew to my computer. My first instinct was to invoke Mrs. Whitmore's hands: dusting, mopping, and pruning. But fifteen minutes into it, I pulled back. The lead for the drowning story was the mothers, how they wailed. This story was more about a boy failing at manly pursuits—driving and fishing—in the absence of his father.

The boots seemed like a better metaphor, something cocky the teen had put on, trying out a new identity. All teens experiment a little. What made it deadly for Peter? Not having a dad present to rein him in?

I paged through the diary, scanning for anything that dealt with his parents' breakup. The entries started angry, then turned despondent. He'd found some new friends spring semester. Apparently Darnell Kellan had stepped into a mentoring role with him at the school. But the details of Peter's day-to-day life were crowded out by increasing self-loathing.

The problem was that Peter wasn't especially articulate. At his darkest moments he quoted song lyrics from Black Sabbath and David Lee Roth. I thumbed past a series of pages that were completely black, one thin ballpoint pen line after another. That must have taken hours to fill. If I had had more time, that would be a nice detail to work into the story. But I didn't have time. I had to find useful passages and get them into the story fast.

Use what you've got, I told myself.

What I had was the box.

⌁

Pat Whitmore's hands trembled on the lid of a Lyalt boot box. Her 16-year-old son, Peter, got the boots shortly before killing a man while driving drunk, then just days later Peter skipped school to go on a fishing trip that would take his life.

Pat Whitmore said Peter changed rapidly in the six months before he and his friend Mason Carnegie drowned. She said she thinks he became despondent after his father left her for another woman.

"He was a teenage boy. I think all the sadness and grief that he couldn't express, I think it came out in recklessness."

Pat Whitmore can't bear to open the lid of that box to find out for sure.

"Be careful. That's all that's left of my baby," she pleaded as she handed over the box she pulled from under Peter's bed.

Inside, snapshots of happy teenagers nestled against a journal that told a darker story. Why did Pat Whitmore allow a reporter to open the box?

"This could happen in any family," she said. "People have no idea how hard divorce hits kids. Peter went from getting mostly As and Bs at school to Ds in everything. He started drinking. He was so sad, but he couldn't talk about it. He didn't have the words."

Pat Whitmore said she would give anything to be able to hold her son again, but since she can't, she wants other parents to know what her boy went through. "Nobody would want the life I've had this past year," Pat said and began to rock in the same chair she had used to nurse Peter 16 years ago. "I wish I had known how much pain he was in," she said. "I would have done something."

Peter's father, Raymond Whitmore, fought with Pat about money and how to divide their belongings. But on one thing, he agrees with his ex: They should have paid closer attention to their son.

What can parents do? Psychologists say each child experiences divorce differently. What was hard for Peter, according to Pat Whitmore, was that his dad said he would always be there for him, but then didn't have time for the things they used to enjoy doing together, like fishing and fixing cars.

Peter said it this way in red marker on January 23: "He says he loves me but he's never around. He says that's easiest for Mom, but what are we supposed to do? Talk about all the same things we always talked about? Over lunch at McDonald's? We're there all of 20 minutes, if that. His girlfriend doesn't want me around. If I touch anything in their apartment, she comes back and straightens it two seconds later. He says she'll get used to me over time. I want to punch the bitch. I want to punch him, too, slap some sense into him."

I gave Kim my seat so she could read the story on my monitor. "What do you think?"

She nodded as she read the words on the screen. "This is really good," she said when she finished, "but you can't call someone a bitch in a family newspaper."

"I'm not saying she's a bitch. It's just how she looks through the boy's eyes."

Kim shook her head. "It portrays her in a negative light."

"I don't name her."

"Anybody in town could figure out who she is. It's a libel suit risk. I understand what you're shooting for, but this really is airing dirty laundry."

"No, it's one family that is an example of a public issue: How divorce changes kids. One man and two kids are dead, arguably because these two parents were too focused on themselves to notice what was going on with their son."

"I don't think you can make that argument."

"I don't. The mom does."

Kim re-read it. "I'm not saying it's a bad story. Just the opposite. It's great. I can't believe that you got that diary. But it's not the kind of story that we run."

"The town mothers need to know."

Kim swallowed hard. "To make it in this business, you've got to compromise. Frank won't put the word 'bitch' in the paper. And it would be best not to mention the girlfriend at all, unless you give her a chance to comment."

Keep your eyes on the Silverton, I told myself. *The girlfriend isn't important to the story. If that little change gets the story in the paper, it's worth it.*

I pulled my keyboard to where I was leaning against the desk.

The deletions left a shorter quote on the screen. *We're there all of 20 minutes, if that. . . . I want to punch him . . . slap some sense into him.*

"That's better," Kim said, "but the father comes off looking pretty bad, too."

This I had thought of. "I got a release," I told her, pulling my notepad out of my bag. I found the page signed Raymond P. Whitmore. "See? Consent."

"How in the world did you get that?"

"The man is turned inside out with grief. He had no idea." I flipped to the page with Mr. Whitmore's quotes. "'I thought we were doing pretty well maintaining the father–son thing.'"

"Did you show him the diary?"

"He didn't want to look at it. He said he wanted to respect his son's privacy."

"But he was okay with you putting it in the newspaper?"

"It wasn't his decision. The diary wasn't his property."

"Did you tell him the gist of the story?"

"That the divorce precipitated a big change in Peter's behavior? Yes. He wanted it in the paper as much as his ex did."

Kim seemed surprised but also pleased.

I said, "You know what's funny? When I was scheduling the interview with Mr. Whitmore, I thought he was the villain. But he was just clueless. He said he thought everything was fine with Peter."

When Frank came back, Kim had him read the story. "This is like something from the *Ladies Home Journal*," he complained.

I said, "Do you have a problem with stories that appeal to women? Over fifty-one percent of the US population is female, you know. Not half—fifty-*one* percent."

Kim cleared her throat. "When Jed was up, he mentioned the chain's market research shows advertisers want their ads next to stories of interest to parents. He said women make most of the purchases in most families."

Frank perked up. "Jed said that?"

"When you were on a phone call, yes he did."

Frank twisted around to face me. "It just looks like people's personal problems to me. Why do you want to blame the kid drowning on his father? The kid was a truant who ignored a clear warning sign. That's the whole story."

Kim cleared her throat again. "The personal is political," she said, "when it's part of a trend. Half of marriages end in divorce now. Parents should know what might happen to their kids if they split up. I'm a parent. I want to know."

Frank rubbed the back of his neck. "We've got nothing else for the front page." He turned and pointed his cigarette at me. "But from here on out, stick to facts."

I said, "These are facts: accurate quotes and entries from the boy's journal."

Kim hissed in my ear, "Don't push it."

I wanted to finish copying the diary, but since I'd been working since eight a.m., Kim sent me home. She walked me to the door and promised to call when the paper was done. "Since you didn't want a cake, I'll take you out for a beer."

The first thing I wanted to do was tell Blue about my story. But when I called over to the firehouse, Curtis told me he was out of town again.

Blue called back minutes later. I could hear traffic in the background.

"What do you need?"

I wanted to tell Blue I had hit a story out of the park. But that didn't fit the "just sex" compartment I had for him. So, I said, "I wanted to know when we could go over that information for the feature on antique firefighting equipment."

"Oh." He paused. "I'm on a pay phone. I'll be back in a few days."

A recording of an operator came on and demanded fifty cents. Blue didn't have it. "We'll talk soon," was all he managed before the line went dead.

⚓

So, my celebration was that beer with Kim.

"These are both on me," she told the bartender at the A-OK. She seemed as happy as I was about the story.

"Thanks for backing me up with Frank."

Kim raised her glass. "To a Silverton contender."

I said, "It was only by sticking together that we got it in."

"You've just got to know how to navigate Frank," Kim said, and we clinked glasses.

⚓

I took the boot box back to Mrs. Whitmore first thing the next day. It seemed like the right thing to do, to build trust. I could get the diary again later if I needed it. Mrs. Whitmore asked me to mail her a copy of the story.

"I had to let go of my subscription."

I didn't tell her, but I didn't subscribe either.

⚓

I went into the office to pick up some copies of the paper for my clip file. Kim met me at the door. I could tell from the look on her face that something was wrong.

I grabbed a copy of the paper from the wire single-issue rack next to the front door.

Frank had changed the lead, inserting a deflating waffle word.

Pat Whitmore's hands trembled on the lid of a Lyalt boot box. Her 16-year-old son, Peter, got the boots shortly before a man was killed in an alleged drunk driving incident, then skipping school for the fishing trip that would take Peter's life.

I wanted to, as Wassle would say, pour maple syrup on the damn thing. It made no sense. Frank's waffling passive verb made it unclear that Peter was the driver in the fatal DUI, and then the gerund in the phrase about the fishing trip was weird. He took out the line about her rocking in the same chair she had used to nurse Peter when he was a baby. There were other changes, but it was the lead that took my story out of the competition for a Silverton.

"Sorry," Kim whispered.

I looked at the desk where I had turned on the afterburners to get that story done in an hour.

It was a good thing Frank was out on Charles's boat, because at that moment, I wanted to punch him. I also wanted to tear off his keyboard so he could never ruin another lead.

Chapter 22

When I went in for my shift, Kim said, "About the apartment . . ." She walked me through the swinging saloon-style doors back to the layout room.

"I couldn't fit this in the Weekender classifieds." She winked.

The tiny ad she pointed to on the light board said *Fisherman's paradise, $200. Baited pier. Pets negotiable.*

The landlord sounded hesitant on the phone.

"It's pretty rustic."

"If it has water and electricity, I'm interested."

We met in front of the small white structure that sat close to the road.

"It's mostly been a fishing camp. I don't know as it's a place for no woman."

Inside, I was so overcome that I had to sit down. It was just one room, a big octagon. It had an apartment-style kitchen on one wall and a couch and reclining rocker against the wall closest to the road.

The landlord blushed when I said I loved it.

"I built it from a yurt kit," he said. "But the extra windows were my wife's idea."

Because the house was built at the top of a steep ravine, the windows looked right into the tops of the trees. While the landlord apologized that there was no dishwasher, I was gazing out at a robin feeding her chicks in a nest three feet away.

"I'll take it."

"I want two hundred a month."

"Including utilities?"

He rubbed the back of his neck. "Do you have a boyfriend?"

"No."

"You planning to entertain a lot of houseguests?"

"No."

"It's yours."

As soon as the landlord was gone, I raced down to my pier on the river, counting each step as I ran. I was delirious with the knowledge that I'd found this wooded retreat, three acres of tall trees and flowering weeds, less than five minutes from town.

I sat on my pier for a long time, taking in every cattail and log. There's something really special about Indiana, and people who have not lived in the state can't begin to understand it. Yes, there's beauty in mountains and oceans. But the pink of an Indiana sunset, reflected in repeating ripples on a river? That's the softest, most comforting color there is.

Blue was all business when I showed up at the fire station. "There was a bomb found in the night dispatcher's mailbox. When the incident report comes back, it's going to say it was a pipe bomb, like the ones kids make with gunpowder. It wasn't. Whoever made that bomb knew what they were doing, and they could have killed someone."

When I saw the way he looked around to see if any of the other firefighters were listening, I made sure I wrote down every word.

"Why is the police report going to say it was a pipe bomb?" I asked.

"Because one of those monkeys wrote it," he said.

Later, I called Blue and invited myself to his place for dinner. I wanted to find out more about the bomb, but after running through my 5W questions twice, I could see I wasn't going to get anything more from him than what he had said at the fire station.

"Set your pad down," he said, pushing back from the table. "Do you like Olivia Newton-John?"

He got out her *Have You Never Been Mellow* album and played the title track.

We stood together and I swayed with him, feeling the questions sear even though her voice was as delicate as spun sugar. When she sang the line about letting someone else be strong, Blue squeezed me.

"What?" I asked in response to the gesture.

"Lean on me. I know people here. Let me introduce you. I could make your job a lot easier,"

I wrapped his arms around my torso and pushed my back into him. When the song was over, Blue softly rubbed his bristly chin on the back of my neck.

Chapter 23

The incident report on the bomb took a couple days to come through, and then it was vague on every detail. I asked Sugar if the intended victim was the night dispatcher. She fixed me with a stare.

"What makes you think it was for the dispatcher? Probably her kid pissed somebody off at school."

Kim had the evening off to go to a parent-teacher conference, so it was Frank who edited my bomb story.

"I'm not interested in a story with an unnamed source," he fumed. "Some kids made a pipe bomb. So what?"

"It wasn't a pipe bomb."

"How do you know?"

I had written around that question. My story, admittedly, was as vague as the incident report, which Frank said was dated. He buried the story on page seven, then stalked over to my desk.

"I'm tired of this crap. There's always some reason you don't come back with a story. The superintendent's wife froze you out. The secret source doesn't want to go on the record. You've got a degree in journalism—didn't they teach you at that fancy college that you're supposed to go out and get a story? You don't come back to the newsroom empty-handed with some explanation that defies logic.

Frank stabbed the air with his cigarette. "Count: We've got two news reporters, you and Charles. Kim covers the city council and the county board, but that's only once a month for each of them. We print eight pages. Eight. I'm not paying you so I can run press releases and wire service copy. I want two stories and a photo with a caption every day. No more of this tried-and-failed. If it's not in the paper, it's not news. And if there's no news in the paper, we can't sell ads."

I said, "You seem angry."

"Damn straight I'm angry. I can't believe we've sunk so much money into you!"

I think I would have reacted more strongly to Frank's diatribe if I hadn't been so looking forward to seeing Blue.

My mind kept flashing on his hair, his hands, his arms. He was strong, which I suppose all firefighters are. The upper body strength requirement is how a lot of fire departments keep women out. But in him, I imagined, strength was more about not letting go. If Blue found you in a burning building, he would not let go until you were safe.

I kept sketching in details like that, which was not my usual MO.

I called him at the firehouse and said I could come by "to work on that feature."

Blue must have heard me coming up the firehouse stairs because the TV was off when I entered.

"Where is everybody?"

"Most of them are checking for a gas leak at a house where it's never really a gas leak. I suggested it would be a good time to give the trainee practice with an elderly paranoid. Curtis is doing laundry."

I smiled and Blue grabbed my hand. Without a word, he led me toward the storage room.

When we got to the door, he pulled me close to him. I could smell smoke and canned corn as his eyes searched my face. "Is this what you want?" he asked.

I stayed in character. "It will be a fascinating story."

Blue said, "There's nobody else here," then quickly looked away. "I was hoping . . ." He was trying for a glib tone, but it didn't sound natural. "Make yourself comfortable," is what he finally said. "I'll be right back."

How do you make yourself comfortable on a trampoline? The first time we had entered that room, we were so lit up, any surface would do. But now I had time to look carefully at the trampoline. The fabric had yellowed. The red X was faded, but it still seemed to shout, *If you have to jump, this is a safe place to land.*

I imagined the young women at the Triangle Shirtwaist Factory, locked in as fire raged around them. Had there been a trampoline? Was anybody there to catch them?

The stretched material wasn't thick, and yet, pulled taut, all that tension transferred from the springs could save lives.

I surveyed the room. Ordinary discards like file cabinets and torch lamps stood next to long-handled hatchets and oxygen tanks. The room smelled like rubber boots and sweat.

I could smell Blue coming in. "Polo."

"You don't like it?"

"It's fine. You just don't seem the type."

"It's what was in the cabinet," he said.

There was a fumbled moment. I should have told him the cologne smelled good. I should have said I liked it. We stood there, each contemplating how we would get on the trampoline. I remembered from gym class that you don't touch the springs. I hoisted my body up with my arms, then swung my legs up to the metal frame. Blue had a more fluid movement.

He stood, shaky at first, then stooped to pick me up. We fell together, hair flying, to the center of the trampoline.

"X marks the spot," he said.

It sounded like a line. "You've said that before, haven't you?"

"We all have."

"We who?"

"Firefighters, darlin'. It's one of the benefits of the job. Women like us."

Suddenly creative, daring, and sexy started to feel like somebody else's cliché. "So, others have done what we're doing now?"

"The tramp does figure heavily into firefighter lore, yes."

I heard footsteps on the stairs and sat upright. "This is not a good idea."

"That's just Curtis. He is not going to bother us."

"Technically, I'm still at work," I whispered.

"So am I," Blue whispered back. "But as far as Curtis is concerned, you're a reporter having a private conversation with a source."

"You really think he won't come back here?"

"I know he won't. If the storage room door is closed, no one comes back here."

The words just kind of hung in the air. Blue got to his knees and unbuttoned his shirt slowly. Then he brought his face close to mine and brushed my hair out of my eyes. "You wish you were the only one, don't you?"

"There's no good reason, but yeah."

"It may surprise you to learn that, in Green Meadow, I'm a hot ticket."

"Are you dating other women?"

"I've got a couple of aunts who like to set me up." He pulled me close to him. "But if you want exclusive rights, just say the word."

I did want exclusive rights, but I didn't know why. Logically, I could see that wouldn't be fair. I was planning to be gone from Green Meadow in one year. I didn't tell Blue that. Instead, I said, "I barely know you."

"My heart is an open book."

"You said 'heart.' The saying is, 'My life is an open book.'"

He pulled me back down so that we were both lying on the trampoline again, then he wormed in close, pressing his head under my arm. I ran my free hand over his head and scrunched his hair between my fingers.

"I feel like I've known you forever," I said. "But I don't know a lot about you."

He moved to put his head on my shoulder. It made the trampoline bounce.

"What do you want to know?"

"Your name, for starters. Why are you Blue?"

His face fell, but he answered. "This is a small town. We tell everyone how wonderful it is here, but some of the things you assume about small towns are true, okay?"

"Tell me," I probed.

His eyes went somewhere else. "When I was a kid, the other kids at school called me Red. I didn't know why they called me that, but it sounded like an insult. That's the way they were. For instance, there was this kid Melvin. He had bad asthma, so any kind of physical activity was an ordeal for him. When he came in last in the school's Field Day race, behind all the girls, they started calling him Swifty. And it stuck. Right up to the day he shot himself."

I said, "I proofed his obit. Melvin 'Swifty' Daubert. When I asked if the family wanted us to use the nickname, Charles said no one would know who it was if we didn't say 'Swifty.'"

"Yeah, names stick," Blue said. "I didn't like Red, so I started dressing all in blue. From my high tops to the sweatband I wore in gym class, everything was blue. Blue jeans, blue shirt, blue coat in the winter. When kids called me Red, I said, 'Are you color blind? Everything about me is blue. Call me Blue.'"

"And it stuck?"

"Not at first. But I was determined. I kept dressing that way, and after my dad died when I was in junior high, I put on a lot of weight. Some of the kids had seen the Beatles movie *Yellow Submarine*. One of my less-kind classmates said, 'He looks like one of those fat Blue Meanies.' The Blue Meanies were the villains."

"I saw the movie."

"I thought I could forge my own identity, but those kids found a way to make even the name I chose myself into an insult."

"You could change it again."

"Nah. Enough time passes, it loses its sting."

Blue took my hand in both of his. "It's my turn to ask you a question," he said. "When are you going to take me to meet your parents?"

I should have told him then that our relationship, if you could call it that, was just a temporary thing. But the truth was that my parents were somewhere in Africa and I would not see them for a year, maybe longer. So, I told him that.

"You're not close?"

I pulled back.

"Okay," Blue said. "But when you want to talk, I want to listen." When he said that, I turned to the X on the trampoline. I felt I could wrap myself in Blue's unquestioning compassion and never move again. It was a beautiful feeling, but it was new to me and I didn't know what to do with it, so I went into interviewer mode. "Why did they call you Red?"

"My mom was Indian."

"You're Native American? What tribe?"

Blue shook his head. "You've never heard of us."

"I took Native American Cultures with Jack Weatherford at Mac."

He laughed. "Then you're the expert."

"I remember there were Potawatomie and Ojibwa people in Indiana."

"Yes, there were. And there still are. My tribe was very small, and it isn't recognized by the federal government."

"Is that a blessing in disguise?"

Blue closed his eyes for a moment, then looked up at the ceiling. "No." The slowness of his gestures, the way he seemed to be trying to create distance from some heavy thing in his mind, reminded me of the day I first saw him go down to the river at that fatal fire.

I reached out and stroked his forehead.

It took Blue a while to find the words. "There's the history that kids get in school. There are the stories guys like your anthropology professor record. And then there is the truth that only the people who were there understand."

"I'm a good student. Try me."

Blue paused again. I think he was trying to decide how much to tell me. We were full-on in a lot of ways, but I had to remind myself that he barely knew me—in the conventional sense of the word.

He settled on the tourist-brochure version: "The French trappers that came to the area called us the river negotiators in their language. Our village was on the bank of the river and we were known for trading. We were an Algonquin-speaking tribe, but the French name they gave us stuck and then got shortened to Riv'nego."

"Your tribe lived on the same river that cuts through town? The one that was dammed to make Long Lake?"

Blue drew a sharp breath. "Yes."

Just then there was a tap on the door.

I grabbed my shirt. "You said no one would come back here."

Blue cleared his throat.

Two more taps.

Blue said, "Can it wait, Curtis? I'm being interviewed."

Curtis's voice came timid through the door. "Actually, I wanted to talk to Hallie. Cujo bit Scooter Mayfield after the DARE presentation up at the high school."

Blue froze.

I tried to calm him. "It's just a dog bite. How bad can it be?" Then I called to Curtis, "I'll get the incident report from Sugar. Thanks for the heads-up."

Blue said to me, "There won't be an incident report." He seemed to be making more calculations. "His mom is Dora Mayfield, the night dispatcher. She's not the most popular person at the police station."

"If the DARE dog's dangerous, it shouldn't be in the schools."

Blue said, "That dog is probably the most highly trained member of the police force."

It wasn't going to be a big story, but I had to keep the town mothers in mind. They would want to know a child got bitten by a dog inside the school.

Kim wasn't in when I got back to the office, so I had to talk to Frank.

"A dog bite? You want to do a story on a dog bite?" He took off his glasses and rubbed his eyes. "You complain that we don't do hard-hitting journalism, then you want time to write about a dog biting someone? My wife's cat scratched me last week. Is that page one?"

"The dog was Cujo, the dog the DARE officer takes into the schools. And it happened in the high school."

"Oh. I guess that is news, although the kid probably had it coming. Do a brief on it from the incident report."

"There's not an incident report."

"Talk to Sugar. She's the record custodian over at the cop shop. I thought you'd know that by now."

"There won't be an incident report."

"How do you know that?"

"The boy's mother is the night police dispatcher."

"If it's not a serious enough bite for her to file an incident report, it doesn't belong in my newspaper."

I chose not to hear that.

I called the high school principal. "I understand you had a dog bite."

"We're looking into it. Don't put anything in the paper, okay? He's a good boy."

"When a German shepherd chomps a kid in school, I wouldn't call that dog a good boy."

"I meant the Mayfield boy, Scooter. He's a good kid. Honor roller."

"I didn't say he wasn't. Did it break the skin? I imagine Cujo's up to date with the vet, so no need for a rabies shot, right?"

"You haven't seen the boy?"

"I'd like to come and get a photograph if there's anything to take a picture of."

"No. His mom would have to sign a release for that. I'm sure she won't do that. She doesn't want this to blow up."

—

When I saw Sugar on my beat check, I asked about Cujo. "Is he a drug dog?"

"Cujo is the second officer in the DARE program," she joked.

"But did he go through special training to sniff out drugs?"

"Those dogs are expensive. And the officer has to go in for training, too. Department couldn't afford that."

"So how did you get Cujo?"

"Same way Darnell got the Camaro. We seized him."

"So Cujo is not a trained K-9 unit dog?"

"You best not let Darnell hear you questioning his dog. He's kind of sensitive about Cujo." Sugar leaned in. "I think because the chief is his father, Darnell don't trust that anybody who is nice to him actually likes him. But Cujo loves him. Darnell gets a steak, Cujo gets half. He takes him right into restaurants."

Darnell seemed to be improvising an awful lot in his police work.

Chapter 24

Suddenly the steady rhythm of our bodies on the trampoline stopped.

"Why'd you quit?" I demanded.

Blue was wearing the antique fire helmet. When he sat up, the dark suspenders, flat against his chest, drew my attention to the sweat glistening on his skin. Everything about him said full speed ahead, except his expression.

Blue pulled off the helmet.

I said, "No more bouncy-bouncy?"

That soured his expression even more.

"What did I say?" I asked.

"I think it was slam it to me. 'Slam it to me, rock it, baby,' then you were on some riff about a rocket to the moon."

"And?"

"It's lonely over here, Hallie. I'm trying my best to keep it casual, try things your way. But I don't want to roger you. And I don't want to slam you or ream you. What were the other ways you said it?"

"Okay," I said, baby voice, "me no talk dirty anymore. Can we go back to—"

"I want to make love with you, Hallie. I want to tickle your soul with my soul. I want to make you want to come back for more."

"I do want more."

"More me! I want you to want more of me. I want you to want to know me better. I want you to think I'm sweet."

I gave him a lascivious once-over. "You *are* sweet."

Blue found his shirt. "Sweet in a *love*-me way. Not just a . . . whatever-this-is way."

I didn't want what Blue wanted, but I had to hear him out. "We're not just negotiating the terms of fuck here, are we?"

He flinched. "I don't like that word. It's not used by quality folk in Green Meadow."

"It is over at the cop shop."

"You make my point. But I was talking about us. Do you even want there to be an 'us'?"

"It's complicated."

He took my foot in his hands, probably because he knew I'd pull back if he took my hand. I wanted to connect with him, I really did. There was this undercurrent with him, and I wanted to let it take me out. But I *knew* how to surf to a certain kind of girlgasm.

"Why is it different with you?" I asked and immediately felt I had revealed too much.

He searched my face with his eyes as if his very life depended on the answer to that question. "Don't shut down," he begged. He kissed my forehead, his big hands hot brackets on my temples. "What's going on in there?"

"Too close." I scooted away.

"Careful," he cautioned as I made my way off the trampoline. "I love it that you're wild for firehouse sex, but don't you want to play house too?"

"Playing firehouse is pretty much my only fantasy."

A smile washed over Blue's face. "I'm safe. You can do this firehouse stuff because I'm safe. You *trust* me. Did you *trust* your boyfriends at McDonald's College like this?"

"Macalester."

"Whatever. Could you risk telling them you had this fantasy?"

"I didn't have this fantasy then."

He smiled even bigger. "Then it's me, not the uniform."

That may have been true, but I had a goal, a prize, literally, that I had to keep my eyes on. Blue was not part of my plan. I was going places. Blue was rooted here like an oak tree. Solid, waiting to drop little acorns. We certainly did not talk about that, but I could feel in his breath a love for life as he pumped into me that wasn't dirty at all. It was sweetness, an awesome goodness that was completely foreign to me.

It felt like an ultimatum: Me or love? Me or some vague pleasant—okay, *strong*, direct pleasance. Was *pleasance* even a word? I was becoming ungrammatical. I didn't know this Hallie, and I didn't trust her. I did not know what she would do next.

I said, "I'm putting my clothes back on."

Chapter 25

As I drove to Sandra's house, I realized that it was the first time anyone in Green Meadow had asked me to lunch. Sandra was cool. Okay, she was a home schooler and a fundie, but she didn't shove that down my throat.

I had been there once before, that brief visit on Memorial Day. Walking up to the house in the daylight, I saw the paint on the porch was peeling.

Sandra greeted me with a dishtowel tucked into the waist of her jeans. Her son scooted his chair back from the table and made his way over. "Pleased to make your acquaintance," Matthew mumbled. Behind his round glasses I could see he had Sandra's dark eyes. His dark hair stood up in a crew cut.

"What a charmer," I whispered to Sandra.

She gave me a tour. It was the house her husband had grown up in. His childhood bedroom was now Matthew's, complete with a model solar system hanging from the ceiling.

"Do you like outer space?" I asked him when we returned to the dining room.

"I've never been, but I'd like to go." He winked at me. Winking must have been a new thing for him, because it appeared he did it with great effort.

I asked, "How old are you?"

"Ten and six twelfths."

Sandra said, "Can you reduce that?"

"Yes, I can. Ten and one-half."

When Matthew left to wash his hands, I turned to Sandra, "This is a kid who was getting bad grades?"

She nodded. "Sometimes I worry I'm not smart enough to teach him much longer. We've blown through most of what our little library has to offer. I'm thinking about getting a P.O. box in Indianapolis so we can check out books there."

She ushered me to the table, laden with whole-wheat spaghetti topped with a Neapolitan puttanesca sauce. Sandra said she made it with tomatoes from her garden.

After the dishes were cleared, Sandra and I got on the porch swing.

"How high can this go?"

"So high it'll fly off the hooks," she laughed, and we started pumping hard.

"You ever flown off the hooks?"

"Once."

"Did you get hurt?"

"Nothing hurts when you're seventeen and in love."

"Was that with Matthew's dad?"

Sandra said, "Yep," and pressed her lips together. I could feel the intensity with which she savored the scene in her mind.

"Remind me what he does."

"Did. He was a Marine. He was killed in Lebanon when Matthew was little." It came out as just an unhappy fact of life.

"Neither of you went to college?"

"Nobody from Green Meadow goes to college," Sandra snorted. "The girls get pregnant on prom night and the boys do the right thing. Can't we talk about the food? Or the weather?"

"The food was wonderful," I said, pushing the swing back with my feet. "I don't think I've ever actually liked capers before. Is that really what you want to talk about?"

"No. It's just that you have this way of zeroing in on the big stuff. Like with Matthew. How did you know to ask about space travel?"

"He's got a solar system hanging from his ceiling and a space shuttle that he made out of balsa wood. It's just like when you go into somebody's office. You look for the things that repeat. Owl figurines or pictures of themselves skydiving."

"What repeats in Frank's office," Sandra sneered, "pictures of former route carriers lining up to sell plasma?"

"The only thing that repeats is the TR-7—four pictures of that car, one of himself holding the keys on the day he got it, and a little model he pushes around."

Sandra said, "TR-7s are expensive."

"They say men get sports cars to compensate—"

Sandra laughed.

I asked, "Why do *you* hate him?"

"I hate him vicariously for you."

"That's not the correct way to use vicariously."

Sandra stopped pumping and the swing made a crazy lurch. "You know, people hate it when you correct their grammar."

"I'm not correcting your grammar. I'm correcting the way you used the word vicariously."

"You corrected me when you knew darn well what I meant."

She seemed to really be mad.

"It's just something I do. I'm a word person. It's like Matthew prattling on about the space shuttle."

"Matthew's a kid, if you hadn't noticed."

"But you tolerate it. If you can tolerate his weird kid stuff, why can't you tolerate this thing with me?"

"I do tolerate it. But if we're going to be friends, you should know I don't like it. And for the record, Matthew works really hard on his issues. He has trouble gauging how interested other people are, so he's really polite and he actively tracks when they change the subject."

"You changed the subject," I said. "Why do you hate Frank?"

"You know I was a carrier, right?"

"You were a *Daily-Observer* carrier?"

"You should see your face. You look like I just dropped from lower-middle class to lower-lower class."

"It does seem beneath you."

"What other job can you do in your pajamas? I was done, showered, and able to make Matthew a hot breakfast before eight every morning. Those routes were a good way for parents to earn three hundred bucks a month. A lot of families depended on that."

"But Frank—"

"Yep. New Year's Day. When the carriers got in to load our papers, there was a stack of envelopes on the circulation manager's desk. Frank was there. He tapped the pile and told us to come back to the building when we were done with our routes. When we got back, Frank asked us each what our name was and then the circ manager handed us an envelope."

I could see from Sandra's face that she was still bitter.

"I got out to my car and ripped that thing open, thinking it was the bonus we didn't get at Christmas. But it was just a two-paragraph letter stating that I would no longer be working as a carrier and I was ineligible to file for unemployment."

"I thought I was the only one who had a problem with Frank."

"No, everyone hates that guy. Get this: The second paragraph invited us to join the *Daily Zero*'s 'family of postal subscribers.'"

"Wow."

"He gives tours, he brings school groups and people from the Chamber of Commerce in, stands right where we load the ZIP bundles on the pallets, and says what a cost savings it was to eliminate the carriers. Every single person who's working as a stuffer used to be a carrier." Sandra's hands curled into fists. "He doesn't recognize us. We were just a red number on a spreadsheet to him."

"I hate the bastard," she said, voice dropping low. "That was Matthew's college fund."

I looked at my watch. It was almost time to go in to work. But when I thanked Sandra for the meal, it was clear there was something she still wanted to talk about.

"The reporter who left was working on a story with my brother-in-law, Luke," she said. "I told him I would find out if you were trustworthy, to see if he could talk to you about it."

"I never called him," I confessed.

"I know."

"But you invited me anyway. What's the story?"

"Ask Luke. Something at the truck factory."

"Trojan is part of Charles's business beat. He's pretty territorial."

The fact that Sandra was trying to get me to do a story made her invitation make sense. But even if I wasn't going to write the story she wanted, I still wanted Sandra as a friend. So, I decided to go deep. "I need some sex advice."

"From an old widow?"

"From someone who lives in Green Meadow."

"The Bible says you should wait until marriage."

I raised an eyebrow. "You didn't."

"Touché. What do you need to know?"

"This guy is really hot."

"And he lives in Green Meadow?" she yucked. "Alert the media!"

"We've been sneaking around."

Sandra recoiled. "He has a wife?"

"No. I wouldn't do that to another woman. Sneaking around because it's fun. Sex in unusual places, no subjugation . . ."

"What?"

"Nobody's being dominated. We've just played around with some stuff at the fire station. Suspenders, uniforms—"

Sandra shot up from the swing. "Oh good lord, what's his name?"

"Blue—"

"Do not tell me another detail!" She pressed her hands to her head. "Oh my God. I'm going to have to wash out my ears."

"Um, you're making me feel kind of sleazy."

"Blue is my cousin!"

At that moment, I understood what people meant when they said, "It's a small town," as if that explained everything.

Chapter 26

I met Blue behind the fire station.

"Let's go to your place for a change," he said.

"I like your place."

His face clouded over. "You've never brought me back to your place. It's like we only exist in my apartment and sneaking in a quickie at work. Maybe we're not real. Maybe we should just—"

I turned to face him head on. "What is this about?"

"I feel like you're ashamed of me."

"I can't let people at work know. But I am not ashamed of you."

He put his hands on both of my shoulders. "Let me in," he pleaded.

"Tell you what," I said. "I'll make you dinner. But no judgment."

We drove to my house in separate cars. As I rushed to fold the couch bed in and take the dirty clothes off the recliner, I saw that I had almost nothing: a lamp the landlord left that dated from the 1970s and two dirty plates soaking in the sink.

Blue didn't knock. When he stepped across the threshold his hair grazed the lintel. I watched him walk clockwise around the room, stopping at every window.

"You live in a hogan."

"I've never thought of it that way."

He kissed me with his whole body, wrapped himself around me, no asking, no hesitation. "Why didn't you want me here?"

I looked down at the floor. "I don't really have the equipment for entertaining. I've got one pillow. I don't own any sheets."

He lifted my chin with the gentlest touch. "Did you think I would care?" His eyes raced back and forth. "Who are you? Where's my Hallie?"

I pulled back. "I can make pasta. If you want sauce, we'll have to go to the store."

"What would you have if I wasn't here?"

"I'd cook corn on the cob in the microwave and squeeze lemon on it."

"Then let's have that."

Blue watched with fascination as I wrapped the two ears of corn in a wet dish towel and put them in the microwave.

There was the awkwardness of the table. I had only one chair, and even if we moved the table over to the couch, it was too low to be comfortable for eating. Before Blue could find a silver lining, I said, "Let me show you something."

With an ear of corn in one hand and his hand in the other, I led him outside and down the three hundred stairs to my pier. The sky reflected pink on the surface of the water. As the moon closed in on us, I could see Blue for who he really was—so able to see the good in me.

＊＊＊

I stopped by the cop shop late to talk to Dora Mayfield. "Did Sugar forget to give you a report or something?"

I said, "Actually, I came to talk to you."

Dora's eyes went dark.

"About the dog bite."

Dora shook her head. She seemed to be afraid of something much bigger than me. "He's going to be okay. He'll be back at school in a few days."

"What happened?"

Dora looked away. I could see her profile in the reflection in the security window. She bit her lip and then closed her eyes, rocking almost imperceptibly. When she turned back to me, there was none of the usual zipped-up-source animosity I was expecting.

"This is my job," she said. "I'm trying my best to hang on to it."

"Do you think they'd fire you if you made a complaint against Cujo? If the dog is that dangerous, he needs to be retired. Or put down."

Dora ran her hand across the switches on the dispatch console. They were all down. "It wasn't the dog," she said. "No offense, but you've got to get out of here."

I wrote down my phone number. When I handed it to her, I said, "Other kids could get bitten, you know."

As soon as I got home, the phone rang.

"Dora called me. She said you came by on her shift," Blue said.

"She wouldn't tell me a thing."

"Of course not. She's a police dispatcher. Listen, you can't put anything in the paper. Dora's afraid you're going to write a story about it."

"A dog that's brought into the schools as part of the DARE program bites a student so badly that the kid has to miss school? If the dog is wild like that, you better believe I'm writing a story."

"That dog is the most highly trained member of that police force."

"That may be a joke around the fire station, but I asked Sugar about Cujo. He's just a guard dog they seized."

Blue cut me off. "I'm working on getting Dora to talk to you. I think it's a bigger story than a dog biting someone."

"This isn't making sense. Why did Dora call you?"

"Do you remember I told you I was a member of an Indian tribe? Dora is a member, too."

My judgment was clouded. I see that. Blue asked me not to write a story, at least not right away. He was the only person in Green Meadow I felt I could trust absolutely, and my gut told me he would not abuse that trust. But what would cause a DARE officer to let a dog attack a student?

There was something there. I tried to think of how I could fit the interviews I had done into a bigger story. Darnell, the chief's son, in a job that was too big for him, was really the same problem I saw with Mrs. Quidley. Darnell was so ineffectual as the truant officer that two kids drowned during school hours. And then the dog he supposedly had complete control over attacked an honor student. Frank would not let me use the word incompetent, but I could lay out these parallel stories and let the readers decide whether nepotism was a good thing in their schools or on the police force. *Scooter Mayfield*, I thought, *might have some choice words on the subject.*

I got up early to see if I could catch Scooter Mayfield on his way to school. I found his photo in the *Daily-Observer*'s copy of the Green Meadow High yearbook while I waited outside the school in my Chevette. He had his mother's dark hair and high cheekbones. His class had voted him "most studious," which augured well for me. Smart kids and kids who got good grades were usually pretty compliant when I wanted to interview them.

A dark-haired boy, tall, with his wrist in an Ace bandage, passed by.

"Scooter Mayfield?" I called out the window, trying to sound authoritative.

The boy turned. "He's up ahead. I can get him for you."

I got out of my car and the tall boy disappeared beyond the line of yellow school buses. When I saw him again, he was pushing another dark-haired boy in a wheelchair.

"She's probably with the DEA," I could hear the tall boy saying as he wheeled Scooter up.

Scooter held up a bandaged hand to me. "I didn't do anything. I don't use drugs. I don't sell drugs. It wasn't me."

This happens sometimes. You go to interview someone about one thing, and before you even identify yourself, they tell you about a story you didn't know about.

I thanked the tall boy and told him he could go. Scooter looked like he didn't want to be left alone with me, but when the bell rang, the other boy sprinted.

I counted six large gauze pads on Scooter's neck, hand, and arm. "Can you tell me what happened?"

"The DARE guy—"

"Officer Kellan?"

"We just call him Darnell," Scooter said, a note of derision in his voice. "He was walking with the principal, leading the DARE dog down the hall and the dog stopped in front of my locker. I was coming out of the bathroom and I saw them. Darnell said, 'Do you smell something, Cujo?'"

Any kid who was caught with drugs in his locker would try to make up a cover story. I tried to gauge whether Scooter was lying. The story sounded like he had told it many times, but he didn't blink a lot or do any of the gestures that can indicate a source is lying. Quite the opposite. The boy's eyes widened as he said, "I walked out of the bathroom and the principal saw me. I said, 'That's my locker, Darnell,' and Darnell said to the principal, 'There's reasonable suspicion here.'

"The principal says, 'This has to be a mistake.' And I said, 'There's no drugs in there unless you put them there, Darnell.' He got right in my face. He said,

'Nobody talks to me like that,' and then he did something with his hand and the dog—"

The boy reached for his neck with the hand that wasn't in bandages. When he touched the place where a black suture stuck out, he winced.

"Is that what happened, the dog attacked you? Did you provoke the dog?"

"Are you kidding? That dog can kill you."

Scooter pulled up the leg of his pants and peeled back one of the large gauze pads. It was yellow with lymph. I counted four sets of bite marks surrounded by sickly yellow bruises.

"The doctor said I was lucky that my arm got the worst of it. I can't untape that. If the dog had gone for my neck first like they're supposed to, the doctor says he would have killed me."

"Were you in a wheelchair before this incident?"

"God, no. I'm in the marching band." He caught himself. "I *was* in the marching band. They don't know how bad the nerve damage is going to be in my hand."

I said, "You don't seem like the kind of kid who would deal drugs."

"No kids deal drugs in this school." He paused again. "Are you going to ask me to turn state's evidence? I can't wear a wire. I don't know anybody who uses drugs."

"I'm not with law enforcement."

Scooter drew back. "I thought your car looked pretty crappy for an undercover agent."

"I'm a reporter."

His face went white.

"It's okay. I believe there were no drugs in your locker." I was violating a basic rule of interviewing, but this kid had been through so much, I wanted him to know I wasn't another enemy. "Why do you think Darnell planted drugs in your locker?"

From the way Scooter pursed his lips, I could tell that he didn't want to talk to me. But a reporter doesn't stop asking questions just because someone is uncomfortable. "Other kids might get hurt, too," I said. Then I repeated, "Why would Darnell Kellan plant drugs in your locker?"

"Do you know who my mother is?"

"She's the night dispatcher."

"Ask her," he finally croaked.

"I already did. She won't talk to me."

"If she said no, I can't talk to you either." With inexpert motions, Scooter sawed his wheelchair around.

I said, "I need your help, I just have a few more questions."

He shook his head and didn't look back. "Lady, I've been in more trouble this week than in my entire life up to now. I am not getting in Dutch with my mom, too."

I knew since Scooter was under eighteen, I couldn't use the interview. But I was on the road to something. He thought the DARE officer planted drugs in his locker. Was he saying it was part of a fight between his mom and Darnell? The boy seemed scared but honest. And the principal, who had said Peter Whitmore was a good kid, had characterized Scooter the same way.

It was hard to just file it all away, but to turn it into a Silverton contender, I would have to be patient.

Chapter 27

Blue and I were having what he called a "talking date" at Tony's Place. Tony's had minestrone soup that didn't have meat in it. And there was the one vegetarian entrée, spaghetti with marinara sauce.

We had the dining room to ourselves. In retrospect, I suppose Blue was trying to slow things down, or divert us down a different path. He asked about my parents, why I never talked about my family. I told him I was the only child of kind but controlling people and it was easiest not to be in touch.

The candle on the table flickered. "For good?"

I said, "I don't know. I just don't want their advice on everything I do."

He asked me again how old I was; that seemed to help it make sense to him. "It's hard to lose somebody in your family."

"Are you talking about your parents?" I asked.

"It was hard to lose my dad. I don't remember my mom at all. But I was thinking of my extended family. There are only nine Riv'nego left. Four of them are seventy or older. Then there's only Dora and Scooter. We had a falling out with our other cousin."

"That's eight. You said there were nine of you."

"My cousin has a kid. She lets me take him fishing once in a while, but that's about it. He and Scooter meant the world to the old aunties."

"That's Sandra, right? What was the fight about?"

"She converted to Christianity when she got married. I didn't care. God knows we all pretend we're church people. It makes it easier to get along."

"That's not right. If you have your own native religion—"

"That's what the old aunties said. There was more to it, but basically they boiled it down to Matthew is one of two living Riv'nego in his generation and his mother was as bad as the white law that terminated us if she wouldn't let them take him to ceremonies."

"What did you say?"

"I was about as young as you are now. You have to remember that. Both my parents were dead. The aunt who took me in, she's—how did you describe your parents?"

"Controlling?"

"She's controlling, judgmental, unforgiving. She could nurse a grudge until it died of old age. But she was all I had. She and the other three had introduced me to this secret history, and I belonged. For the first time in my life, I wasn't the weird outsider. I was somebody important."

"So you didn't stand up for Sandra?"

Blue looked down. "Sandra said she had a right to raise her kid in any religion she chose. She said she was the parent, not them. I didn't defend her."

"I don't know that you were wrong, but I can tell that you think you were wrong."

"We lost them both. There are only nine of us and we lost two."

Tony brought the food out and Blue wiped his eyes with his napkin. "This isn't what I had in mind," he said, fumbling to reposition the napkin on his lap. "I wanted to talk about you." He cleared his throat. "Do you have a religion? Any hobbies?"

"I am a confirmed agnostic. I don't really have time for hobbies, but I am interested in firefighting technology of the past."

Blue's face fell. He had disclosed something deeply personal, and I was being a smartass. But he shifted like an automatic transmission. "Why did you decide to—what's our euphemism?"

"Date? Why did I decide to date you?"

Blue said "Do you remember that day in the firehouse, when I gave you my number? Why didn't you call?"

I remembered that day very well. "I meant to."

"Meant to? Couldn't you feel the electricity jumping between us?"

I nodded, not wanting to give that memory over to words.

"So?" he probed.

"I know this is creepy," I stammered. "I did think you were really hot that day. But something about you didn't make sense. Why would someone like you stay in a backwater town like this?"

"Did it occur to you that this is my home? That I love people in this little backwater?"

"It didn't then."

"Why didn't you ask?"

"We were all spark. Words were not necessary for any of the things I had in mind."

Color rose in Blue's cheeks and he shifted in his chair.

The meal was mostly done. He threw a twenty on the table and called a goodbye to Tony.

As we walked to the door, I grabbed the back of his jeans and whispered, "Do you want to go back to my place?"

Blue removed my hand. He said, "I want to walk with you through this quiet neighborhood like a proper couple out for a stroll." But once we were through the door, he pulled me close to him. "You don't make this easy on a man."

We just breathed each other in for a few minutes. Then when we started walking again, he returned to his line of questioning.

This neighborhood, unlike mine, had sidewalks. The houses were small. Neat.

"You said you did something creepy that day. And that you were planning to call. What creepy thing did you do instead?"

I confessed, "I followed you. After the false alarm at the restaurant downtown. Do you remember what you did after the false alarm?"

"I probably did what I always do after a false alarm. I probably went for a run."

"Why do you run?"

He took a deep breath. "I don't know if it's the same for women, but for a man, when you get all that adrenaline pumping, rushing off to a fire call where you might, literally, be the difference between life and death for somebody, you have to talk yourself up for it. It's not exactly praying, but it's sort of like that. You say in your mind to whoever's in danger, 'Hold on, I'm coming.' And you hold that thought, that will to find whoever's in there. When it's a false alarm, to get that revved up for nothing—we really do risk death when we run into a fire, and to have somebody be so disrespectful, to waste our time and effort, it makes me angry."

Blue recomposed himself. "I have made it a point in my life not to be angry, but I'm still a man. I've still got that adrenaline going through my veins. So, I go out and run until I'm not angry anymore."

"Why do you go to the game lands?"

When I said game lands, it seemed to click for him. "So, you were there in the woods." He nodded slowly. "That is creepy, but it's actually nice to know. I try not to overemphasize intuition, but I felt so connected to you, I couldn't shake it. I was up all night, thinking you'd call at any minute."

"It's funny that you say all night. I had a wet dream about you that night."

"You've got a dirty mouth."

"It was there, in those woods at sunset. Do you want me to tell you about it?"

"No," Blue murmured. "I want to act it out. Meet me there at sunset tomorrow."

⚲

The anticipation made it hard to focus on anything else, so I went early to the game lands. The sky wasn't even beginning to pink when I got there. If anything, it was graying over. *Might not be the best sunset.*

As I took off my shoes and tried to move into my dream world, the real world tightened its grip. I was much more aware this time of the way the dust in the air made me want to sneeze, how the gravel in the parking lot poked my feet.

The path itself was really two parallel paths formed from the ruts of an old service road. Some parts were covered in clover. Other parts were shiny pools of mud that squished up between my toes when I stepped in them.

I walked on the inside path. It looped around a clearing where I saw a doe and her fawn, then four more deer. They regarded me briefly and apparently decided I was not a threat. I walked two laps before I heard Blue's car.

I'd spent close to twenty-four hours thinking about nothing but that dream. But the reality of this wild place seemed so much sweeter. How much did I want to act out the dream? I wasn't sure. Part of me wanted only to walk side by side with Blue on the parallel paths.

Blue apparently thought we should stick to the script. He came flying, his hair wild. When he saw me, he stopped.

"I thought you said you would be hiding."

"I was in the dream, but how would you know where to find me?"

All seriousness, Blue said, "Don't worry, I'll find you. Take two."

He returned to the parking lot, then started on his run.

As soon as he was out of sight, I leaned into the crook of the big birch in the copse of trees where I had hidden before. The leaves were full now, green hearts turned toward the sun.

When Blue ran by, they shook.

"Over here," I called and stuck my head out between the branches so he could see me.

He let out a snort and stopped. He said, "I thought we agreed that we would not talk. I thought you said I came up behind you and pinned you against the tree."

"When you say it that way, it sounds like a scene from a fifty-cent bodice ripper."

"It was *your* dream."

This wasn't going the way I had imagined. "Just come find me on your next lap, okay? I'll be right here."

Blue shook his head. When he started running again, I leaned against the birch tree and waited to hear his feet on the path.

Apparently I hadn't stressed how significant to the dream the noise of his feet was because soon, without any sound at all, he was behind me, pulling me hard against the tree.

"This is too weird." I broke away.

"I did everything that you told me."

"I'm sorry. But just consider the politics of it. It's like I'm waiting for a man to make my dreams come true."

Blue conceded that was not in keeping with what he knew of me. "I need to run a couple laps, okay?"

I climbed onto a low branch and watched him. The consternation on his face brightened when he approached on the second lap. He stopped and squatted on the ground near where my muddy feet dangled below my perch.

"This is a special place," he said, looking up at me. "I'm glad to be here together with you."

"You mean to be here together *again*."

He laughed. "I don't know what I was thinking we might recapture." Then, earnest, he asked, "Is it good for you?"

"What?"

"Us."

"Are we an 'us'?"

Blue's face went dark.

No, no, no. I got down on the ground with him and stroked his hair.

He said, "I like the ways that you're different, but I don't know if we even have the same picture of what 'we' are."

I wanted to comfort him, but I could not make promises. I picked a clover blossom and gave it to him. "It was sweet of you to want to act out my dream," I said. "Do you have a dream you want to act out?"

Blue said, "Yeah, I have a dream. It's set right here . . ." but then he stopped and looked away.

I knelt in front of him and laid my hands on his shoulders. "How kinky can it be?"

He raised the clover, as if he wanted to give it back.

An owl hooted, way up in a tree, and then the sky threw heavy raindrops down on us.

Blue asked if I wanted to go home. I said no.

He got up and flicked the water off his face, then led me out of the trees and onto the side of the road.

My hair felt like seaweed against my neck. My wet T-shirt stuck to me like a second skin. I started singing the chorus from a Neil Sedaka song. Blue seemed to know where he was going, so I just followed along, splashing him on the downbeat.

Just a few yards in from the road stood an odd three-sided structure with wide and very short windows cut into the wall that faced into the clearing.

"What is this?" I asked.

"It's a deer blind. The state had to put it here to provide access for disabled hunters. But I don't think any hunters have ever used it."

I made a wary step inside. "Have you used it?"

"I've waited out some rainstorms in it. And at dawn you can sit in here and watch the deer waking up in the meadow."

"Or bears?"

Blue put his arm around me. "Don't worry. They'd only be black bears. Nothing to be afraid of if you don't get between a sow and her cubs."

We sat in a corner and dripped a puddle on the plywood floor. The rain on the roof was the only sound until a car slowed and then turned into the parking lot. I heard the engine shudder.

"I thought nobody ever came out here."

Blue said, "It's complicated," and then a distressed woman's voice that somehow sounded familiar called, "Blue?"

Blue didn't appear to be surprised. "I have to go talk to her."

I tried not to wonder how whoever it was knew to look for Blue here.

He kissed me, a soft kiss that did not fit the situation. "I'll be right back."

I reminded myself that I had bristled at every bid for commitment that Blue had made. And he had made a lot of them. I would be gone in less than a year. And it was crystal clear that he was deeply rooted in this dirt-bag town.

I leaned into the pressboard. The deer blind was made of glue and sawdust, but it stood. For now. How many things in my life were like that? The fishing shack that was barely high enough for a hobbit but looked out onto that gorgeous view of the trees and the river. Or my pier—every second board was rotten, but I knew where to step. "I'm comfortable working with available material," I told myself, but my wet clothes were starting to make me cold.

Blue reappeared, sharing an umbrella with a skinny woman. I was relieved that she wasn't a stunning piece of arm candy, and then I was immediately ashamed that I had thought that.

It was Dora Mayfield, the night dispatcher whose son was mauled by the DARE dog.

Blue said, "Hallie, this is my cousin Dora."

I said, "We've met."

Dora looked drawn.

"She may have a story for you."

The night dispatcher gripped tight on the umbrella handle. She didn't pick up Blue's prompt, so he said, "They said they'd fire you, Dora. We don't have much to fight them with, but Hallie could put a story in the paper."

A dispatcher? Getting fired? Was this what Scooter had hinted at? I had to hide my enthusiasm. She was situated to know everything that went on at the cop shop. And if she really was about to be fired, she might be in a mood to spill.

"Why are they firing you?" I asked, trying to calm her with my tone.

"I had to take leave."

It didn't sound like a story. People think it's news when they lose their job. I'd had half a dozen people call me to give me the big tip that they were being fired. You listen politely, because it's possible there might be some news there, but most of the time there's nothing.

"Was there something unusual about your needing to take a leave?" I asked.

"My grandmother was dying."

I tried to remember the Family and Medical Leave Act poster in the break room. It said you're entitled to unpaid leave to care for a sick child or spouse or parent. I didn't think grandparents were on the list.

"How long did you need to take off?"

"A month. She had cancer bad. By the time she agreed to let them go in, it had spread from her stomach to her lungs and her kidneys. The doctor said she could go at any time, but she lasted four weeks." Dora's voice cracked when she said this, as if her grandmother's whole life had been cheated down to one short month.

Blue put his arm around Dora, that familiar way he had with anyone who was in need. Nothing about his gesture suggested he was self-conscious about being soaked to the skin.

I didn't have a notepad with me, but despite my appearance, I tried to project a professional persona. "Have they already fired you?"

"No, but they're going to. Chief said I lied when I called in sick."

Keeping my voice even, I explained that a story in the *Daily-Observer* might not get her job back, but people would understand her situation a little better. "It might lead to a discussion on the conflict between paid work and the unpaid work women do in the home."

"Women's work," Dora said and made a weary one-syllable grunt. The creases on her face suggested decades of deep unhappiness.

I said, "You never made a report about your son being bitten by the dog at school."

"I work with Darnell," she replied. "There was no reason to put it in writing." From Dora's expression I gathered that she hadn't allowed herself to really think about the dog bite until that moment. Her eyes were focused on a bitter scene only she could see. "I've got fourteen years in with the Green Meadow Police. Now I'm not going to get my pension."

There was something there, but Frank was going to be pissy about another "*Ladies Home Journal*" story. I had to figure out a way to use the FMLA angle to get at workplace retaliation. It wasn't an easy connection to draw. I needed time to prepare for the interview.

I said, "If you're going to be home tomorrow evening, I could come by and talk to you."

Blue told Dora, "We'll take care of you."

If I was part of that *we*, Blue had far more faith in the power of the press than I did. And so did Dora, because she nodded.

Chapter 28

Mayfield was spelled in green letters on a shiny mailbox by the edge of the road.

The dispatcher lived in a trailer set behind a row of pine trees. Her garden, lined by painted bricks, took up nearly as much space as the trailer.

Dora offered me a lawn chair. I sat and took in the view. Vapor trails in the sky were just starting to catch the light.

There's a pinkness to hazy days in Indiana that is unlike anything I have ever seen. The ag dust participates in the sunset, makes it start earlier and makes the colors more intense. I was only beginning to see how the things that make Green Meadow ugly at noon make it beautiful as the horizon strives to keep the sun for one more hour.

Dora's gaze was focused past the end of her lawn chair where an orange kitten tumbled in the dirt. Dora dangled her fingers beside the chair and the kitten came running over to pounce. She picked him up by the scruff of his neck and held him up against the sun.

"I've got so many babies here, I can't leave," she said. "And this place is paid off. When you get to my age, that means a lot. Chief can't take this from me."

She set the kitten on her lap. It seemed to be fascinated by a strip of leather tied around Dora's wrist.

I picked up my notepad. "Could you spell your first and last name for me?"

"You want this on the record?"

"It can't go in the paper if it's not."

Dora paused. "This is hard. There are some good people on that force. Some of them are like family to me."

"But they didn't respect your family obligations," I said, grasping for something that would draw out the real reason why she was getting fired.

"Respect? I was the one who got the bomb in her mailbox."

I tried to remember the date on the incident report about the bomb. It had been weeks old when I got it.

"Are you saying your mailbox got bombed because you used Family and Medical Leave Act?"

Dora touched the strip of leather knotted around her wrist. She was a striking woman: long dark hair with white strands catching the pink light of the sunset. Probably from all the gardening, she had well-defined arms. She was wearing dress-up clothes for the interview and the knotted leather, like something a kid would give as a friendship bracelet, looked out of place with her crisp white blouse.

"I'm going to tell you everything," she said. "The chief and a few of the officers wholesale cocaine."

That second, the sky turned magenta. I gripped the lawn chair, felt how thin the webbing was that held me up.

Dora said, "It's gotten out of hand. I mean, they went after my *son*." There was a note of horror, but she quickly composed herself and described how the police involved in the drug ring arranged for cocaine to be shipped into Chicago in compartments in new Trojan trucks. "The feds can't track them because each truck only carries coke once."

If what Dora said was true, it was bigger than anything I had ever covered. My hands flew across my reporter pad, recording every word. When Dora paused, I wrote out my 5W questions. *Don't forget the basic stuff,* I told myself.

"How long has this been going on?" I asked.

"Probably for years."

"How long have you known about it?"

"I've heard rumors for a long time. But really known they were true? About three months. You remember that cruiser that got totaled? That was one of the officers who sampled the merchandise."

"He was driving while high?"

"Yep. That alone cost the department forty thousand dollars," she said.

I asked her how she found out about the operation.

"The chief's son, Darnell. They never should have hired him. He's dumb as a box of rocks."

"You mean Darnell Kellan, the truancy officer?"

"Is that what they're calling him now? He's not qualified to write parking tickets."

"It's his dog that bit your son."

"That's why I have to talk to you. The bomb in my mailbox and siccing Cujo on Scooter, that's Darnell's clunky way of warning me to keep my mouth shut."

"But you're not keeping your mouth shut. Why not?"

"They're not as careful with information as they should be and that has meant—" she paused, "collateral damage."

"You've got to spell this out for me, Dora. What do you mean by collateral damage?"

We were all alone, but she dropped her voice to a whisper. "I think they've had to take care of some people who found out."

I was writing as fast as I could, wishing I had a tape recorder.

"You're saying they've killed people?"

"It's the cops who write the reports when a body is found," she said. "Have you noticed there are a lot of single-car fatalities in this county? More fires than other towns have?"

"Can you confirm on the record that they have killed someone?"

"I have no firsthand information about that. But I've heard talk."

"What gives you reason to believe the talk?"

Dora shuddered. "I know what the Kellans are capable of."

"What do you know firsthand? How do you know about the cocaine?"

"Conrad Kellan just can't face the fact that his son is—let's just say, less than gifted. If you needed someone to transfer a load of cocaine, would you pick him to do it?"

"No, he's—how did you put it?"

"The dumbest rock in the box."

I laughed.

"So, I get a call at home, early in the afternoon. I think Darnell thinks all dispatchers are like Sugar. She didn't have one good parent. I don't hold it against her. But, damn, she gives dispatchers a bad name."

"But the phone call?"

"Right. It was a couple days after them two boys drowned. Damn shame. Darnell calls and he wants me to help him unload some boxes. It's the middle of the day. I said to ask Sugar. He said it wasn't police business. And I said, 'If it's not police business, why are you calling me at all?' I said there's plenty of people out of work in Bryce County. Hire a temp."

"What did he say to that?"

"He says, 'The cash in this operation ain't on hand right now.' I go, 'Unload your own damn boxes.' He said, 'I can't. Someone's got to watch the road.'"

Dora shook her head remembering it. "That's when I knew. I mean, there had been talk about drugs moving through Bryce County for a long time—but I never thought *Darnell* would be involved.

"And then, get this, he said, 'Can I talk to Scooter?' I don't know what was in my mind. I guess I'm a mother first. I said, 'Don't you dare try to involve my son in your drug operation!' and hung up."

"So, you just put two and two together. You'd heard talk, and then you got a call asking you to do a loading task that wasn't part of your job and wasn't police work either, so it had to be drugs? That's not—"

"There's more. Darnell came by the house the next day. He was pretty upset. He begged me not to tell his father that I knew what was going on. He said his father would kill him."

"Did you promise?"

"What kind of fool do you think I am? Of course I'm not going to tell Conrad Kellan one cross thing about his son. But I started asking around and a shirttail relative of one of my cousins had seen the compartments at Trojan."

"Has that relative seen cocaine?"

"Yes."

"But you have not?"

"No."

"So how sure are you that this is an ongoing thing and not just Darnell doing something one time?"

"I sit on the dispatch desk at night. I see them come in and have to clean their uniforms, but nothing gets put in the log. If there is a report filed, it's months late. It's always the same officers. And the fires. This is 1989. Everybody knows not to smoke in bed."

"Have you talked to Blue about this?"

"I was a member of that force for fourteen years."

"Does that mean you never told anyone?"

"You're the only person I've said a word to. Blue thinks you're here to talk to me about my FMLA complaint."

I hesitated.

"What?" Dora asked.

"Do you mind if I tell Blue what you've told me about the cocaine?"

Dora leaned in. I could see her trying to read my face in what was left of the light. "It's going to be in the paper, so why not? You're pretty close with Blue. Some of the old aunties won't approve, but we're stakin' in for a long fight. You might be able to help."

Dora had two stories, really: one about the cops running drugs and another about being fired from her job as a dispatcher. The second one was simple to write. She had tried to take FMLA time to care for her grandmother who had cancer, but the chief told her she couldn't use the time that way.

Back in the newsroom, I remembered the indignant way Dora had said, "How did they expect me to not be there when the woman who raised me was dying?" I turned to that quote in my notebook. It would be a minor story, but I hinted to Kim that I would have a big enterprise story soon.

She didn't ask what it was about.

"It's a major story," I repeated.

"Frank thinks I don't keep a tight enough rein on you when it's just me and you working in the evening. He was pretty clear after the drowning aftermath story that he doesn't want enterprise stories from you. He wants spot news."

I was taken aback. "Do you remember that man in Tiananmen Square who stood up in front of a line of tanks?"

"What about him?"

"If a person armed only with a couple of shopping bags can be so fearless, can stand up for what's right, you and I can certainly stand up to Frank."

Kim said, "Frank is not the enemy. Frank is our boss. If he says he wants school and police coverage, that's what you give him. He called down here after he left today to make sure I told you to do all your beat checks. Do you know how that feels, after being here for seven years?"

"He sure can micromanage."

"Why do you insist on setting him off? He's not that hard to work with. Just do as you're told."

"Wow." I didn't want to fight with Kim. "You're going to love the story."

"I hope I do, but we've got a paper to put out now."

I had faith that once Kim saw the cocaine story, she would apologize.

Blue called when I got home. "Somebody's going to call you tomorrow with a news tip. Take them seriously."

"I've got something serious to tell you," I said and told him what Dora had alleged about the police wholesaling cocaine.

Blue took a while to react. He said, "That explains some things. I wish she had told me."

"She fears they'll come after her for telling people. That's why she wants it in the paper right away."

"Can you do that?"

"There's not enough there to support her allegations. I'll use the quotes she gave me, but I have to corroborate what she's saying first."

"She should have gone to the DEA."

"Nothing is firsthand. All she said was she was pressured to unload packages and when she surmised it was cocaine, Darnell begged her not to tell the chief. I trust her judgment, but on their own, her allegations aren't enough to be the basis of a story."

"Your job is harder than I thought."

"There are a few rules, yes."

"What are you going to do next?"

I laughed. "Kim promised she would nominate me for a Silverton Award. I'm going to find the piece of paper she signed promising to nominate me and put it on my mantel where I'm going to display the award I'm going to get for this."

"I like your confidence, Hallie. But you do know these people are brutal?"

"Drug dealers don't kill reporters."

"These drug dealers are cops. And their MO is to make their hits look like accidents."

Chapter 29

When I picked up the phone on my desk, I did not recognize the male voice on the other end, but I knew not to ask who was calling. "It's going to be parked at the truck stop just before the county line. It will still have Trojan factory stickers on it," he said and hung up.

I flew to the door.

"Where are you going?" Kim called.

"News tip. Probably nothing."

She hoisted herself up. "You can't just run out of here like that," she said. "Take a camera! If it does turn out to be something, we'll want a photo."

I grabbed the camera and made it out the door before Kim could ask what the tip was about.

<hr />

Passenger cars were parked in front of the truck stop. The big rigs were parked in back, each one slanting at the same angle as the next. There were probably a dozen of them, dusty and spattered with mud, except for the silver silhouette of a busty, long-haired woman, gleaming from many of the mud flaps.

I scanned down the row. There was no new truck. I guessed I was too early.

My eyes swept the edge of the woods that lined three sides of the truck lot. I saw nothing, so I went through the automatic doors. Smoke pushed into my lungs, heavier than in any bar I'd ever been in.

Seat Yerself, a hand-lettered sign instructed.

I surveyed the room.

The hostess said, "Last decent place to eat before Chicago." Truckers filled the booths. I looked for a window seat with an unobstructed view of the truck lot outside. Unfortunately, the only empty tables were far from the sightline I needed.

I eyed the fiftyish man sitting alone in the booth I wanted and walked over. He had on one of those caps that's like a baseball cap, but with padding that rises up higher on the front. It was embroidered with the Peterbilt logo.

"What's a pretty girl like you doing in a place like this?" he asked.

Trying hard to sound flirtatious, I said, "Looking for a guy like you. May I sit down?"

He eyed my legs, which I had not shaved for at least two weeks. "Please don't tell me you're one of those she-males with a trucker fetish."

"Nope."

He laughed. "Even if you're lying, have a seat."

I said, "Nice weather."

He said, "It's beautiful. But there are bad storms west of here."

The waitress came by. "Is this guy bothering you, honey?"

"Oh, I'd love to bother her," the trucker said.

I ordered coffee and a side of coleslaw.

"You're strange," the trucker said.

"Do you know much about Trojan trucks?" I asked.

"A regular Chatty Cathy. I like that. I think Trojans are made somewhere near here. I see the trailers with the factory stickers still on them when I drive north to Chicago. Their tractor's got a bumpy ride. A lot of guys will pair a Trojan trailer with another make of tractor, if they're owner-operators."

"Are you an owner-operator?"

"I don't have the get-in money just yet. I pick up contracts driving company trucks."

Seeming to gauge my lack of interest in his response, he chuckled. "Are you, how shall I say it? Working here?"

"No, I just need a favor. If anybody asks, I need you to say I was sitting here for an hour."

He sized me up, as if he had misestimated the first time. "If you're on the wrong side of the law, you better watch out. Green Meadow cops are ruthless. Old truckers say they'll pull your teeth out just so you'll remember where you got pulled over."

Through the window, I saw a truck with "Trojan Truck" stickers pull into the lot.

I got up and tossed a twenty on the table—the last of my grocery money. "One hour. I sat here for one hour."

Once I got outside, the shiny new Trojan truck slowed and then the driver got out, opened the rear door of the trailer, and walked into the building.

I looked around to see if anyone was nearby. Not a soul.

I darted to the open trailer. I had to jump up, supporting my weight on both hands, to get in.

The roof was made of some kind of translucent plastic, so I could see quite well. But what was I looking for? A box marked cocaine? There was nothing. The truck was completely empty.

I took a few pictures, just in case I might figure it out later, but as best I could tell, I was inside a regular truck.

I looked down at my Doc Martens, as worn out as the vinyl seats of the booths in the truck stop. Maybe there was nothing. All I had on the record so far was from a compromised source.

Still, the adrenaline coursing through my veins was shouting that I was onto something.

"Hunches are for chumps," I said out loud and then quoted Professor Wassle: "You can't attribute something to a hunch."

"Who are you talking to in there?" a voice at the end of the trailer asked.

Shit. It was the trucker I had shared the booth with. "I've got a slipped disc," he told me. "I can't flop up there the way you did."

He pulled down the ramp, then walked up it.

"Takes your breath away, don't it?" Running his hands along a line of rivets, he said, "When I do buy, I'm gonna buy one of these."

"Are they really all that different?" I asked.

"They're taller," he said. "Let's round up and say the trailer's ten feet wide and the full fifty-three feet long. That's about sixteen cubic feet more that I can haul. With the lower fuel costs because the ceiling material is so light, that's a week I won't have to work every year."

"You really think this is fifty-three feet long?" I asked.

"They all are. A trailer company couldn't compete if theirs ran short."

I walked, knocking on the long side of the trailer. Nothing. When I got to the end, I kicked the short wall.

"Whoa, honey. You kick the tires; you don't kick the walls."

"Why not?"

He stopped and thought. "I suppose it's respect for whoever buys it. Like you don't let a woman tattoo your name on her butt unless you're serious about her."

"You're comparing a truck to a woman."

He folded his arms. "In many ways the truck is superior. She's sincere. When a truck sings, it ain't to distract you and take your money."

I kicked the short wall again. "It's a thing," I said. "Women are not things."

"Honey, you just moved that panel."

"Shoddy construction?"

"You want to get out of here," he said with a severity I could not question.

I spun around to see two men in black pants and sweatshirts walking out of the woods toward the truck.

The trucker waddled as fast as he could down the ramp. "Hurry up," he shouted.

I said, "Just put the ramp up."

He looked at me like I was crazy, but he did it.

The two men started running toward the truck.

"What were you doing in there?" one shouted.

"Oh it's a beaut," the trucker good-ol'-boyed. "I'm gonna get me one of these one day."

"You were talking to someone. Who?" the tall one demanded.

The trucker turned away from them and fingered his pants as if he were zipping his fly.

"Oh," the bald one said.

"I've never done it in a brand-new one," the trucker said.

Crouched in a corner of the trailer, I pressed on the back wall beside me. It was not reinforced aluminum. It felt like plastic. Maybe a painted version of the material the ceiling was made out of.

"Come out of there, you stinkin' whore," the tall man shouted and pounded on the outside of the wall like he was flushing out an animal.

I walked heel to toe along the side of the trailer toward the rear opening. It was hard to be sure I had counted right, but if I had, the trailer was just under fifty feet long. That told me a lot about the bald man yelling through the open end of the trailer.

"What the fuck are you doing? Are you a whore or a stowaway?"

It seemed to make him mad when I did not respond. "I should arrest—" He caught himself. "I should have you arrested."

"I didn't do anything," I said.

"No?" the tall one sneered. "That makes this your fuckin' lucky day."

"That's no way to talk to a lady," the trucker said and gave me a hand down.

The tall guy looked me up and down. "You want that?" he asked. The other one just shook his head.

I was struck by their ordinariness. If my source was right, these two clean-shaven guys in black oxford shoes were going to stow pounds and pounds of cocaine in that truck. The camera was in the bottom of my purse. I didn't dare get it out, but in my mind, I memorized their faces.

After I finished my otherwise ridiculously ordinary shift, Blue came over and I told him what I had seen at the truck stop. His first question was, "When is the story going in the paper?"

I explained that I didn't have enough yet to meet the journalistic standard of truth.

"But they've seen you."

"I didn't recognize them."

When I described the two men to Blue, he said they didn't sound like anyone he knew in Green Meadow. "Chief Kellan is probably working with cops from another town."

"You think it starts at the top?"

"Poison apples are all that falls from that tree," he said. "I'm worried about you."

"I'm always careful."

"No, you're not," was his come-on.

I fell asleep piecing together what I had to do next. I didn't have actual evidence that cocaine was smuggled in the truck compartment, but my task had moved from trying to find out if Dora was right to trying to nail down the details that could get it in the paper. Thinking about it was exhausting. The Silverton medal glimmered in my mind as I drifted to sleep.

—

Blue bumped the foldout as he groped for his clothes on the floor, and it woke me up. I said, "You don't have to go."

"'I shall foot it,'" he said, "'in the silence of the morning, see the night slur into dawn.'"

"Who is that?"

"Carl Sandburg. I asked the librarian to help me find a book of his love poems, but when I told her what you're like, she said you'd like his *Chicago Poems* better."

"Stay."

"I love you but—" He caught himself. He'd been working the word love in a lot. "I love being with you." "You make me feel like love is possible." But I hadn't reciprocated. He had said it and I had not.

"That's why you leave, isn't it? I don't say 'I love you.'"

"I'm your boy toy. It's not the job I applied for—"

"But you do apply yourself," I growled.

Blue ignored that and zipped his pants. When he got to the door, he said, "You're too young to know this, but it can get better. A lot better."

Slowly, deliberately, he reached for the chain lock. "You've never offered to make me pancakes. Where's the new toothbrush in case I want my own?"

"And the white picket fence and the two-point-five kids?"

"I'd like to think that's a possibility, yes."

"Blue, I like you because you're hot and you're smart. But I don't want to break a beautiful heart like yours."

"So, you'll just suck on it for a while?"

"I am what I am."

I don't think I'd ever seen him get angry before, not at me.

"You don't have to be such a—" He stopped himself.

"What?"

"You're a caterpillar! You are crawling around on the ground, but you could fly, really fly, with me."

"Is that a metaphor for sex?" I purred.

"Stop it, Hallie. Yes, sex gets better. But you've got to get into a cocoon to grow your wings."

"Wings for what?"

"For love. For everything. You've got—" He caught himself again.

"Finish your sentence."

"You've got child-bearing hips. Breasts like yours—"

"Are for babies? You want to have *babies* with me? I am on the verge of breaking the story that is going to win me the Silverton and you choose this time to talk about having children?"

"Believe me, I have been doing my best not to have this conversation. But if you ask a person what he is thinking, you have to be prepared to hear the truth."

"Okay, here is my truth: I've got an editor who would prefer I just rewrite press releases, and two cops who know I was banging around inside a truck they will use to ferry coke into Chicago. I am the only person in my class who got a full-time job in journalism, and somehow I am going to make it, even at this stinking chain paper that is barely a step up from a shopper."

Blue's face wasn't mad anymore. "The way you're locked onto getting this story, it just makes me want you that much more. There's never going to be another woman like you in Bryce County. I want you for real. Permanent." He knelt down on the floor next to the bed and stroked my hair. "Can we at least take it one day at a time, agreeing that it could become permanent?"

"Let's go back to Carl Sandburg."

I wanted the Silverton. I wanted to get out of Green Meadow. But I also wanted him.

Chapter 30

It was a little after four when I parked behind the office. I had done the police and fire beat checks. I had just a few minutes to sit in my car and brainstorm how I could connect the police to the compartment in the truck I saw. Yes, those guys in black were cops. But I didn't know their names or which town they worked for, so I couldn't call them cops in the story.

Everybody thinks investigative stories are just one good interview and finding the right documents, but really, there is a lot of strategizing required. You've got to list everyone in a position to know what's going on and then list sources who already trust you to see if you can triangulate an interview with someone who knows the truth.

Blue knew about questionable fire scenes but didn't have lab results yet. I guess since he'd asked for the tests as a favor, he couldn't demand a rush job. Dora had told me everything she knew firsthand, but on its own, it wasn't enough. I wished that I knew who it was that had tipped me about the truck. I put him on my list as Mr. X.

There was a rap on my windshield. I slammed the notebook shut.

"What are you doing?" Frank demanded. "The courthouse closes at four thirty. Have you checked for new filings?"

I said, "I have three beats—cops, courts, and schools. If I get to the court by 4:22, I get everything filed that day. I will walk out our front door at 4:16 and make it in time. If I go any earlier, I have to call to make sure nothing was filed after I left, which would be wasting precious time on the clock."

Frank looked at his watch. "Then you've got two minutes to get going."

When I got back from the courthouse, Kim called me to the back of the newsroom.

"Frank wants to have a talk."

Once I sat down, Kim started. "This is hard, because we really like you and we really want you to succeed."

"Don't sugarcoat it," Frank snapped.

"Hallie," Kim said my name with measured kindness, "this is a community newspaper. And this is a small town. Subscriptions don't pay our operating costs; they don't even come close."

"We run on ads here," Frank interjected. "In journalism school, they probably told you about a wall between advertising and editorial."

"Of course. It's the bedrock—"

"It's bunk," he sneered. "We are here to draw readers' eyes to the display ads. Our number-one customer is the Green Meadow Chamber of Commerce. I've gotten a lot of complaints about you."

"From whom?"

Frank said, "From Mrs. Quidley, for starters."

"She's not qualified to teach special ed," I protested.

Frank said, "She's the superintendent's wife."

I appealed to Kim. "You've got a kid in those schools. People should know."

Kim looked down.

Frank barked, "As far as I can tell, you hardly cover them."

"You told me not to put in extra hours."

"I told you to use the press releases they send out."

I kept looking at Kim, but she avoided my eyes.

Frank continued, "It seems you're willing to believe anything bad that people say. That's not the kind of newspaper we run here. This is a community paper. If you want to run people down, go back to the Twin Cities."

"Is this about the bomb?" I asked.

Kim perked up. "What bomb?"

"Forget about the bomb." Frank glared at her. "This is about Hallie's refusal to do the kind of journalism we hired her for."

Then Frank fixed on me. "We're putting you on probation."

Kim set her teeth close together. Frank took a drag on his cigarette.

"You're just not fitting in," Kim said. Even though she did not raise her voice, it felt like she was yelling at me.

Frank said he had noticed a lot of dated police reports. He hinted that he thought I was not doing beat checks every day. I said that I stopped at both the cop shop and the fire station every day and went over for court news on all the filing deadlines. "I told you that in the parking lot."

Frank shook his head. "You're on probation. Every day, I want every incident report, every fire call. Don't dress them up. Don't go looking for secret sources who might or might not know anything. If you quote somebody, it had better be somebody with authority. And I want you to catch us up on births, deaths, marriages, and divorces."

Oh God. Vital Records. The woman before me had never done them. Nor, as far as I could tell, had the woman before her. There was at least a two-year backlog of babies, marriage licenses, and the most mundane civil court rulings waiting for me in the clerk's office.

Do you know what a Trash 80 is? It's a portable computer sold by Radio Shack. It only weighs about five pounds, has a two-line screen, and runs on D batteries. The next morning—Frank let me come in early to be there as soon as the clerk's office opened—I hauled the *Daily-Observer*'s Trash 80 and two sets of batteries down to the courthouse to record the backlog of vital records.

To my dismay, there were three Junes in the backlog. As I copied in bride after happy bride, I began to ask myself why I was typing for Jennie Annabelle Bateman and Mary Louise Brighton, now hyphenated to Brighton-Beech, an announcement they'd already sent out on parchment to anyone who cared. If they saw the "Vital Records" column at all, I imagined it would not merit space on their refrigerator doors.

It wasn't fair. No one mentioned the Vital Records column in my job interview. We only ran the column because publishing court rulings, births, deaths, marriages, and divorces qualified our tiny tab as a newspaper of record under Indiana law, and that meant the *Daily-Observer* could take legal notices, a lucrative advertising stream.

I imagined the columns we would run with two-year-old marriage license announcements in five-point Helvetica. What a waste of paper. Of my life.

When the clerk came back to tell me she was closing the office for her lunch break, I realized that I had not gotten very far, even though I had been hunched over the miniscule Trash-80 screen for four hours.

Out in the hall, I rubbed my eyes, then I looked up, taking in the repetition of the balusters that supported the railing on the balcony outside the criminal court room.

There a woman stood ramrod straight. Her afro was pulled back in a headband, except for one frantic puff that escaped above her ear. Everything else about her was fastidiously groomed. She wore a pale blue suit and black shoes that were identical to my pinchy flats, except hers had been polished.

If she was a criminal defendant, based on her expression alone, I had missed a big story.

I ran to the docket posted near the front entrance. There was only one woman's name, Theresa Parker. The charge was transportation of a controlled substance with intent to distribute.

Parker did not look like a drug dealer to me. She looked like a schoolteacher or a Mary Kay saleswoman, somebody's mom.

I dug my reporter pad out from under all the batteries in my purse and climbed the stairs to the second floor. There was nothing else except DUIs on the docket. If the judge had found probable cause to detain Parker, she'd be in cuffs.

"Miss Parker," I said in my most respectful voice, "I was wondering if I could ask you a few questions."

She turned on me, rage behind her eyes.

"I'm from the newspaper. What happened in your case?"

She said, "The charges were dropped."

"Where are you from, ma'am?"

"Not here."

That was all she would say.

I skulked back to the stairs. An older African American woman was making her way up, breathing hard from the exertion. I stood at the landing and listened to the exchange that echoed off the marble.

"Why didn't you just drive home?"

"They cut my car seats all the way down to the springs, Momma. They pulled off all the foam."

"How long have you been here?"

"Since Friday."

I saw the prosecutor swing in through the revolving door.

"What's the story with Parker?" I asked.

He had to think for a minute. "Routine drug stop."

"Were there drugs?"

"No. That's why we dropped the charges."

"But she was kept in jail for four nights."

"She should have considered that possibility when she refused the search."

I didn't know Parker or her mother, didn't know a thing about the stop, but I was starting to think I had missed a lot by focusing on police and fire instead of looking for stories at the courthouse.

When the clerk's office reopened, I surveyed the shelves of criminal files. If I had taken time at the courthouse, could I have found a story worthy of a Silverton in one of those cases?

The files for 1989 were all thin. I pulled down four of them. Waddell, Whitlock, Wilkinson, Williams. None of the names were familiar. The first one I opened, LaShawn Waddell, Black male, 26, from Chicago, pleaded guilty to one count of possession of a controlled substance with intent to distribute. I opened the other three folders. Except for their ages, the information and plea agreements were exactly the same.

I had just pulled down folders that were together because of where the defendants' last names came in the alphabet. What were the chances that four defendants who were near each other alphabetically had the same demographics, the same charges, and the same outcome? And if they really were drug dealers, why had I never seen an African American man at the A-OK Corral? There weren't that many places in Green Meadow where people who might want drugs would go to buy them.

I pulled out another set of files, Abbington, Addison, Armstead, Askew. Same demographics, same charges.

I had missed something big.

It was still early, so I went directly to Sugar's apartment and pounded on her screen door.

"Are there police calls that don't get reported?"

"I'm getting ready for work, but I love unexpected company!"

"Answer me," I demanded, "are you giving me a report on every police call?"

Sugar seemed flummoxed, but she smiled and ushered me in. "I give you every report I get," she said, "but not every thing they do gets written up. For instance, welfare checks. They don't bother writing up the welfare checks."

"You mean public benefits fraud?"

"Huh?" Sugar asked.

"Incidents involving people misusing their government money, food stamps . . ."

"Oh, no, I'm not talking about that."

"What exactly is a welfare check in Green Meadow?" I asked.

Sugar got a bottle of Coke out of her refrigerator. "They're really nothing. The officers stop cars to check on the welfare of the people inside. Usually it's a white woman riding with a black driver. The officer will offer her a safe ride home."

"Why would he think she's not safe?"

"Are you kidding? That guy could be out wilding! Or the poor girl could be about to get sold into white slavery. Pimps in Chicago recruit farm girls from this area."

"If it's such a problem, why doesn't anyone ever talk about it?"

"We don't let it get to be a problem. Not in Bryce County."

"Because of the welfare checks?"

"Yeah."

"How many welfare checks are there in a week?"

Sugar thought for a minute. "Maybe three?"

"And from those, how many kidnapping arrests are there?"

"We haven't had a kidnapping arrest."

"Crossing state lines with minors?"

"They wouldn't cross until Illinois."

"So, what comes from these stops?"

"If there's probable cause," she said, "the officer will search for drugs."

"That's never on the scanner."

"I don't keep anything from you, Hallie. The cops don't write incident reports on welfare checks. It's just routine."

It didn't seem like Sugar was lying to me, but I wondered if she was lying to herself.

Before my regular shift, Blue had me meet him in the parking lot of the game lands. He didn't seem to know what to do with his hands. "This isn't a—what do you call it?"

I said, "A booty call?"

"Right, this isn't a booty call."

I tried to fill the void I felt between us. I told him about what I had found in the criminal case files. He wasn't surprised.

"They have to keep up the appearance that they're fighting the war on drugs. To get the federal grants, they have to show they have an active anti-drug campaign."

I didn't know what was off with Blue. Not holding hands or anything, we just walked along the trail where I had spied on him. I reached down and touched the ground his feet had pounded. "You've worn it smooth."

"Things wear down, yes. Let's go somewhere else."

We walked, not speaking, for about half a mile along the side of the road until we came to a subdivision. Finally, he said, "I've been reading the *Daily-Observer*. You had four stories in yesterday's paper, and every one of them was a piece of crap."

"Frank said he likes my productivity when I write stories from press releases. Maybe if I can make it a full year, he'll write a reference letter for me."

Blue pointed to a forlorn Irish setter on the front steps of a tract house. "That dog hates me. She hates anybody who wears a uniform—firefighters, mail carriers, cops. She can smell us whether we're in uniform or not."

The dog laid down against the door.

"I know this because one time a mail carrier who is a friend of that family showed up early for their Super Bowl party. The guy let himself in and the dog tore into him, almost as bad as what Cujo did to Scooter."

As we got closer, the dog's body remained impassive. The only motion was the wind riffling her hair.

"She doesn't look dangerous."

"She's not," Blue said, "not now. Instead of getting rid of the dog, the family installed an electric fence. But they might as well have put her down. The dog they have now is completely broken."

"Shock collars are cruel."

"They put you on Vital Records. They yanked your chain, Hallie."

"You have no idea."

"Oh yes I do. I have been put in my place by people who could never have gotten their jobs if they weren't related to somebody important. I know what it's like to work for small people in a small town. But you were good at your job."

"Were?"

"Yes, were. Past tense. As in, 'You were our best hope, but now you aren't.'"

Blue turned to face me. "Where's my bitch? Where's the Hallie who would tear you a new one if you said girl instead of woman, didn't matter if you were the fire chief or the mayor?"

"That approach didn't get me very far."

"Oh no. It got you very far. Why do you think Dora talked to you?"

"Random chance."

He shook his head. "You are good at what you do, and you've got to start doing it again. I gave you information. I gave you an introduction. But I'm sorry to see you're not using it."

He wasn't accusing or blaming or anything I could push back against. "Write the story," he implored.

"I don't have enough information to say the police are doing anything illegal."

"Then go get it."

Chapter 31

On my way in to work, I stopped to see Terrence, one of the kids I had interviewed for the drowning aftermath story.

"Was Peter Whitmore involved with drugs?"

Terrence looked at me like I was crazy and walked away. But shortly after I got into the newsroom, my phone rang.

"Miss Linden? This is Terrence." His voice was chalky. "Scooter Mayfield said I should call you. I need to tell you something about Peter Whitmore."

I looked at the clock. I had fifteen minutes to get to the courthouse for my beat check. Thankfully, Frank was in his other office. "Go on."

"I lied to you. Well, I didn't lie, but I didn't tell you the whole truth. That's how they say it, isn't it? The whole truth?"

I could feel the hairs on the back of my neck stand up.

"What did you leave out, Terrence?"

"I didn't tell you that Officer Kellan said to tell Peter he was looking for him."

"On the day Peter and Mason drowned?"

"Right."

"Why are you telling me now?"

"I don't like the way kids have been talking about Peter. I'm not criticizing your writing. But people are saying it was his dad's fault that Peter got so—"

"Got so what?"

"I don't know. Fast? How did you say it in your article?"

"I said he became despondent. That he was depressed, and he became reckless."

"Yeah, he started drinking. It was like he was throwing his life away. But here's the thing: Peter was a good person, and he wasn't stupid. He knew it was dangerous to walk across that bridge. But I just keep thinking, what if he knew the danger but decided to do it anyway?"

"You're saying it was a calculated risk? Do you think Peter knew he could drown, but he did it anyway? Why would he do that?"

"It wasn't his parents' fault. Of course he was mad at his dad. He was mad at his mom, too. But there's other kids whose dads left. They don't all go and drown."

"So, whose fault was it?"

"It was a accident. But it was a accident that Peter put himself up for because he was a good person, not because he was stupid."

Frank came back in the newsroom and looked at his watch.

I ignored Frank. "You're going to have to spell this out for me, Terrence."

"He didn't want to talk to Darnell."

"Of course he didn't," I murmured, trying to sound reassuring. "Darnell's the truant officer."

"He didn't want to talk to Darnell because Darnell said Peter owed him for him not getting charged with anything in the crash. You know those boots he was wearing when he drowned?"

"The Lyalt boots?"

"Yeah, with the metal on the toes. Those are drug dealer boots."

"So, Peter was mixed up with drugs?"

"No! Peter didn't want to be involved with drugs in any way. He was a good kid!"

I could hear someone in the background. Terrence said, "Nobody, Mom," and hung up.

Ignoring the way Frank was drumming his fingers on his desk, I dug the copies I had managed to make from Peter's journal out of my bottom drawer. If I remembered the interview with his mother correctly, he probably got the boots sometime in April.

Paging through the sheets, I scanned for Darnell's name.

There it was: *Officer Kellan said I can call him Darnell. He said he's sorry my dad left. That's the first time an adult has said anything about it.* That was April 17.

Then on April 19, *Darnell said he's got a job for me. He said it's easy and he'll let me drive his Camaro. I don't really like Darnell. He creeps me out, but I would do anything to drive a Camaro. I'm going to own one someday.*

The next day, Peter wrote, *The job working for Darnell is in the middle of the school day. He says I don't have to worry about being arrested because he's the truant officer. He gave me a pair of boots. I am so dumb! I wore them! I don't think I can give them back now. I don't want to miss school because my GPA is B+ and Mom says I'm smart enough to go to college, but that's thousands of dollars. I'm such a putz! I wish I was good at basketball or football. It doesn't matter how dumb those guys are, they can go to college on a scholarship. I'll be lucky if I can go to community college.*

The next entry was about working: *I thought the job was going to be cleaning or moving things around at the police station, but Darnell drove me out into the woods. We sat in the Camaro for a long time. When I said I wanted to sit in the driver's seat, he called me a pussy. He said you've got to earn it. We waited for about an hour and then a van drove up and I took the boxes out of the van and put them in Darnell's trunk. That's it. Darnell stood out at the road. When I told him I wanted to be paid in cash because I want to go to college, he said you've got a 300 dollar pair of boots to work off first. I don't see why he can't load his own damn packages. The guys in the van didn't offer to help at all. They weren't friendly. Just the opposite.*

The next mention of Darnell was at the bottom of the last page I had copied. *Darnell is a creep. I dropped a box on a rock and he pulled his gun on me. He said don't do that again. I'm embarrassed to even write this, but I wet my pants. The guys in the van were disgusted. They said the cracker boy wet himself. That's nasty. I don't know what I was thinking, but I said, You'd piss too if a cop had a gun pointed at you. Darnell yelled at me to shut my mouth. The guys in the van wanted to go. He's got his gun up like he really is going to shoot me, but he's begging them to stay, promising them all sorts of things. He kept his gun on me the whole rest of the time. Nobody's ever, I mean, you just don't do that! My dad taught me, never, never point a gun at a person, loaded or unloaded. Never. I was so nervous, I dropped another box. It broke a little and I could see inside—*

That's where it ended, halfway through the entry. I had to get the journal again.

Mrs. Whitmore didn't look happy to see me when she came to the door.

"I thought there would be more stories," she said. "I thought you'd come around to talk again."

"You've been lonely, haven't you?"

Pain swept across her face. "After people read your story, they said it was my fault. Well, more Raymond's than mine, but they stopped coming by."

I didn't want to diminish her feelings, but I wasn't surprised. "That happens to everyone who loses somebody. People don't understand how deeply it hurts to lose a child."

She gave a cautious sigh. "Is that what you come to talk about?"

"Actually, I might have gotten something wrong in the story. Those boots—"

"The Lyalt boots that we buried him in?"

"Where did he get them?"

"I thought his father gave them to him. That's what divorced dads do: They buy expensive presents as if that compensates for the time they're not spending with their kids."

"Was that Peter's usual taste?"

"Fancy dance boots? No."

"Have you been able to bring yourself to read Peter's journal?"

"No, but Darnell Kellan came by for it the day after your story ran."

"You're kidding."

"No. He said since I loaned it to you, I had to give it to an officer of the law."

———

I called and asked Blue to get Terrence Dunn's telephone number from Scooter. Blue laughed. "It's 583-2196. His dad runs the basketball pool."

I said, "Everybody knows everybody here."

"And we're happy to help. I mean that, Hallie. Lean on me."

I cut the conversation short because I needed to talk to Terrence while Kim was still out on her dinner break.

Terrence sounded timid on the phone. "Miss Linden, I'm sorry I hung up on you."

"That's okay, Terrence. Sometimes a person just has to go. When we were talking, you were worried about something, that by not telling me about the truant officer, people might have assigned blame to Peter's parents."

"Officer Kellan pushed him. I don't mean pushed him into the water, I mean pushed him to be part of something that Peter didn't want to be part of."

"I think you mean drugs."

"Yes, ma'am."

"How do you know?"

"Because he's pushing me now."

That quote nailed it. I needed a few more details, but my story was no longer just based on Dora's inference. I had a witness. But I had a responsibility first.

I said, "Terrence, you didn't ask me for any advice, but I'm going to give you some. Tell your parents what's going on. Do not go into the woods with Darnell. Do not do any work for him. Don't accept any gifts from him, and if he says you owe him, don't believe him."

"It's cocaine, Miss Linden. Peter saw it when a package broke, and I saw it when Officer Kellan was testing it in his Camaro."

"So you have worked for him. How old are you, Terrence?"

He said he had just turned eighteen. I could quote him in the paper without his parents' consent. But there was a right thing to do.

"Terrence, do you understand that as far as I am concerned, this interview is on the record? I plan to use your name."

"That's the only thing that will keep them from killing me for talking about this with you, isn't it, ma'am? You have to put it in the paper."

Chapter 32

With Terrence on the record and what I had seen at the truck stop, I had support for what Dora had said. I could also use the Xeroxed pages from Peter Whitmore's diary. Blue was the only one who could say they killed someone, but he was still waiting on the lab report from the fire at the River Road house.

I knew everything in Green Meadow would change once the story ran in the paper. There would be criminal charges. The Drug Enforcement Agency would do its own investigation, but there would be immediate changes at the cop shop.

I expected that my life would change, too, and quickly. I would not have to wait a year to get out of Green Meadow. With that clip, I could write my own ticket.

Knowing that, I was in no rush to get up the next day. I was with Blue in his bed. When I smiled, he said, "Me too."

He sometimes seized these quiet moments to make little speeches.

"I've been thinking," he said, getting my hand between both of his. "There's a fundraiser for the fire department. It's the social event of the year for us pole-and-ladder types."

He said pole because that was his one holdout tease, the one thing I'd wanted to play on at the fire station that he said was strictly off limits.

I said, "Pole?" and he was off.

"Think of it as a chance to debut—"

"Is it black tie?"

"It's organized by firefighters. It's no-tie."

"And the women wear?"

"Wear anything you want. It's mostly jeans and T-shirts. The rich guys from Sir Splash-A-Lot wear cowboy boots and those T-shirts with a collar."

"Polo shirts?"

"Yes. We all play polo after dinner. Actually, it's Wiffle ball."

"With ponies?"

"They're donkeys. We hold it at Bud Kraemer's farm." He squeezed my hand. "Will you come with me, darlin'? It really is the most fun we have all year."

"I'll probably have to cover it."

"Let Charles cover it. I want you on my arm."

"As a date?"

"You are one strange kind of shy," he said, running his eyes over my body.

"Can't."

He rolled his eyes. "Why not?"

"The story!"

"You're telling me you can't get too close to a source? Hallie, if we were any closer, we'd be walking around in each other's skin."

"You're not a source exactly," I said, "but you're on a side."

"A side? Which side? The anti-fire side? The people-should-live side? There is no other side."

"It's the appearance—"

I could tell from his face he wasn't buying it. "It's the pole, isn't it? You want me to give you everything, even the one thing reserved for honeymooners by the Green Meadow firefighters' unwritten code. Okay. I'll do it. Every man is going to be at the fundraiser. I'll take you down the pole then."

"What's the catch?"

"Afterward, you will go with me to the fundraiser as my date."

⚞⚟

I was supposed to have Saturday off, but Frank called me at home.

He cleared his throat. "Could you please come in today? Charles is sick."

"This will not violate the ban you put on me coming into the newsroom when I'm not scheduled?"

"I wouldn't have asked you if I didn't want you to come in."

"And I'm off probation?"

Frank made his stupid harrumphing noise. "Yes, you're off probation. I need you to cover the fire department fundraiser."

~*~

I took my dinner early to go over to Blue's place and tell him I couldn't go after all.

"You promised."

"This is what's it's like to date a reporter. I'll see you there."

He grabbed my waist and pulled me close to him. His kiss sent me to a place I did not know existed. I wanted to ditch work and ditch the fundraiser, too.

"Look for me there," Blue said.

I tried to re-compose myself. "I really will be working."

~*~

When I got to the farm an hour later, the fundraiser was already in full swing. An ear of corn and a Solo cup of beer were free with admission. I flashed my press pass and the guy at the gate shouted to the beer pourer to give me two.

I declined. "Workin' tonight." I realized I was good ol' boyin'. I knew these guys, most of them, by sight. They were mostly good guys. Guys who would talk down a suicide and never mention it. Guys who would patiently help old men find their medication in the back corner of a cabinet and politely tell them that although *they* understood it was an emergency, that wasn't really what the county wanted 911 to be used for.

There was a dunk tank with a firefighter in old-fashioned gear, including one of those sloping red plastic hats. He was yelling insults at people in the crowd, trying to get somebody mad enough to want to dunk him.

It seemed like almost all of the people knew each other, but the firefighters were taking their roles as carnies quite seriously, hawking and busking.

I let them pose for pictures at their booths. At the game where kids could toss a ping-pong ball into a fishbowl, the firefighter manning the booth confided, "Every kid's a winner." I counted a dozen children walking excitedly with goldfish in plastic bags filled with red- or blue-tinted water.

"It's all-natural food coloring." It was Blue's voice behind me. "I told them you'd do an exposé."

"He did warn us." The guy in the booth laughed.

Blue grabbed for my hand.

I flinched. In a low voice, I said, "Working, remember?"

"I want to introduce you to everyone."

"I already know most of them."

"I want to introduce you as my girlfriend. Womanfriend."

I said, "I can introduce myself," and the guy in the goldfish booth said, "Ouch."

Blue turned away. He had changed into a western shirt with ribbons that came down in two tails off the yoke in the back. I imagined that if he could see how they were fluttering in the wind, he would cut them off.

"Miss—" the firefighter in the goldfish booth leaned over as if he was going to tell me the secret to winning, "he's one quality guy."

I walked away. There was more going on than I understood, but I didn't have time to figure it out.

I took pictures of kids with fish, kids with corncobs, parents with kids on their shoulders holding giant stuffed animals. It seemed that everybody had won. Except me.

At eight o'clock, the people who weren't an obvious part of a family unit gathered for what was listed on the program as Wiffle ball. But there was a twist: The players on the team at bat rode donkeys.

This was the sort of thing I had imagined that I would be covering when I took the job: sweet small-town life. I thought I would hold a mirror up so this town could see itself. And I was doing that. But I did not know how many of the people here would want to look in that mirror in a few days when my big story about the cops came out.

I decided to savor this last quirky assignment. Soon I would not be an anonymous reporter, interchangeable with a long line of women who had held this job for a year or less.

I saw a crowd forming behind the bleachers. People stood ten deep in two separate lines to wager on the game. The first line was to bet on who would win. The other was to guess on which base the first pile of poop would land. One of the firefighters running the betting had a spreadsheet listing the records of all the players. I peered over his shoulder. Blue's stats were impressive.

The farmer who owned the land came out to the pitcher's mound to give the rules. "No sliding," he joked. "If you tag the donkey, you've tagged the player. And, ladies, keep your panties on."

The stands erupted. "There's no rules on us," one woman yelled.

When the names of the fire team members were called, they rode out on their donkeys in front of the bleachers.

The women howled and made panting noises. "That one's gonna be mine!" an intoxicated fan yelled. The firefighter she favored tipped his cap and she started fanning herself with her hands as if she were going to faint.

The camera gave me an excuse to squeeze into the front row. Behind me, I could hear two elderly women talking. "We need to get him settled down," one said. "He says he's got somebody. Said he was going to introduce me to her tonight, but if that's true, where is she?"

My attention went to Blue. As soon as the announcer said his name, the loudspeaker was drowned out by whoops and whistles.

"Ride it, honey, ride it," a woman in my row yelled.

Blue looked magnificent on the donkey. While the other riders were flopping around or lying against the necks of their mounts, Blue's back was straight. He seemed to trust his mare.

I don't think he knew I was in the bleachers.

As the crowd surged forward, I saw Sugar getting kicked off the diamond as she tried to give something to the catcher.

She lit up when she saw me, "We got some nice prospects this year." She issued a giddy-up noise from her frosted pink lips. She had shimmery eye shadow all the way up to her brows.

"Hallie, you've got to get you one of them," Sugar said, pushing herself in onto the bench next to me. "You want a fireman or a police officer?"

She explained that all the single men on the police force and in the fire department played the game and women bid on date packages afterward.

I said, "It sounds like a slave auction."

"You got a kinky mind," Sugar said. "I can only afford one this year, and it's going to be that catcher." When she pointed she caught the man's attention. Staring at him, she pulled the neck of her shirt low.

I asked her to let me out. "Working."

Sugar said she'd save my place.

I headed back to the midway where I took pictures of everything. I felt so alone. I wasn't one of those parents carrying a goldfish home for a sleepy toddler. I wasn't in the stands hoping to catch a foul ball. I wasn't part of anything. I was just acid running to the cracks. Knowing that hurt because I genuinely liked these people—the firefighters I knew through Blue, Sugar, the moms I had interviewed trying to crack the school beat.

But I knew that at the end of the day, when they went home with their families, I would go back to the newsroom.

I ducked into the port-a-potty. Just then, a thunderclap shook the walls and rain started pouring down hard, hitting the door and coming in through the plastic mesh screen. In the mirror, though, I could see it was tears, not raindrops running down my face. I leaned into the door, heaving.

"Are you okay in there?" a voice asked from outside.

"It's nothing."

"It doesn't sound like nothing. Look, nobody's out here. They're all watching the game. Come out and we can talk about whatever's troubling you."

He was a Green Meadow firefighter; I could tell by the compassion in his voice. I didn't want to talk to him. I didn't want Blue to find out how torn up I was.

"I'll be all right," I managed.

"We've got the Jaws of Life," he threatened. "Don't make me cut you out."

I didn't laugh.

"What if I told you I need to use the john?"

I apologized. *Buck up,* I told myself, *you're working.*

When I dried my eyes, the thin toilet paper left little paper boogers on my face. I didn't care enough to remove them.

"Sorry you had to wait," was all I said to the firefighter as I scurried out.

On the midway the guys in the booths hung blue tarps over the stuffed animals and headed for the Wiffle ball diamond. I put up the tiny Totes umbrella I took everywhere and went there, too.

The rain let up. Even though there were only six innings, the game was slow agony. The batters mostly bunted. That usually got them to first because the fielders didn't want to get too close to the donkeys, lest they get kicked.

It was the fourth inning when I saw Blue get up to bat. There was a runner on every base, or as close to the base as the donkey would stand.

"Oh baby, knock me home," a woman at the top of the stand yelled as Blue rode up to the home plate. Blue laughed and turned. "This is for you," she yelled.

Blue shook his head, but in an instant, a pair of hot pink panties were sailing toward him. They hooked on the donkey's ears. "You can ride me later," the drunk yelled.

That's when Blue saw me in the crowd.

"It's not—"

"Play the game," I mouthed.

The drunk turned her attention to me. "I'm buying him," she yelled and started clomping down the bleacher steps waving a wad of bills in her fist.

My eyes went from her to Blue. "Sorry," he mouthed, noticing too late the plastic ball sailing toward him.

"Strike," the umpire called.

The crowd booed.

I didn't know the rules. I didn't know if it was a fair call.

The drunk woman was almost to the bottom of the bleachers. I didn't know if I even had a right to be angry. *I've told him a hundred times I'm not permanent.* I said to myself. *Why do I care if some woman I don't know wants to throw her panties in the ring?*

Blue was looking at me, not the pitcher, who was winding up, as if that would propel a Wiffle ball any faster.

Male voices in the crowd were yelling at Blue to focus. The women were starting to chant, "Fight, fight, fight, fight."

You'd think with all the police around, people wouldn't do that. But the cops were down by nine and their pitcher seemed ready to exploit the fact that Blue was completely fazed by the scene in the stands.

Blue was saying something to me and pulling the panties off his donkey's ears. I put the camera to my face, as if to say what I had said earlier: *I'm working.* That's when the drunk woman fell. She made a sharp conk on the aluminum stairs and every eye went to her. Half a dozen paramedics rushed over.

"It's just a flesh wound," the woman yelled, and then at me, "He's mine."

Her money had fallen out of her hand when she went down, and now she was demanding that the people who had picked it up for her give it back. "I'm countin' it. I had two hundred dollars for that stud. Cops're all over. I'll have you arrested."

One of the medics insisted on putting the woman on a backboard. As he strapped her in, I could hear her slurring, "I want me a brown-eyed guy this year."

The pitcher seized the moment to throw the ball. It came slow, but Blue's yellow plastic bat waved two feet short.

The crowd jeered as the cops took the reins from the firemen on the bases. "Keep your head in the game," a man shouted at Blue. "I've got money on fire."

They played two more innings. I could tell Blue was trying not to look at me.

Sugar found me in the crowd after the game and pulled me back to the bleacher seat next to her.

"What was all that?"

I told her it was nothing, but all around us women I did not know slapped me on the back and told me I was lucky the drunk woman got carried out on a backboard.

Then two cops brought out a wooden box and centered it in front of the crowd. "No touching the merchandise," one yelled, "until it's paid for."

"Sugar, how much money do you have?" I asked.

"I've got a hundred and forty."

"Can I borrow it all?"

Sugar looked torn.

I said, "If he likes you, he'll take you out, anyway."

"But what if he don't like me? No. I can't. You're my best friend, but it's been a year."

Keep it together, I told myself. *Just be a reporter for a few more minutes.*

But I couldn't keep it together. Blue was the first on the block. The auctioneer said that even though Blue hadn't made it to first base all night, he came into the game with the best record in the history of Green Meadow Donkey Wiff. "It's time to put him out to stud," the announcer intoned.

When Blue stepped onto the box, I could see that the blue and white ribbons sewn onto his shirt had not fared well in the rain. Their tails stuck forlornly to the damp fabric.

"Is there anything you want to say for yourself?" the announcer asked him.

Blue pushed away the mic. "Just get it over with."

With the pink panty drunk gone, bidding started low. "Come on, ladies," the auctioneer shouted, "Thirty dollars? He went for one hundred sixty last year."

One of the yentas behind me bid forty. "It's for a friend."

The thirty-dollar bidder yelled, "Must be present to win," but the older woman stood her ground.

Then her companion chided her, "That's a lot of money. If you're serious, you better make sure he really is single."

The bidder called to Blue. "We didn't think you were going to be playing tonight. Are you really single?"

"I don't know, auntie," he said. And then he looked at me. "Hallie? Say the word and you can take me off this block."

There was a silent moment. Then the crowd turned on me, angry women whose makeup had run in the rain. I'm not a photojournalist, but anyone could see that picture told the whole story.

I don't know what Blue did next. I just heard the winning bidder's friend say, "It's for a good cause."

I took two photos of the next guy on the block grinning and flexing his muscles.

"That's more like it," the auctioneer said and started the bidding at a hundred dollars.

I felt like shit, but I had my story. I'd go back to the office and write it, then figure out a way to make peace with Blue.

Chapter 33

In my rearview mirror, I checked my face. I didn't want to look like I had been crying because I didn't want to discuss the evening with Kim. I kept a bottle of Visine in the ashtray, so I stared up at the car ceiling and put two drops in each eye.

But my clear eyes gave me no privacy. As soon as I rounded into the newsroom, Kim was on me.

"Is Blue a source or is Blue your boyfriend?"

I said, "Excuse me?"

"Charles told me all about it. Whatever that display was, you're the talk of the town."

"Charles was at the fire department fundraiser? I thought he was sick."

"Don't change the subject. The last girl in your job ran off with the prosecutor. We've got too much invested in you to let something like that happen again. Whatever's going on between you and Blue, call it off."

"I'll take that under advisement."

"This isn't friendly advice. Frank said you've quoted Blue in three different stories. I don't think you're seeing the seriousness of the problem. While I think you might be able to remain objective, Frank thinks you're compromised. He was this close to taking you off fire," she said, holding up a thumb and forefinger barely an inch apart.

"Who would you put on fire?"

"That's what I said. Charles won't work weekends and you've finally gotten into the swing of things with the police."

"Let me get this straight. You and Frank had a conversation this evening about my job duties based on what Charles alleged was said at the firefighters' fundraiser?"

"The new dispatcher has been cackling about you on the scanner for an hour. Blue has been the most eligible bachelor in donkey Wiff two years running. Couldn't you have chosen someone with a lower profile?"

I wrote the story leaving out what apparently was the biggest news of the night.

I drove to Blue's house as soon as I was off work. I felt like I was carrying a rock in my heart.

When he opened the door, I saw that he had changed out of the shirt with the ribbons.

"What happened?" he asked.

"I have to call it off."

Blue looked stricken. "I pushed too hard."

"No." I buried my face in his chest and cried.

"Your terms," he pleaded. "Whatever you want."

I said it wouldn't work. I didn't tell him what Kim had said. It was my decision. I could choose my job or Blue. I couldn't have both, and there was no other job for me in Green Meadow.

I groped for words. "Was that really your aunt?"

"She's a cousin of my grandmother. I gave her money back."

"You don't talk much about your family."

"I want you in my family."

"Can't," I cried. "Take her friend out. She's probably nice."

Blue grabbed my hands. "I don't want nice. I want you."

I pulled my hands back and covered my face. It hurt too much to keep hurting him, so I turned and walked out the door, small steps I did not want to take. I drove off his street and then parked. Through my windshield I could see the moon, indifferent to my tears.

It was quite a while before I felt safe to drive. When I finally got home, the round room was cold and much too big. My answering machine flashed three, two messages from Blue that I fast forwarded through and one from Kim apologizing, saying it was so hard to be both my boss and my friend, but she really did have to say what she had said, Frank had told her to. As I deleted that, my phone rang.

Amber.

I started to apologize, aware that I needed at least one friend in the universe, but she cut me off.

"Life is short. You sound like hell."

I told her everything. Amber took my side, called Kim a bitch. When I asked her if she thought I was compromised, she said, "Who cares? You work for an editor who can't write in a town where cops wholesale cocaine."

I said, "Professor Wassle would probably see it differently."

"That's why I called. Norm Wassle's in a coma."

I didn't think I could feel any worse, but I did. "Is Norm going to make it?" I croaked.

Amber didn't answer.

Chapter 34

The next day at work was tough. Kim seemed to understand. She said, "Let's both just eat here so we can leave early."

She made popcorn in the microwave and offered me some. It wasn't much of a dinner, but I had not packed anything. We went out back to the picnic table and Kim nattered about Norton's latest transgressions.

This is all that's left for me here, I thought, and resolved to get the story nailed down as soon as possible.

⌁⌁

The phone woke me up early Tuesday morning. I thought it must be a telemarketer. Everyone who knew me knew I worked late.

Blinking against the light, I heard a man's voice tell my answering machine to be at Trojan at ten-thirty a.m. "Someone you can trust will show you."

I jumped out of bed. "Show me what?" I was yelling at the machine when the phone rang again.

"Hallie? It's Sandra. I'm sorry for calling so early. I need you to watch Matthew. My mother-in-law was in a crash. I don't know how long I'll be at the hospital. I can't reach Luke."

"I don't know anything about kids."

"Mattie can get really keyed up when there's stress. I need you to do this for me."

"It will take me half an hour to shower."

"He doesn't care what you smell like. He's waiting on the front porch."

"You left him alone?"

"My mother-in-law is dying. Matthew would pick up on that and it would be pandemonium in the hospital. Get there as quick as you can."

***

Matthew sat rigid on the porch swing, staring down at the space shuttle model in his hands.

"You broke the speed limit," he said as I walked up.

"How do you know?"

"Mom said to stay still and count to eighteen hundred. Eighteen hundred is the number of seconds in half an hour. But I wasn't even to six hundred. So, you broke the speed limit. That means it's serious, right?"

"I suppose I might have broken the speed limit."

"You changed the subject. It's serious, right?"

"Does your mom have you count very often?"

"You're doing it again. That means you don't want to tell me, so I can deduce it is pretty serious. Mom thinks I would cause a fuss at the hospital, but she's wrong. I can count in the hospital, too."

"Do you want to go inside?"

"I have to finish counting. That's the rule. I count and I don't move."

"Okay, well I'm going to go in and get some cereal. Have you had breakfast?"

"Mom made me an egg before they called about Grandma."

Inside, Sandra's kitchen betrayed her rush leaving the house. A frying pan and spatula jutted out against the orderly row of canisters. I poured a bowl of cereal and topped it with soymilk.

When I went back outside, Matthew was almost to nine hundred.

"Can I talk to you while you count?"

"Yes, but I can't really talk to you back."

"But you could nod yes or no?"

"I think by don't move, my mom means don't get up and go anywhere. I think if I nod my head, that's okay."

He resumed his string of numbers. When he got to nine hundred, he said it louder, but at exactly the same tempo. "NINE hundred Mississippi. Nine hundred one Mississippi. Nine hundred two Mississippi."

I said that since he was supposed to count until I arrived, it was probably okay to continue counting in my car. Matthew nodded in agreement and followed me.

I didn't know if Sandra would have approved, but I wasn't likely to get another chance at Trojan if I missed the 10:30 appointment.

Behind a chain-link fence, the plant was a grim series of battleship-gray buildings.

"Why are we at Uncle Luke's job?" Matthew asked as we rolled into the parking lot.

"I've got to work, Matthew. But maybe we can find Luke. He doesn't know your grandma's sick."

"She's not sick. She was in a car accident."

I sighed and told him to come in with me. We stepped through the doors into the lobby where a semi dominated the huge showroom. A set of wooden steps led into its trailer.

Matthew ran up the steps and began pounding inside the trailer. A janitor polishing the tractor's grille looked up. I'd never seen Matthew this wiggy, but I guess he'd never been under stress when I was around.

"Can I help you?" a severe man in a business suit asked.

"I need to find one of your employees, Luke Tenney."

Where I was standing near the fancy wooden stairs, I could see Matthew standing stock still in the truck. The janitor had moved so that I could see him. He slowly shook his head no.

The man in the suit was a little to my left. "What exactly do you want, miss?" he asked.

The janitor made a slit-your-throat motion. Maybe he knew Luke. Maybe having a kid show up at work got you fired here.

"One of your employees is giving a tour," I lied. "This little boy was supposed to be on it."

"We don't give tours," the showroom employee said. "Why are you here?"

Matthew came flying out of the truck. He leapt down the stairs and hugged me with the ferocity of a bear cub.

"We're here to see my Uncle Luke. He's the FOREMAN in the paint room!"

Suit went to the counter and picked up a phone. A minute later, Luke appeared in paper coveralls.

"Mattie! My man! What are you doing here?"

Luke took us back to the paint room. As soon as the door closed, his smile disappeared.

"Are you crazy?" he asked me.

I apologized. "Sandra's mother-in-law is in the hospital."

"Grandma was in a crash!" Matthew yelled.

Agony registered on Luke's face. "A bad one?"

I smoothed Mattie's hair and said, "Probably she just got a little shaken up in a fender bender."

While Mattie examined the whorls of paint on the floor, Luke mouthed the word "Really?"

Slowly, I shook my head no.

"I should never have . . ." Luke seemed to blame himself.

I said, "She wasn't very old, there's no reason she should not have been driving." I was trying to placate him, but he looked at me like I had no idea what I was talking about.

"There's no turning back time," he said. I could see that Luke was really torn up, but he continued, "You're probably wondering why I had you called here. You're working on a big story on the trailers, aren't you?"

"How do you know that?"

"Sandra told me when she invited me to be in a prayer circle for you."

This surprised me because I had not told Sandra about the story. I had been very careful not to mention it to anyone. I thought only Blue and my sources knew what I was working on.

"Who is in this prayer circle?" I asked.

"I don't know. I'm not in it. That stuff's a big time suck. I just said I'd help if I could. But here's the thing: I think the," Luke looked at Matthew, "the, uh, wholesalers might know you're looking into their shipping practices."

Luke motioned for me to lean in. Instinctively, I put my hands over Mattie's ears.

"Dora's my neighbor," Luke whispered. "Somebody went in her house and killed her cat this morning. Left it in the dish drainer. You know how far her trailer sits back from the road? I could hear her screaming from my place."

He said Dora and Scooter had moved out of the county "until things blow over."

I pulled Matthew close to me. "How long will that be?"

"That's pretty much up to you."

Luke asked if I'd brought a camera. I had not. He thought the showroom had a Polaroid they used to take pictures of new owners with their trucks.

"Mattie and I are going to go borrow it," Luke said. "While we're getting it, take a careful look at the short panel in the interior of that trailer." He gestured to a trailer that looked just like the one I'd seen at the truck stop.

I walked up the ramp into the trailer. Stepping my feet carefully end-to-end, I came up with the same length I had for the one at the truck stop. Once I got to the short wall, I examined it carefully. There was no handle that I could see to open the compartment, but when I pushed the cardboard back of my reporter pad into the molding, I was able to wedge the panel up. A gasket no thicker than a rubber band ran the length of the interior of the molding.

Behind me I heard a rattle. Luke was back and hurrying up the ramp.

"Got the camera!" he called.

Matthew dashed up the ramp behind him.

"It's a pry panel," Luke said.

Matthew rushed to where I was crouched down at the other end of the trailer.

"Let me help," Matthew demanded.

"This is important," I said to him. "I need you to hold still and count Mississippi as quietly as you can."

"Did I do something wrong?"

"No," I said, "it's like your mom telling you to stay on the porch this morning. It's important to do it right. No running. No yelling."

While Matthew counted, Luke pointed to a series of hex-head screws. "We rivet in this factory. Nothing we build is meant to be modified by the purchaser. But this—" he pounded on the short panel, "this looks like it could be removed with an Allen wrench."

"How big is that compartment?"

"Three by ten, all the way up to the ceiling."

"A lot of nose candy could fit in there."

We slid the panel up again using a screwdriver. Luke took three photos that peered in, giving a sense of the space.

"Why are you helping me with this?" I asked him.

"It will keep the prayer ladies off my back if I can say I did my part."

I glanced at Matthew, then whispered to Luke, "That's not a reason to blow the whistle on an interstate drug ring. Aren't you afraid?"

Luke faced me head on. "It's got to be pinned on the cops. There are rotten apples in this factory helping them, but it's the cops who are at the top. I'm counting on you to get that right in your story. Otherwise, when the feds figure it out, the cops will point to us."

"Do you really think the DEA will figure it out?"

"Operations stepped up this year. I used to see a truck with one of those panels once a month. Now there's one every week. As you said, that's a hell of a lot of nose candy. If there really is a war on drugs, that kind of volume is going to attract attention in Chicago."

Matthew stopped counting. "You made a swear."

"I can keep Matthew," Luke said.

"Don't you need to go see your mom in the hospital?" I asked.

Luke didn't answer. Instead, he looked down at the floor of the trailer. "I think I can keep Matthew safe here. I'm not sure he'll be safe with you."

⚓

Kim called me at home before my shift started.

"Can I come over?"

I had mixed feelings. I didn't want to tell Kim about the story before I turned it in. *This would just be a social call*, I told myself, *maybe a chance to get Kim on my side if Frank wanted to take out the unnamed source.*

I had to let go of my anger at Kim for telling me to call it off with Blue. Kim was right; Blue and I had gotten too close for him to be a source. The fact that the reporter before me had gotten involved with the prosecutor didn't change the standards. Gripping the receiver, I tried to think of Blue in an appropriately distant perspective. With any luck, he was going to be a source on the follow-up cocaine story when the lab report came in.

Kim cleared her throat. "Can I come?"

"Sure. Come over."

I straightened up my living room and dusted my award shelf. The only thing on it was Kim's note promising to enter one of my stories for the Silverton.

Kim stood back from my door. There was a wistfulness on her face.

"Have I ever shown you my pier?" I asked.

As we walked down to the water, I pushed back the boughs of the pine trees that grew right up to the sides of the concrete steps.

Kim said, "I know it's been a rough haul for you. I'm sorry Frank put you on Vital Records. I'm sorry about your firefighter friend, too. It has to be lonely, this just being your first year in Green Meadow."

Kim apologized again for me being put on probation. "See, the thing is, we've got two editors for two reporters, a photographer, and a sports stringer in a town where nothing ever happens."

"I wouldn't say nothing."

"Frank thinks corporate is going to tell us we're going to have to let somebody go next quarter, and I can't allow that to be me."

"Are you saying ordinarily you would have backed me up in that meeting?"

"Forgive me. I know you do beat checks every day. I know you're analyzing those reports and looking for patterns in a way no other reporter we've had ever did. I know you're building sources. You are doing everything right—I always mention that in the Tuesday morning phone conferences with Jed."

Hearing that helped.

Kim said, "What it's come down to—and maybe this is something I got out of conversations with you—is that I can't tolerate Norton's drinking anymore. He's setting a terrible example for Misty. I put my foot down. I told him he couldn't be drunk around her anymore. I gave him a month to sober up, but if he doesn't, I have to be able to make it on my own."

"That's why you didn't stand up for me?"

She reached for my hand. "I have to stay on Frank's good side."

Maybe in planning ahead for what would happen if she had to enforce her ultimatum, Kim realized I was a pretty good friend. I don't know if I was just choosing the path of least resistance, but when she squeezed my hand and said, "Friends again?" I squeezed back.

Chapter 35

As soon as Kim left, I sat down at my kitchen table and listed what I had to build my story: Luke had buckled to fear at the last minute and said I could not use his name. I knew under the law I had a right to quote him since he hadn't said anything about the interview being off the record when we started. But the law isn't all you consider when deciding whether to name a source.

I had the measurement of the trailer interior. What's the carpenter's adage? Measure twice, cut once. I had measured in two different trailers. I had seen the compartment and had a polaroid picture. That, combined with Peter's journal, the quotes from the night dispatcher, and the Terrence Dunn interview, was almost enough. I just needed a response from the cops.

I called Sugar.

"Do you know how you said you could set me up on a date with Darnell?"

"Yes! Let's double."

"No, I want to get to know him on my own first."

"I forgot, you didn't get anyone at the bachelor auction. I'm sorry I couldn't loan you my savings. I really am."

"You set me up with Darnell, that will more than make up for it."

"We'll get you some action, you dirty girl."

When I hung up the phone, I hand wrote a fill-in-the-blank story, leaving space for the obligatory denial I would get from Darnell.

What was this really about? I asked myself. In the war on drugs, the word "drugs" evokes a general fear that people who take them will go crazy or commit violent acts. But I'd been at parties with people who were high, and they weren't much different than drunks.

I wrote a lead: *Contrary to popular belief, the real danger with drugs isn't in the taking, it's the brutality of the illegal trade that gets the drugs to the user.*

Ugh. Too abstract. And, really, I was editorializing.

Write what you know, I told myself. I knew Darnell tried to get three different people involved in loading cocaine. That's drama. Everyone in town knew how Peter Whitmore died. Lead with his journal entry and they'll sketch in the pathos.

Some people believe Peter Whitmore became reckless after his father left the family. But one of his Green Meadow High classmates says Peter died trying to get away from the school's truancy officer, who was trying to force the boy into work as a drug trafficker.

On April 28, 16-year-old Peter wrote in his journal, "Darnell drove me out into the woods. We sat in the Camaro for a really long time. . . . We waited for about an hour and then a van drove up and I took the boxes out of the van and put them in Darnell's trunk. Darnell stood out at the road."

Peter wrote that Darnell assured him he would not be arrested for truancy, but there were other dangers.

"I dropped a box on a rock and he pulled his gun on me. He said don't do that again. . . . The guys in the van wanted to go. He's got his gun trained on me like he really is going to shoot me, but he's begging them to stay, promising them all sorts of things. He kept his gun pointed at me the whole rest of the time."

Peter's friend Terrence Dunn said he has firsthand knowledge of a wholesale cocaine operation that the truancy officer pressured Green Meadow teens to work in.

"He's pushing me now," Dunn said. "It's cocaine. I saw it when Officer Kellan was testing it in his Camaro."

Kellan quote here _____.

A former Green Meadow Police employee confirmed the story. Dora Mayfield, who worked as a night dispatcher for 14 years, said Kellan asked her to do loading work as well, and when she refused, he asked for her son.

I had to take that last phrase out. She only said Darnell asked to speak to Scooter. Asking to speak to someone is not the same as offering them a job in the coke pipeline.

But I could use the truck allegation.

Mayfield said, "They arranged for it to be shipped into Chicago in compartments in new Trojan trucks. Drug agents can't track them because each truck only carries coke once."

Interior measurements of two different Trojan Truck trailers were 50 feet, but the National Highway Traffic Safety Board length standard for trailers is 53 feet. A false back wall, easily removed with an Allen wrench, creates a 3' by 10' compartment in trailers allegedly used to ship cocaine into Chicago. A source at Trojan Truck demonstrated one compartment was sealed with a thin rubber gasket to prevent contents from being detected by drug-sniffing dogs.

Luke was an unnamed source, but even Frank would have to allow that for this story. Just to convince Frank, though, I added, *Mayfield said she blew the whistle on the operation because she fears for her life.*

"I was the one who got the bomb in her mailbox," she said. "They've already tried and they'll try again, I reckon."

It was Mayfield's son Scooter who was savagely attacked by the DARE dog Cujo. Although Kellan takes Cujo into schools and restaurants, the German shepherd is not trained to detect drugs. Instead, Cujo was seized from one of the officer's competitors in the drug trade.

The irony there seemed a bit over the top. I changed it to, *Instead, Cujo was seized in a drug raid, as was the Camaro Officer Kellan drives.*

It was pretty good. If Blue got the lab reports on the fire victim back in time, it would be a slam-dunk for a Silverton. Then it wouldn't just be one cop coercing kids into the drug trade; it would be cops plural killing someone who found out about their drug operation.

⚔

I kept mum about what I was working on. After I touched all the bases to complete my shift on Wednesday, I headed out to meet Darnell.

I didn't think it was possible, but the Top Hat was even skeezier than the A-OK Corral. It was smoky and dark, but not dark enough to hide the fact that the floor looked like it had not been mopped in a long time, maybe not ever.

Darnell greeted me with a belch. There were six empty glasses next to his keys on the table.

"You're late," he said. "That's gonna be a spankin'."

"Do they still allow corporal punishment in Indiana schools?"

"Corporal who?"

"Spanking. Do they still allow spanking in the schools here?"

"How would I know?"

"You're the truancy officer."

"I'm the DARE officer, too. Dare you to take your shirt off."

I bit my tongue. *Remember why you're here*, I reminded myself, *the Silverton*. "This isn't that kind of bar."

"But you're that kind of girl." When Darnell patted the seat next to him, the thick gold chain around his neck sparkled.

I chose the chair across the table.

"Hard to git, huh? Sugar said you was different. But I know girls all want the same thing." Darnell licked his lips. "We're gonna get real close. I got sixteen hours off with nothin' to do but do you."

I cleared my throat and got out my reporter pad. "Tell me about your work with DARE," I said. "Drugs are a real scourge on society."

Darnell pushed out his lower lip and fumbled with his cigarette pack. The beer seemed to be doing most of his thinking. "At least tell me you smoke."

"Those are Kools," I said. "I didn't know they were sold around here."

"Don't know if they is or ain't. Took 'em off a drug dealer. Cigarettes are 'spensive."

"Did you get a pair of boots off a drug dealer, too?"

"I'm sure I did at some point. Boots. Leather jackets. Stereos. Drug dealers have lots of nice stuff." He leaned in with a drunk's compulsion for full disclosure. "I actually don't do the seizing myself. Dad gives me the stuff."

"Your father is Conrad Kellan, the police chief."

"Why are we talkin' 'bout my daddy? Sugar says you's hard up. Do you want to get lucky or not?"

"Not. What I want is to know if your father knows you're using high school kids to transfer cocaine."

Darnell slammed his hand against the tabletop. "Goddam it, how do you know that?"

"Everybody knows," I said, holding his eyes.

"But nobody talks about it. Daddy makes sure of that."

Don't react, don't react, I told myself.

I threw my shoulders back. "There's a fine line, Darnell. It's one thing to enrich one's income when working on a low public servant's salary. It's another thing entirely to abuse a position of authority."

"I'm not following you," Darnell said, struggling against the alcohol.

"Did you give Peter Whitmore a pair of boots and then tell him he had to work them off by loading cocaine?"

"That kid's dead," he said, without a trace of emotion.

I closed my notebook. "If you can't give me a quote, I'm going to have to ask your father. What's his home number?"

Darnell winced. "Don't call my dad. Please. You have no idea what he is capable of." As if he could explain away his involvement in the drug ring, Darnell said, "We were down a man after Ricky got injured in that rollover. It was supposed to be a temporary thing."

"So you're not denying it?"

Darnell cocked his head as if he was having trouble understanding my question. "Ain't that what you call a double negative? Could you ask it again?"

"Are you part of a cocaine wholesaling operation using compartments built into Trojan Trucks?"

"Who talked at Trojan?"

"Are you going to answer my question?" *Upper hand. Upper hand.*

Darnell's face changed again. He looked very young. And afraid. There was a gulpy quality to his voice when he asked, "Are you going to call my dad if I don't?"

"Yes."

"But you won't if I do?"

From his question I realized I really did have the upper hand, and it wasn't because of the alcohol.

"All right," I said, "not tonight. I won't call your dad tonight if you answer."

Darnell exclaimed, "No comment!" and slapped his leg like it was the funniest thing he'd ever heard.

"That's not an answer," I intoned. "I have to get an answer from a police source tonight. That can be you or your dad. It's your choice."

I kept my eyes locked on his as he thought about it.

"I don't deny it," he said. "That's a double negative, too. Ain't a confession, though. And you can't say it means I do it all myself, either. I never see the money."

"So you're working off the Camaro?"

"Practically the whole force is working off a car or boat or something. But that's off the record. 'I don't deny it' is the only thing you can put in the paper. And only about the Whitmore kid."

I got up.

"Are you going to put this in the paper?"

"Of course."

"Sugar said you was cool, but you ain't cool," Darnell said, downing the last of his beer. "You've got to understand, it's not just me."

"Is that what you want in the paper?"

Darnell blanched. "God, no. Daddy'll fire me if I say there's others involved."

I started to say, "What your father does is the least of your worries," but maybe that was not true. Would Conrad Kellan pull out his own son's teeth to teach him a lesson? Would Daddy let his pride and joy take the fall for the whole ring?

Those questions would have to wait for my follow-up story. I had made a deal; I had my quote.

Darnell was so drunk that he wasn't thinking straight. From the way his head kept bobbing down, I thought he was probably going to be out cold in a matter of minutes. He didn't have his gun with him. At least for now, he was no threat. But until the story was published, my continued corporeal existence had to be a primary concern.

Darnell reached for my ass as I left, but his muscle coordination was shot. One of the barflies said, "She's not from here," as I walked out the door.

⚊⚊⚊

It was way past midnight when I let myself into the newsroom. The paper had already gone to the post office. I was completely alone in the building when I sat down to finish the story.

It seemed too easy. Darnell had pretty much admitted the whole operation existed exactly as Dora had described it. And yet, when I moved my cursor to fill in that blank, I had a real dilemma: I had let Luke take his interview off the record retroactively because he feared for his life. Darnell had spoken to me in a public place, a bar, so every word was fair game. I had lured him there under false pretenses, but there was no way, even as drunk as he was, that he thought we were on a date one minute into it.

Still, the same people Luke feared might kill him could go after Darnell.

I didn't like Darnell. In my mind he was a criminal who abused the trust of kids. He knew he was on the record with the non-denial, but in an act of charity, I worded his comment in a way that did not suggest Darnell had told me other officers were involved in the operation.

Officer Kellan did not deny Dunn's allegation is what I wrote in the blank.

I read over my completed story. It was journalistically conservative. Every allegation was supported, the major ones by more than one source. There was nothing for Frank to nitpick, no typos, nothing vague or unclear. It was a Silverton contender for sure, and it would run three days before the publication deadline. Maybe there would even be a chance to include a follow-up story if Blue got the lab reports back.

Triumphantly, I hit send to put the story in the news queue.

Chapter 36

I was surprised that my story wasn't already on the galleys when I got in Thursday afternoon. Kim only had time to tell me that Frank and Charles had left together to get an early start on the Labor Day weekend when her phone rang. I could tell by the way her shoulders went rigid that it was Norton.

Before she had the handset back in its cradle, she was sobbing. "I have to attend to a family matter. Will you be all right without me?"

I assured her that I would be. But I was angry that Kim's rapist drunkard husband had her attention so completely. I wanted to know how the story was going to be featured. I wanted to make sure Frank had not fiddled with the lead when he edited it. Instead, I was alone for hours with no access to the computer queue where my prize contender awaited publication.

I decided to do the police beat check by phone, just in case Darnell had talked about our encounter.

Apparently, he had not.

"How did it go?" Sugar asked.

"I'm not one to kiss and tell."

Sugar laughed and said it must have been pretty good since Darnell hadn't shown up for work. "That boy is sleeping you off."

I really did hope that Sugar was right. But fear sometimes keeps you alive, and fear was what hit me when I hung up. Fear and the enormity of the story. Darnell would lose his job, that was a given. Darnell would probably also go to prison.

It seemed likely that after the investigation, Ricky and the chief would be indicted too. Sugar would probably never forgive me for that. But then we were just work friends, I told myself. And part of being a reporter is writing things that may hurt sources that you like. *That's why we keep boundaries.*

Kim was morose when she returned.

"Norton went ballistic when I told him I had to fill in for Frank at noon. He said he's entitled to eight hours of sleep, as if I had *chosen* to have to come in early."

"Was he drinking?"

"Yep. He was supposed to take Misty to the water park today, but I couldn't risk that, not with him in that condition."

I found no Kleenexes in the supply closet, so I got Kim a brown paper towel from the women's restroom.

"Misty hates it when Mommy and Daddy fight," Kim sobbed. "I can just see her with her face buried in her pillow. This is the last week of summer vacation and I've ruined it for her. We've got a family press pass to Sir Splash-A-Lot's. She should be there today."

"Norton ruined it." I said, but Kim was already starting a bad-mommy spiral.

"I left my daughter alone with a drunk."

Kim sat staring. Faced with this situation a few weeks earlier, I would have talked it all out with her. But I had a different agenda. "Frank's left us alone on a Thursday. I guess that means you've been promoted to managing editor."

Flattery will get you everywhere. Even with catatonic editors.

Kim said, "I went through Frank's evergreen queue. He used pretty much everything."

I edged behind her. While she thumbed through the press releases in Frank's in-basket, I leaned in and saw that my story was not in the queue for the typesetter. *Frank must still have it in news,* I thought.

I put a hand on Kim's shoulder. "You need to go back and talk to Misty," I said. "Take a long dinner. I'll cover for you."

She flashed her biggest smile. Even though it usually signaled some very unprofessional request was coming, I realized I had missed that smile.

"Let's leave early instead," she said.

That was a lot to ask. It meant I would have to get the rest of the beat checks done fast and split the editing.

I could see how much Kim wanted to plow through so we could leave at eight. I wanted to say, *It seems like bad journalism*, which it would be, but instead I said, "The drunk drivers tend to die racing home late at night."

She said, "*Drunken* drivers."

"Hamilton College must have had some English Department. You're the only person who says it correctly."

"Frank changes it in my copy, but I persist."

"You should be managing editor."

She said, "No, thank you. Not since they merged it with the publisher duties. Church and state."

"Mr. Gorbachev, reinforce this wall."

Kim laughed and the sweat on her cheeks sprinkled down onto her blouse.

She told me she usually voted Republican, but she hadn't been able to pull the lever for Reagan. "The guy took more naps than Misty. He was just a figurehead. It was probably Nancy and her astrologer running the country."

"Is that really any different from what we have here?"

"I don't mind doing the editing so Frank can have a long weekend."

"Bullshit."

Kim said, "Charles has to bring his boat in for the winter. They wanted one last hurrah."

As Kim turned back to Frank's monitor, I got a gleam of an idea: Sisterhood might be powerful tonight.

"Go see how Misty's doing. Take two and a half hours for dinner. Tuck her in. Tell her it's from me."

"Really?" Kim said. "What about your dinner break?"

I held up my brown paper bag. "Go."

She hesitated. There was the matter of the front page.

"Do you think you can drum something up while I'm gone?"

When I said, "I've never let you down before," Kim grabbed her purse.

"We've got big holes on one and three," she called over her shoulder.

I plunked down in Frank's chair and spun around. His desk, for a managing editor, was surprisingly empty. It looked like the desk of an insurance executive—nothing but an old-fashioned blotter and the inbox.

I lifted the velvety blotter paper. There was no list of passwords under it.

I unfolded the document holder Velcroed to the side of his monitor. There was a list, but it was just phone numbers—the mayor, the school superintendent.

He had a home number for the chief of police. I copied that down, annoyed that he hadn't given it to me months ago.

I pulled the handle of each of Frank's desk drawers. All locked. *The lengths he goes to keep anyone from taking batteries for a Walkman,* I thought. But then I realized Kim must have a key.

Searching Kim's desk was a different exercise. She had three school pictures of Misty in frames and an award from the state chapter of the Society of Professional Journalists teetering on a stack of reporter pads. Competing for attention were about a hundred pieces of paper, many of them marked TOP PRIORITY or DO FIRST. I had to be careful poking around looking for the key lest I knock one of her piles to the floor.

And sticking out from the bottom of her monitor? A yellow Post-It.

I unstuck it and was thrilled to see Frank's even cursive. "Evergreen password: D-OEG1989." Frank was one of those people who used initials for passwords! I lunged to his desk.

The orange cursor blinked. I tried "D-ON1989" for the news queue.

Yes! Slowly the list of slugs scrolled up the screen. Most of the stories were coded with a T, which meant they had already been sent to the typesetter. I recognized the slugs of all of last week's news: water park final summer concert, high school football preview, Kiwanis fundraiser.

There it was, police—cocaine.

Frank had coded it DNR. I had never seen that coding before, but given how long it had sat in his queue, I figured DNR probably wasn't good. So, I deleted those three letters.

I quickly ran through the story, my eyes searching for any clue about why he had not sent it to the typesetter already. Frank had dinked around with the lead, but after the fourth graf, there were no edits. In the note section at the end, all he had written was "TT Connie." I deleted that, too.

I switched the lead back to my original, then read the story again. The nut graf was tight. The quotes sizzled. There were no problems, except maybe length.

The next thing I did was not in keeping with my normal personal code of ethics, I'm aware of that.

I walked over to my desk and turned the volume on the police scanner all the way down, then I went back and read my beautiful story one more time.

My mind kept flashing on what it would be like to give my acceptance speech at the Silverton Awards. I was picturing a banquet hall full of reporters all wondering how somebody at a newspaper like the *Daily-Observer* could win. That's when I remembered Professor Wassle's annoying habit of asking, just as I was turning in a story, "Is that the best that you can do?"

I took one more look at my masterpiece. The answer was no, it was not the best I could do. For one thing, I could tighten the lead.

Rewriting that night, my fingers flew on the keyboard, adding more quotes, more visual detail.

Because I had been worried about getting the story past Frank, I had only written about Dora as a source. I had left out how torn she was about speaking against her coworkers on the force.

But tonight, I was writing for Kim.

I put the night dispatcher in as a character. After an hour and a half, it included a more fully rendered portrait of her as whistleblower. And I described in detail the trailer compartment I had seen, how the panel clicked into place, how a gasket no thicker than a rubber band would keep the odor of drugs away from police dogs.

"They tested it with the DARE dog Cujo," she said. I was glad I found a way to work that quote in. It would make everyone whose kid had come home talking about the DARE presentation realize their children had been in contact with the very people involved.

At six forty-five, I read the story through from beginning to end. There was nothing more I could add from what I had in my notebooks. It was a magnificent story.

But when I conjured Wassle asking again, *Is that the best you can do?* I thought of something else my old professor had said: "You pull your punches, somebody else will get the prize for the follow-up."

I had not included the most damning allegation in my story because I could not verify it. But there was someone who could.

My fingers dialed Blue from their own kinetic memory. His voice, deep and throaty on his outgoing message, said, "If it's a fire, call 9-1-1. But if you're just burning to talk to me, you've got to leave a message."

I left the office number.

In less than a minute, Blue called back. I picked up on Frank's desk phone.

Blue said, "I thought you told me never to call you there."

"This is strictly business," I said, trying to ignore the melting feeling that was my autonomic response to his voice.

"Where have you been?" he asked. "I didn't think I would never hear from you again."

I was breathing hard. This was too difficult.

Keep it together, I told myself. *I've got a job to do, and not much time.* "Can we not talk about us?"

He agreed, but only if I would meet him for lunch the next day. Then his voice went into a minor key. "I think I know why you're calling. The lab report is taking longer than usual—"

"But you're convinced?"

"They did it, yeah. I think they must have drowned the guy who lived on River Road, then put him in the bed and set the house on fire. There was no smoke residue in his nostrils. He was dead before the fire started. And there were those cigarettes. I asked around at Trojan. The guy didn't smoke."

"Can you say that on the record?"

"The report should come in the mail tomorrow. I can't bring all that wrath down on my head when the document will say it without my name. What's the rush?"

"I might be able to get the drug dealing story in tomorrow's paper. Monday's the publication cutoff date for the Silverton Award. The homicide would add the journalistic equivalent of Ansel Adams's true black."

He repeated my words "true black," then he paused for a while and I tried to imagine him standing there, weighing the risks.

I wound the curly phone cord around my finger. I wanted to touch Blue, to smell the smoke that never left his hair. The phone was cruel in that it gave me the low purr of his voice, but not his eyes, not his arms. "Are you wearing suspenders?"

"You said that part of our relationship was over."

"Sorry. On the record, can you say that the police killed him?"

"No."

"Can you say what you said about there being no smoke residue in his nostrils?"

"They'll kill me, Hallie. They'll kill you, too."

"Not if it goes in the paper. Not if everyone knows."

"My first call when I see that autopsy report will be to the attorney general. I love you, sweetheart, but—"

He had said he loved me a dozen times before and I had shrugged it off. But now I knew that I loved him, too. I knew because there was a professional thing to do: I should push him to go on the record. I should say that when the story came out, the cops might go after anybody who knew anything, and they might kill another witness. I should push what I knew was Blue's biggest button, saving people, and make him feel he had a duty to go on the record.

But I didn't. Instead, I said, "I know it's too much to ask. But it would have made my story a slam dunk for the Silverton. Still, cops wholesaling cocaine is a contender."

"Write the hell out of it."

"I did. It's done. See you tomorrow."

As I hung up, Kim pushed through the door.

"Why are you at Frank's desk?"

I took my time getting up and smoothing my skirt. I said, "I sent a story to Frank's queue, force of habit, and then realized it should have gone to you. You left his queue open, so I went to get it back."

I had misspoken. She had left the evergreen queue open, but I was in news.

Kim peered at me. "Your voice is quavering." She picked up the untouched lunch on my desk. "Have you had anything to eat? You've got to eat."

She checked the clock and snapped out of maternal mode. "Let's get this paper to bed. What have you got?"

I told her my story's slug, police—cocaine.

"Anything else?"

"No, but it's thirty-four inches. It will fill the hole."

"Not a single fatality?"

"Scanner's been silent," I said as I got up. Technically it was not a lie. "But in that story, a dispatcher says half the police force is running drugs."

"Jesus, Joseph, and Mary. How did you get it?"

"Do you remember that dispatcher who got fired? Frank said it was just a personnel issue and not to do a story? I interviewed her anyway."

"Good instinct. And?"

"It's all in the story."

Kim pushed Frank's chair out of the way and pulled a metal folding chair over to Frank's desk.

As she sat down, I asked, "Do you know a woman named Connie?"

"No. Why?"

I wasn't practiced in deceit. All I could think to do was spill my water bottle.

"Why are you so nervous?" Kim asked.

I said, "This is the biggest thing I've ever written," which wasn't the whole truth, but it was true enough.

Sitting at Frank's computer, Kim hit page down again and again. Her eyes narrowed and her lips moved as she read and re-read what I imagined were the parts that she could not believe.

When she was done, she folded her hands in her lap. "I can't run this."

"What do you mean?" I demanded. "Everything's nailed down. Everything's attributed."

"You're saying Trojan workers put false panels in the trucks to make compartments to hide cocaine?"

"I'm not saying it. The dispatcher said it. On the record. And I looked at two of them. The coke compartments are about the depth of your linen closet."

"Don't they sell that stuff by the gram?"

"Precisely. The scale of this operation is unheard of. And what if I told you they killed a guy who found out about it?"

Kim's eyes went wide. "That's not in here."

I said, "Do you remember that fire by the river on my first day?"

"Where the third shifter died?"

I said, "No autopsy was ordered."

"The bed was completely burned up. They don't waste money on autopsies when the cause of death is obvious. The police chief said he was smoking in bed."

I said, "Nobody asked the fire chief. Blue said there were accelerants."

There was a blank moment, and then it seemed clear that Kim had put the pieces together. "It's too big," she finally said. "Even without the murder allegation, we could be sued for libel. We have to run this by the chain's attorney."

I said, "Actual malice is the standard. There's no reason to believe this is false, and I certainly did not act with reckless disregard for the truth. Far from it. What I could not verify I left out."

I could see from her face that Kim knew I was right. We had both read the briefing on media law in the AP Stylebook. Still, she said, "I have to ask Frank."

"We could win the Silverton with this," I pushed, "but Monday's the publication deadline. We don't have a paper on Monday. There's no mail on Labor Day."

"Frank's probably still out with Charles."

It was a stare down.

"I'd like to put it in tonight," Kim placated. "I'll try calling Frank."

Those words felt like a bowling ball hitting my stomach. As Kim picked up the receiver on Frank's desk phone and pushed in his seven-digit number, I turned around so she would not see my face.

Frank wasn't home, but Kim left a message on his machine to call when he got in.

I creased my brow. "I thought you were a real journalist." I stared off to the side, as if I could not bear to look at Kim.

"I work for a company," Kim said. "So do you. We have procedures for problematic stories."

"Problematic *story?* We've got a police chief at the top of a drug wholesale operation. This stuff kills people, Kim. It ruins lives. Kids not much older than Misty get recruited by gangs to sell it. You know how violent all that is. And we know at least one person was murdered by the police just for finding out about it."

"We don't know that. You say you know, but I don't know your sources."

"I told you, the dispatcher and Blue."

Kim said, "She's a disgruntled former employee."

"And Blue?"

"He's a—"

I couldn't bear to hear whatever she was going to say next. "He walks into burning buildings," I exclaimed. "He's good through and through."

"I told you that you were too close to him."

"And I broke it off. I—" my voice cracked, "I broke it off because it was the professional thing to do. Now there's a professional thing for you to do."

Kim had to know I was right, but she didn't say anything.

I pushed. "Give me one journalistically valid reason to sit on the story."

She couldn't. All she said was, "What's the rush? It's not as if there's another paper that's going to scoop us."

Sadly, she was right. If we didn't run the story, there was absolutely no other news entity that might uncover it. As far as I could tell, the local radio station rewrote *Daily-Observer* stories for their newsbreaks.

"The rush is the Silvertons," I pleaded. "The publication cut-off date is Monday. There's no telling when Frank will call back. They're probably staying overnight on the boat. You may not even be able to reach him in time to put it in Saturday's paper."

I had to make an argument that would convince her to move from number two in the newsroom to number one. I said, "This is the biggest news in the state this year. We don't know what the competition will be next year. Come on, you want this as bad as I do."

"Badly. I want it as badly as you do."

"See? You said it. Imagine how the *Daily-Observer* will rise within the chain."

Kim said, "No paper in our chain has ever won a Silverton."

"No one in the chain has ever won a Silverton because . . ." I trailed off, as if I was thinking better of what I started to say.

"What? Because we're hicks? Small-town people working at small-town newspapers?"

"How can you say that?" I asked. "The fact that you can say something like that points to what the real problem is."

"What is the real problem?" Kim asked.

"It's that you don't believe in yourself. You're the hardest-working editor here. Certainly you've got a better command of the English language than anyone else in the newsroom. But you're like a little girl waiting for Daddy to have the final say on everything. You let Frank butcher your stories, editing them when he's distracted with other things. He edits errors into stories."

Kim sighed. "I hate that."

"And the readers hate that. Certainly the Silverton committee hates that."

"I didn't have a single clean story to enter last year."

I think I had her at that point. She was connecting with my argument at a visceral level. I just needed her to act, to put a T in the code line and hit return. Two little keystrokes to send it to the typesetter. And her hands were already on the keyboard.

I said, "You believed in me when you pushed Frank to hire me. You believed in me when you put me on the police beat first thing. I believe in this story. Everything is nailed down. Everything is attributed. I believe in the story and I believe in you."

I could see her seeing a future in which she was not always checking Frank's mood like she was sweeping for land mines. Her hands made a decisive move on the keys.

I flew to the galleys. "We can get out of here in less than an hour," I yelled and flicked on the waxer. The syndicated features and AP copy were already laid out. When Kim brought in the typeset story, the news hole on one and three matched the story length almost exactly.

I'd never laid out a story with such care. There was no question: This was going to the Silverton committee.

But we couldn't use a Polaroid picture so we didn't have any art. The best we could do was a file photo of the chief.

I made a space for a one-inch headshot on the front page. I was waiting for Kim to decide on the headline when the phone rang.

Kim picked it up. When her voice went quiet, I crept to the doorway between the newsroom and layout to hear what she was saying.

"No, I didn't know. The scanner's been quiet. We were going to lead with a great investigative piece Hallie's got."

Kim was just starting to tell Frank she was running my story on the front page when Frank exploded. I could hear him yelling, even though I was ten feet away.

I rushed back to the light table and pulled the strips off.

"Darnell Kellan drove off the edge of Indian Canyon," Kim yelled "If the wreck is still there, we can send a photographer."

Kim had gotten up and was turning the dial on the scanner at my desk.

"What in Jesus' name did you do to the scanner?"

I could not think of a lie. "I turned it down."

"Why did you do that?"

My X-Acto was frozen under the chief's face. I stood immobile. Knowing there was no excuse for what I had done, tears started streaming.

Kim stormed in and pulled me back from the light table. "We will talk about this tomorrow, but I will NOT have your tears ruining the galleys. Look at the time. Move, girl."

There was no sisterhood. I moved, as told, to my phone.

The new night dispatcher, the one who had replaced Dora, said every officer had been out looking for Darnell since before her shift started, and then the men from the lodge had joined the search. "It was one of the lodge brothers found him. He heard Darnell's dog barking from his boat."

"Will Darnell live?" I asked.

"Honey, he died at the hospital. In a way, he was lucky he was drunk. You don't seize up so much. Aw shit, I didn't just say that. Don't put in the paper that he was drunk. I'll get fired if you quote me."

"Don't worry."

I wrote the story, filling in the details about Darnell's car from memory, and sent it to Kim. She put that on the front page with a lot of white space. A story from a week-old press release on a new mural at the high school went on three.

"What about my story?" I croaked.

"Frank said he coded that do not run."

I'm sure my face registered the anguish I was feeling. Kim pulled me into a bear hug. "You're so ambitious. I admire that, but it's going to be the death of you. What were you thinking?"

I said I wasn't thinking, that Frank had had it out for me from day one. He knew I wanted the Silverton and he'd thrown up dozens of roadblocks. But this was different. This was a major story. This was cops dealing drugs. Whatever Frank's criticism of me, the town was owed this story.

"Your story's probably why Darnell went over the side of the canyon," Kim said.

She promised to talk to Frank and find out what the problem was. She said it to reassure me, as if he probably just needed to get an okay from legal.

But I didn't trust Kim. So, I took the strips of my typeset story when I left the building.

Chapter 37

We hadn't said a place to meet, so Friday at noon I waited for Blue by the birch trees in his woods.

Hair flying, Blue rounded the curve. When he saw me, he sped up, as if he did not believe I would stay there.

"Thanks for coming," he said and lifted me against a tree trunk.

I kissed back, wrapped my legs around his waist. Kim be damned, I knew I couldn't work at the *Daily-Observer* much longer.

Blue said, "Unfortunately, we've got business to attend to."

When I got down, he reached into his back pocket and pulled out an envelope.

"Good or bad news?"

"True black. There was no smoke inhalation. He drowned. They probably beat him unconscious and threw him in the river, then thought better of it and put him in the bed and set his house on fire."

"Was it a gang hit?"

"Oh no. There were three different sizes of Red Wing oxford footprints in the mud by the river that night. It's a pretty safe bet they were police officers."

I ground the crown of my head into Blue's chest.

"I thought this is what you wanted."

"I don't think I can get it in by the deadline. Kim said they'll have to run everything by legal."

"Well, you can enter your contest next year."

"I'm not going to be working here next year."

Blue's mouth moved but no words came out.

I said, "You knew that."

"I guess I had hoped we could—"

"Maybe we could have, but we can't now. I'm done in this town. I fully expect Frank to fire me. He read the story, but he was holding it for some reason. Yesterday he found out I took off his 'do not run' coding."

"That's insubordination."

"It gets worse: I turned off the scanner."

"Why'd you do that?"

"I wanted Kim to need the story."

"So you'll get canned." Blue took a minute to process it. "What's funny is I thought you would grab this report from me and run into your office to add it to the story."

"Frank has forbidden me from working when I'm not on the schedule." I turned around and pounded the tree with my fist. "Why did I ruin everything?" I yelled. "The story's not going in the paper, I'm going to get fired, and I won't have one decent clip to show for my six months in this hellhole."

"People were killed, you know. I've been working for months trying to piece it together. You're not the only one who's losing. Those of us who call this hellhole home, for instance—"

I turned back to him. "You're the only thing that made this place bearable. And then when I couldn't see you, it was like someone switched off the sun." When I said that, tears started rolling down my face.

"You're really going?"

"I can't stay here."

Looking up to the sky, he said, "After you broke up with me, I made a commitment to the aunt who came for me when my father died. I told her that I wouldn't leave, not while any of the four of them who were there when the village was flooded are still alive."

I said, "I love you, but I can't take you away from them. It wouldn't be right."

Blue turned to me. I saw him fully in that moment. He said, "You said you love me."

"Did you really not know?"

There are kisses that bind you to another person and kisses that send you out into the world. This one, I could feel, was meant to stay with me my whole life.

"I'm staking in," Blue said.

"What's that?"

"It's a ceremony. The Riv'nego haven't had one in seventy years. The old aunties have been pushing. You were the last thing keeping me from doing it."

When I walked in my front door, the phone was ringing. It was Kim.

"Is Frank mad?" I asked.

"I told him maybe it was wrong to have you working so many weekends in a row. I told him maybe being tired had clouded your judgment."

"I really appreciate that."

"Did you have the lawyer look at the story?"

"Let's not talk about your story," Kim said, "I actually called to tell you Frank and I agreed you should not come in today. Or for the rest of the weekend."

From Kim's tone, I could tell this wasn't comp time for all my uncompensated overtime.

Late in the afternoon, my phone rang again. It was Sandra. She sounded rabid. "It was a Trojan test truck that hit my mother-in-law. Luke said a witness called him. Those are professional drivers. They don't hit somebody unless they want to hit them. It was deliberate."

"Who's they?" I asked. "Why would someone want to hurt your mother-in-law?"

"They figured out Luke had to know about the coke with all the trailers coming through with compartments."

"Yeah, but why your mother-in-law?"

"For the same reason Darnell sicced Cujo on Scooter! It's a big operation. They can't know who all knows, but if it looks like somebody is talking, they hurt someone that person loves so they'll tell everyone else not to talk."

This did not sound farfetched to me.

Chapter 38

It was late when I finally turned onto Lockehaven Drive. A barn owl, startled by the car, leapt into flight. Its white feathers caught the glow of my taillights. In the rearview mirror, it looked like a messenger from hell, heart-shaped face as red as blood.

I did not know what I was going to do next. Freelance the story to a newspaper in Indianapolis? The *New York Times* wouldn't want it even though I could show the photo of the compartment and that I'd checked everything out. They'd send their own reporter. That was the problem with being so new to journalism—nobody would believe me.

As I pulled in front of the fishing shack, I tried to lose myself in the crunch of the gravel beneath my tires. *No one except me ever drives to my little round shack*, I thought.

And Blue. Blue drives here. Drove here. His tires on the gravel, that's where that positive association came from. That crunch used to mean I wasn't alone. Somebody knew I wasn't just working on high school band concert announcements and stories about Little League fundraisers. Someone knew I was a real journalist.

In the yellow porch light, I found my key and opened the door. Inside, my little house looked empty. Kim's worthless note taunted me from the shelf where I'd planned to display my award.

The fridge was nearly empty, too. I hadn't shopped in a week. All my energy had been focused on the story. Food and sleep and hands I could not hold anymore merged into a blur of details that did not matter.

In the back of the produce drawer, I found half a head of iceberg lettuce. An olive jar had one lone survivor floating in the brine.

That was all the fridge would yield, so I climbed up on the counter to look on the top cupboard shelf for two packets of saltines I remembered saving from a dinner at Tony's. I was rooting around up there when three sharp knocks shook the front door.

I was eye-level with the wall clock. Almost eleven.

No one except Blue, Sandra, and Kim knew where I lived, and it wasn't Blue's knock.

I jumped down. Back in Minneapolis I kept a baseball bat by my door, but when I packed for Green Meadow, I had not thought I would need it. The irony struck me as I pawed through my silverware drawer to find the bread knife I never used, blade sharp in its cardboard case.

There was no peephole in the door, so I left the chain lock on and opened it just a crack, my knife at the ready.

The No-Pest bulb gave a jaundiced glow to the sliver of Kim's face that was visible.

"Let me in," she said. "I need to talk with you."

I didn't widen the crack, but I lowered the knife. "It's really late."

Kim shoved the door. The flimsy chain lock broke. Kim didn't apologize.

"Come on, Kim," I said. I did not care about whatever Norton had done to send her out here so late. That part of our friendship was over.

"Misty's asleep in the car. Can I bring her in?"

"Why doesn't Norton have her?"

"He's going to AA. I was going to ask you to babysit, but I just decided to bring her in to work with me after dinner, given the circumstances."

"The circumstances? That's what you're calling this?"

Kim put her hand on my shoulder. "I'm your friend."

"No, you're not. You're my boss. And I'd say this week, you're so afraid to stand up to your boss that you let the biggest story of the year rot in a queue."

"I'm getting Misty."

Kim returned from her car carrying her daughter. Misty smacked her lips and clutched the yellow yarn hair of her Cabbage Patch doll more tightly, but she did not wake up.

There was a pause that extended into an awkward silence. That seemed to be our thing these days.

Finally, Kim said, "Can I have a glass of water?"

I gave her tap water, not the spring water from the jug.

She settled in on the rocking recliner. Misty, so small for a second grader, lay across her lap. The springs creaked as Kim pushed forward and back, forward and back. "Those were some pretty far-fetched accusations in that story."

"So this is a work meeting?" I tried to keep my voice calm, more for Misty's benefit than Kim's. "Okay, let's talk shop: You've had the story for two days." I said it as evenly as I could. *Try,* I told myself. There was still a chance to resurrect it in time. "If there were holes, you could have talked to me about them. Were there?"

"What?"

Was she listening to me at all? "Were there any holes?" I repeated.

"No," Kim said, like she was annoyed. Misty shifted.

I still couldn't figure out why Kim had come. I told myself, *Talk to Kim the way you talk to a hostile source.*

"You said you'd talk to Frank. You've had time to talk to Frank. When are you going to run the story? You just said it doesn't have any holes in it."

Kim stretched out all of her fingers and examined the backs of her hands. She didn't look up at me. "We don't run stories like that. This is a community paper."

"You sound just like Frank," I said.

"I may not agree with him on every call, but he and I are on the same team."

I stepped in closer. "It's a newspaper, Kim, not a sports team. I've got a dispatcher, a solid source, saying the police are wholesaling cocaine into Chicago. Anybody who doesn't want that on the front page ought to quit, because they're not journalists. It's not a game. It's deadly serious."

"Why don't you sit down?"

"This is my house!"

"Suit yourself," she said in a school-marmy voice. "But let's be clear on the facts. Your source is a *former* dispatcher. She's mad because she got fired."

"It doesn't matter what her motivation is. Everything she said checked out."

"Did you interview the police chief?"

I noticed the hands of the clock lined up, five to eleven. I let that question hang in the air, let it really soak in for Kim, what she was asking.

We stared at each other a full minute. Teammates? We weren't even the same species.

Kim's lip twitched. "Frank talked to the police chief this evening. Frank gave your story consideration, he really did. But he wasn't going to let the whole town get a black eye like that without giving the chief a chance to give his side."

"So that's the hole? Frank needed a comment from the corrupt cop at the top of the operation. Did he get a good quote? Is the story going to run tomorrow?"

"No."

"Why not?"

"I told you, your main source was a disgruntled former employee who had been fired for lying."

"She was fired for taking time off to care for her grandmother who was dying of cancer."

"See? You're defending her. You've lost all objectivity. But just to be fair, Frank asked the chief about it. The chief told Frank that when your source found out she didn't qualify for Family Medical Leave, she called in sick."

"And?"

"That's lying, Hallie. She's not a reliable source."

"You called in sick when Misty had a test for the gifted program."

Kim rocked back and forth and smoothed Misty's hair.

I moved to my next line of defense. "And Terrence Dunn? Peter Whitmore?"

"Frank said they're truants out to get the truancy officer."

"Darnell's dead, so that's not really an issue. The source at Trojan?"

"Anonymous. Frank told you no more anonymous sources."

I looked at the clock. "Norton's probably back from his meeting. Take her home."

"You and I are not finished."

"I've got a dispatcher on the record saying the cops are dealing drugs, I've got it confirmed, but you and Frank don't want to run it."

"You say you've got it confirmed. Frank wants to know who confirmed it."

"So he can tell the chief? Not on your life."

Kim tried to soften her voice, tried to invoke the warmth we had once felt for each other. "Can you tell me so I can tell him it was someone reliable?"

"You've already told me you won't run the story." My understanding of what was going on came into focus. I said, "You need to leave."

Kim said, "I'm your friend, Hallie. Frank's going to fire you."

"You're not going to run the story. Why did you ask who confirmed it?"

Before Kim answered, my mind flashed red. I had to get out of Green Meadow fast. And I wasn't the only one in danger.

Kim sat there measuring her words as I threw the bread knife and all my notes from the story into my backpack.

"Frank told you to come here, didn't he?" I demanded.

"He told me to find out who the anonymous source was, yes," she said. "It was a direct order, Hallie."

"Some friend," I muttered as I gave one last glance around the room.

Kim looked stricken. "I am your friend," she said. Moving carefully so as not to wake Misty, Kim got out of my rocker. "I'm really sorry. I need this job."

I drove to Blue's place.

When he answered the door he had on his sweet sleep face. "You want to make it work? I know this has to be a dream, but hop on in."

"Frank's not running the story. He told the police chief."

Blue woke up fast. "When?"

"Probably an hour ago. Can you follow me to the county line?"

He grabbed his keys from the peg by the door and pushed them into my hands. "Take my car."

I held his keys, confused. "What are you going to do?"

"I'm going to crash yours in a ditch so they think you've already been taken care of."

"Really? They'd do that?"

"They killed Sandra's mother-in-law just to send a message."

I drove the speed limit, checking for Blue in the rearview mirror every few seconds. Near the water park, Blue passed me and pointed his arm out the window, signaling he was going to turn onto the beach.

I stayed on the shoulder with Blue's engine running. He drove my Chevette onto the sand, then put his head out the window and yelled, "Where's the gas tank?"

"Left side."

Blue got out of the car, a reverse firefighter tonight. The moonlight glinted off his shoulders as he unscrewed the gas cap and pushed a paper napkin past the vapor guard. I knew the tank in my car was full of gas, enough to get me past Chicago, probably to Madison. Just then I looked at Blue's fuel gauge, glowing white in the dark. It registered barely a quarter tank.

"Wait," I yelled, but it was too late. The yellow flare of the match hit the napkin and then Blue came running as only he could.

"Go!" he yelled as soon as he was in the car.

Long Lake glimmered in the rearview mirror. It, like Blue's scanner, seemed oddly quiet. But in my head, blood was pounding in my veins. "Drive!" Blue screamed.

Blue's tires crunched. I wanted to floor it, but we agreed the best way to not draw attention was to go the speed limit.

"Don't look back, sweetheart. It's a car. It's just a car."

Blue's well-tuned engine didn't rattle the way mine did. It was quiet in the car for a few miles, then the new officer's voice came on the scanner. "I've got an eleven twenty-five on the beach just north of the spillway. Do you read me?"

Sugar came on. "Loud and clear, sweetheart. Is that an eleven eighty-three? Do you need backup?"

"What's a car on fire?"

"A nine-o-four-A," she said. "It's right there on the cheat sheet I taped to your dash."

He read her my license plate number and then there was a big boom over the scanner.

Blue saw me wince. "That would be your fuel tank exploding."

There wasn't time to be sad. All I said was, "That was my first car."

I kept driving. Sugar came back on, her words halting. "Code six, that means stay away."

The scratchy voice of the chief came on the radio. "It's for training purposes. Sorry you weren't advised."

Another man back at dispatch chuckled, "Yeah, we're going to let that one burn."

I asked Blue, "How much time do you think we have?"

"You're only really going to be safe outside this state. It will take forty-five minutes to get to Gary."

"And how long will the car keep burning?"

"Not that long. Forty minutes."

I counted the other people they might come after now that in their minds I was safely dispatched: Terrence, Luke, Dora and Scooter. Each of them was in danger.

I swerved into the driveway of a farmhouse, shot the gear into reverse, and turned the car around.

"Are you crazy?" Blue shouted. "We can't count on more than half an hour before they know you're not dead."

I said, "I've got ten minutes. Dora and Scooter are out of the county. Luke knows all too well what the Kellans are capable of. But Terrence Dunn's name is in that story, too. He's just a kid, Blue. Frank probably told the chief he was a source."

I was trying to keep my eyes on the road, to drive as carefully as I could, but out of the corner of my eye, I could see Blue was looking at me in a way he never had before.

Chapter 39

I did the shave-and-a-haircut knock on the door next to the *Daily-Observer* loading dock. Sandra opened the door.

"You look like you just saw a ghost," she said.

"Frank told the chief I know."

Sandra's jaw dropped. "You have to get out of here."

"I've got about ten minutes to salvage the story."

"What are you going to do?"

"I'm going to put the story in the paper."

Sandra said, "They'll kill you."

"They think they already have. Listen, I need your help. Keep Kim in the newsroom while I go into paste-up. She's already proofed the galleys, right?"

"They're running way late tonight. She just got the layout done."

"Will you do it? Will you go in and distract her?"

Sandra had one of those mother rings. It had a diamond, her birthstone, and Mattie's. She fingered the garnet, no doubt thinking of Mattie.

I said, "Just have a friendly conversation."

Sandra snorted. "Friendly?" But she headed to the front of the building to talk to Kim.

I followed a few paces back, through the back door to paste-up. After Sandra had gone through the swinging doors to the newsroom, I looked for the galleys. They were in a stack on the slanted light table, waiting to be taken to the pressman. I could hear Kim was on the phone.

"Do you need something?" I heard her ask Sandra accusingly.

"Excuse me, ma'am. I can wait."

I looked at the front page. In the photo, the president of the Rotary club was handing the police chief a check. The headline said, "Rotary Gives DARE a

Big Boost." It would be ironic to replace that story with mine, but Kim always gave the lead story one last look as she carried the galleys in. Better to go on an inside page.

There wasn't much news. Page three was an American flag. Page four was a reader survey. It looked like they were already missing me.

The DARE story only ran for a paragraph on the front page, then it jumped to page five. "Police from A-1." That would do. And the jump was just above the school lunch menus and the Major League Baseball box scores, so a significant portion of our readers would turn to page five.

"Our" readers. *I don't work here anymore*, I reminded myself. *No prizes are coming out of this gig, no reference letter, nothing.* But I was still a journalist. I still wanted the people of Green Meadow to know, on the record, that the rumors were true.

Using an X-Acto knife, I carefully peeled off the jump.

Wax! I hadn't thought to turn on the waxer.

I tiptoed over to where it sat between overflowing trash barrels on an oilcloth-covered stand. The wax was still liquid. Kim must have just finished paste-up a few minutes ago. I wondered what went wrong.

You don't work here anymore, I told myself. *Stop caring.*

I peeked below the saloon doors. Sandra was by Frank's desk. When she saw me, I mouthed, "Make some noise." She screwed up her face and shrugged.

I pantomimed coughing.

Sandra cleared her throat.

"What?" Kim snapped at her.

"Somethin's in my throat. Sorry, ma'am. I'll just—" she skulked toward the front of the office. "I just need to make some copies."

I mouthed, "Keep it going," as Sandra pressed the button again and again.

I pulled the typeset story out of a folder in my bag. I only needed ten seconds to give the strips a pass through the waxer. That sweet smell reminded me of my one and only candlelit dinner with Blue.

The story pieces emerged shiny on one side, sticky on the other. I kissed the pieces for luck.

I laid each column in, being careful to cut at the end of a paragraph because there would be no opportunity to have any corrections typeset. Because of this, the story ran about four inches too long. Should I put it where the flag was instead? The whole story would fit in that space, but Kim might notice. Better to lose some detail, I reasoned, and lopped off the last three paragraphs. Never in my life had I appreciated the inverted pyramid so much.

I heard Kim hang up the phone. I don't really believe in a sixth sense but the air became prickly.

"Do you really think you should be running personal copies here?" Kim asked Sandra.

"I was planning to pay for them, ma'am, I was just about to ask you where to leave the money," Sandra said, trying to sound like her pride had been wounded. "Is it a dime a page?"

Kim said, "Put it in petty cash."

"Ma'am, I wouldn't know where that is."

"Just leave it with me then. You shouldn't be making personal copies on company time."

"We're paid piece rate, ma'am, so until the new issue comes off the press, I think my time's my own. But I wanted to ask you about that paste-up position that was posted. What does that job entail?"

"You'll have to talk to Frank."

"Could you just—"

"I'm really late. I've got late-breaking news. So you'll understand that I can't sit and chat with you now. I've got a daughter sleeping in the car."

"Really? How old's your girl?"

I could hear Kim's chair rattle. She must be getting up. Quickly, I stacked the galley pages in order, making sure "Police from A-1" stuck above my story.

Kim pushed through the swinging doors, her eyes glued to the typeset sheet she was proofing.

I froze.

"Ma'am!" Sandra barked from the newsroom. "I didn't give you my forty cents."

Kim swirled around like she wanted to punch Sandra. "I told you I'm running late. Leave your dimes on my desk."

Sandra must have seen that I was just inches away from Kim's back. Sandra squeaked out, "I need change."

Kim was doing her slow headshake, arms rigid, but she went back into the newsroom. As soon as she was out of paste-up, I darted out to the stuffing area. My heart was racing. Every sound I made seemed to reverberate like a fire alarm.

I curled up against the wall, between a trash barrel and a roll of newsprint. I could hear the mechanical progression of the time clock above me. I figured I still had six minutes. *Collect yourself,* I said to myself. *Calm down. You have time.*

And then there were the backs of Kim's big legs across from me. She turned to the flap where the newspapers should have already been pouring out on the belt. Lifting it, with great exasperation she called in to the press operator. "We've got to scrap the DARE story. There was a fire by the water park."

"Anybody killed?" the press operator asked.

Kim said, "All I've got is that it was a car fire."

"That's a front-page story?" the press operator asked.

"You don't work at the *Chicago Tribune* anymore."

I held still, not sure what I would say if Kim spotted me there on the floor. But Kim was so focused on the press run, she never noticed me.

She went back into paste-up. Through the paste-up room's open back door, I could see her peel my story pieces off. Apparently, she was in such a hurry that she didn't look at them.

That's Terrence's life, I thought.

I moved to the far side of a trash barrel. When Kim came back to the belt area, I was well hidden.

The press operator came out. "Just an ordinary car fire?" he asked Kim.

"Probably. It was a Chevette. Navy blue like the one Hallie drives." There was no emotion in her voice at all. "There's no time to do a proof. Just get it out or we'll miss the post office deadline."

I thought about all the stories with holes that I had written at the *Daily-Observer*, all the fatal fire and accident stories that were missing a W. Who? No ID. I almost never had a why. Readers were left to sketch in "too stupid to live." How many times had that not really been true? The question was too personal to ponder just then. In the official police version of events, I was supposed to be burning to death in my car.

Kim gave the press operator the galleys. He squinted at them as he returned to the press. Kim shuffled back to the newsroom. *It's amazing,* I thought, *the things no one sees.*

Sandra returned to stuffing, whistling "Amazing Grace" really loud.

I stood up. "Is she gone?"

"I don't know."

"Could you go into paste-up and grab the scrapped jump from page five? Those pieces are the only full version of the story."

Sandra nodded and began whistling a new song.

The tune stopped abruptly.

"What are you doing?"

It was Kim, cornering Sandra.

"I was just picking up trash," Sandra said.

"You're not a janitor."

"Ma'am?"

Kim called Frank. I could hear her saying there may be a problem. She asked him if he had laid off the janitor. Apparently, he had.

Kim lit into Sandra. "You need to tell me right now what you are up to."

"I'm not up to anything."

"Stealing trash is a crime."

"I just wanted to see how paste-up is done. For my high school newspaper, the stories were typed and then we stuck them down with rubber cement."

"What were you doing at the copier?"

"Making a résumé?"

Kim's voice softened. "It's not easy to find a job in this town that will work around a child's schedule. Let me see your résumé."

"No, ma'am. You're in a hurry. Look at the time."

"If you did paste-up on your high school paper, make sure that's on your résumé. Did you graduate high school?"

"Yes, ma'am. I was the salutatorian," she said. "May I keep these?"

"Sure. It's basically the same concept as what you did in high school."

⚊▴▴

When Sandra came back, I grabbed my scrapped story.

"Somehow, this has got to get in the paper," I said. "Once she's gone, I've got an idea."

We looked at the clock above the rack of timecards. It was inching to midnight. I guess I had been missed. When I subbed in production, we never ran this late.

"Do you know what happened to the layout guy?" I asked Sandra.

"Cost cutting. They let him go two days ago. They posted an ad for a replacement—at minimum wage."

"You're kidding."

"Nope."

I hesitated to ask what I had to ask. If Sandra said no, I would have to let it go. All of it. The research, the interviews, getting fired. I would just have to leave it all, like I left my car on the beach.

But I had one chance. I had to try.

I held the story pieces in my hands. I wouldn't be winning any awards, I wouldn't even be able to use it as a clip, but this town could be told, on the record, what had been whispered for years.

I said, "I'm about to ask you something. And I know you love Matthew and any jeopardy for you is a risk for him, too. I get that. But when you stuff the late inserts tonight, can you stuff them face down?"

Sandra's eyes widened. "We don't have any late inserts."

"You will."

Sandra nodded slowly. She said, "Use the canary paper. That's what the ad boss Xeroxes his lates on."

She was with me! Sandra was going to do it.

I think she also realized we would never see each other again, because she said, "I'm going to be praying for you."

"Thank you."

"But you need to know, I'm not doing this for you. It's *my* town. My kid shouldn't have to grow up worrying about getting on the wrong side of somebody in the police department the way we all do. When we don't say anything, we're part of the problem. You got me to see that."

She walked back to the front office copy room. After a minute, she called, "It's clear."

I jinked in behind her, clutching the waxed strips of story.

The ad department's Xerox machine was huge. A sign next to the clock admonished the ad reps to unplug it at the end of the day. I'd only used it once. I did not know how long it would take to warm up. I watched the red second hand on the wall clock sweep around. One. Two. Three minutes. "What am I doing?" I said out loud. "I've got to use this time."

I located two reams of canary paper. It would take another case to make enough inserts. Turquoise. Goldenrod. They weren't in alphabetical order. There was canary, next to a case of Coke marked "Do NOT help yourself." Not going to take that advice tonight. The ready light finally came on and I groaned when I realized the machine would have to go through its warm-up sequence again when I loaded the paper.

"Calm blue ocean, calm blue ocean," I said to myself, picturing the lake as I had seen it in Blue's rearview mirror. "Use all the time you have."

The story had been almost a yard long. I cut the columns again to break at the bottom of an 11-inch page and grabbed a pen.

The first headline I tried was too long. I cut a one-inch strip from another sheet of paper and secured it with Scotch tape.

I hadn't done this kind of jerry-rigged layout since we'd spoofed the campus event calendar on April Fool's Day of my sophomore year. I never thought the things I learned in that little prank—line things up against the edge of the page, Magic Tape does not show on a Xerox—would ever be useful again.

Writing the headline with a pen, I could feel all my professional aesthetic sensibilities shatter, everything I had learned in newspaper design: Never let anything be printed that has not been proofread; a line askew tells readers not to bother . . .

There was only one thing that mattered now. And it wasn't professional-looking layout.

I decided on "Police officer killed in crash linked to illegal drug trade." It was fair. It was informative.

Just then the machine blinked "ready" again. I had four minutes left. There was no way the machine could make six thousand copies in four minutes.

I hit copy and went back to stuffing.

Sandra looked terrified. "You've got to get out of here. Kim is still in the office. Are there any copies to insert?"

"Can you pull them off the machine?"

Sandra didn't hesitate. "Of course."

"I'm leaving my baby with you." I hugged her. "You are such a magnificent—"

"GET OUT OF HERE!" Sandra pushed me toward the door by the loading dock.

She went back to the copy room. I looked around stuffing one last time, then headed to Blue's car in the parking lot.

Blue gestured to the back door. "I'm going to chauffeur you to the county line."

He said to lie down and handed a large box across the seat. "I had a completely different scene in mind for giving you this, but here, cover up."

I lifted the lid off the box. It contained an old white wool blanket. When I unfolded it, I saw it had brightly colored stripes on the ends. I wondered what it signified, but we didn't have the leisure of that conversation.

I lay down across the foot wells and pulled the blanket over me, being careful not to let any of my hair stick out.

"Has there been more on the scanner?"

"Sugar figured out it was your car."

We had just gotten out of the parking lot when Blue slammed on the brakes.

"Do you know someone who wears a black apron?"

"Yeah, four of them."

"Well, do you think the one running toward us is friend or foe?"

"Probably a friend."

Blue jerked the car into reverse. When he rolled down his window, the stuffer held out an unreadable sheet of canary paper.

"The Xeroxes are a smear. What do we do?"

"It's the toner," I said. "Sandra's got to take it out and shake it." I looked at Blue. "Do we have another three minutes?"

"Maybe. But not four. They're going to swoop in as soon as the flames go out to make sure you didn't get out."

I didn't know if Sandra had ever opened up a Xerox machine before. I ran back in to find Sandra hitting the button again and again, trying to get a clear copy. I stopped the machine and opened the front panel like I'd seen them do in Kinko's dozens of times. It was the same kind of toner. I took it out and shook it. It felt like there was hardly any in there.

"It's not going to be enough," I said, restarting it anyway. Sandra was behind me. "You saw how I did that. You push the cartridge in, and it clicks. Then you pull down this lever, close the front, and it will go through its warm-up. You can do that again when it starts to blur, right?"

Sandra said she could.

"You might get a few hundred more from that cartridge. Once Kim leaves, you can make copies on the newsroom machine."

"Kim took the key out," Sandra said. "I saw her."

I could not let Kim's stingy impulse defeat the plan. We were so close. "We've got to find more toner," I said, trying to keep an even keel.

The machine hummed through its slow warm-up sequence, indifferent to our fury as we tore through all the cupboards looking for a new toner cartridge.

Finally Sandra lifted a clipboard. "Order toner. It's underlined three times. Dated today."

I wanted to cry. The *Daily-Observer*, a newspaper, couldn't keep an extra toner cartridge on hand.

Sandra had an idea. "There's the coin-op copier in the lobby."

"Do you have six-hundred dollars in dimes?"

She looked at me like I was high, which I suppose I was. I should have been out in that car.

I asked, "Do you have one dime?"

"Kim said I had to wait until tomorrow to get my change. No."

I looked at the clock. There was no telling how long it would take for the machine to warm up. "If I can take one copy with me, there will be evidence in case—" my voice dropped low, "in case something happens."

One thin dime was what we needed for that insurance. I didn't have one. Sandra didn't have one. But over in circulation, there were about twenty single-issue racks shoved into a corner, each with a slender coin canister with a small lock on the side.

Sandra and I went to circulation to look for a key for the coin cans. The locks were no bigger than the kind used for suitcase zippers. I assumed the key would be in a drawer in the laid-off circulation manager's desk. I rummaged around but found nothing. Sandra said she would look for a key rack, but when I looked up, I saw she was taking off her necklace.

"We don't have any time to waste," I said.

"No, we don't," she replied and slid the long end of the cross from her necklace into one of the canister locks. She jiggled it and the lock popped open.

"Thank you, Jesus," Sandra whispered. When she turned the can over, a shower of coins cascaded out.

Hands full of dimes, we dashed back to the copy room. The Xerox machine was still in its warm-up sequence.

Looking at the clock, I saw I didn't have another minute to wait. I had to leave without a copy of the story. Everything was up to her.

Sandra understood. "Go!"

I sprinted down the hall, turning back just once to see the green light bleeding out from the sides of the cover as the camera made its pass.

Sandra held out both hands to catch the paper as it emerged. "Thank you for whatever you're able to do," I whispered to her, to all the stuffers whose hands would make sure Green Meadow knew.

I made my way through the loading dock door, got in Blue's car, lay down on the floor, and pulled the blanket over my head.

The voices on the scanner were going nonstop. Above them, Sugar started singing in an airy, trembling voice, "Girl, You Know it's True."

"That is not professional," Blue said. "Dora would never sing on the microphone."

"No, professionalism is not a hallmark of the Green Meadow Police Department."

"The bad news," he said, "is those monkeys have figured out you weren't in the car. While you were in there changing the toner, I heard one of them say to look for you at my house."

"And then?"

Blue said, "I don't know. But I intend to drive to the county line as fast as I can without breaking the speed limit." He added, "They're going to set up a roadblock at the Interstate."

I could hear Sugar on the scanner again, her words solid. "We've got six squads on the search. Six squads." One by one she spoke to each officer. "Give me your location."

"Sugar's telling us where they are!" I exclaimed. "Everyone's headed north."

We drove west, Blue apologizing for the bumpy dirt roads. When we reached the county line, he gave a little cheer. "No one's followed us!"

Blue sped to where Dora was staying. The woman whose house it was loaned me her pickup, just like that. Blue said I might not be safe in Chicago. He told me to go all the way to Wisconsin and park the truck at the bus station in Madison. He could have someone drive him up to retrieve it once things settled down.

"Cheeseheads are good folks," he said, "but if it seems like someone is following you, go directly to the federal courthouse."

There wasn't time for goodbyes.

I put on a cowboy hat I found behind the seat and drove to Madison without stopping.

In a 24-hour copy shop near the University of Wisconsin, I wrote out everything I could remember from the story on a yellow pad and made copies of all my notes from the interviews. When I called the DEA from a pay phone, the agent I spoke to told me where to mail everything. When she asked how she could reach me, I gave Amber's number.

Chapter 40

So, I moved back to my old apartment. The first day, I went to the hospital where Wassle was and sat next to his bed. I told him I really did try.

The nurses said he probably couldn't hear me, but talking to him couldn't hurt. They said it might be good to hold his hand, so I did that too.

They took him off life support a week later. The loss didn't hit me until I had to take him off my reference list for job applications.

Blue mailed me my box of *Daily-Observer* clips from the fishing shack, but mostly I just send out my stories from the *City Paper*. It's easier than explaining everything that happened.

Kim called a few weeks after I left. She said she just dialed the number on my old résumé.

"It wasn't easy covering the Labor Day weekend schedule without you," is what she said.

When I made no response, Kim tried again. "I imagine you're showing off the boot scootin' boogie on the dance floors in the big city."

"Why are you calling, Kim?"

"I need to know where to send your last paycheck. And there will be the W-4s for your taxes."

"You've got an editor who's in cahoots with a police chief who wholesales cocaine, and you want to know where to send my tax forms?"

She said it wasn't like that. Her words were, "Frank was as alarmed as I was by the allegations in your story." Nothing in her tone rang false. She said she and Frank talked it over. That would have been before she drove over to the fishing shack my last night in Indiana, the night Blue burned my car. She said Charles weighed in, too. He said tourism was the only sector of the economy that was growing.

"We couldn't afford to give the town a black eye like that."

I said, "What do you mean, 'Couldn't afford?'"

"Do you think anyone who has kids wants to take them to an amusement park in a town that is a major part of the drug trade?"

I asked her if the insert made any difference.

"Your little stunt? It got tongues wagging. Somebody sent it to the DEA. They talked to somebody here—maybe your secret source—and now the police chief is up on drug charges."

"Conrad Kellan is in jail?"

"No, he made bail. They set it real high, but I guess he had been saving."

I said, "He was saving money he took out of the pockets of suspects."

"You don't know that," Kim said, and it was true, I did not.

Kim said I would be happier doing advocacy journalism. She didn't say 'advocacy journalism.' She said, "Writing for one of those lefty publications."

The silence stretched long.

"I guess it was just a bad fit, huh, Hallie?"

I did not want career advice from Kim and I didn't want to smooth things over, either. I did not miss her, did not care what happened at the *Daily-Observer*. But there were people I did care about.

"Is Terrence Dunn okay?"

"He disappeared. People say he went into a witness protection program. Just until the trial's over. It's not like on TV. He won't come back with a new face and new fingerprints. Somebody thought they saw him carrying groceries into a motel in Shelton."

"What about Dora?"

"The interim police chief said Dora could have her job back even though she was AWOL for weeks. We ran a story about it, she got an Indian lawyer who threatened to sue the town. Her job's waiting for her, but she's taking her sweet time coming back. Sugar's been pulling double shifts. I hear Sugar on the radio day and night."

"Was Sugar in on it?"

"She wasn't charged. But Ricky was. He could not make bail, he's in jail."

My Xeroxed story with the headline written in black marker had made a difference. I was speechless.

"You there?" Kim asked. "Mrs. Whitmore called to thank you. She said your story cleared her son's name."

"You told her I was terminated?"

"I told her you quit."

I didn't want to argue that point with Kim. I no longer liked Kim, could not trust her. Still, I asked, "Did you know?"

"Heavens no. None of us knew. Not Frank, not Charles. No one in their lodge knew, either. Except for Chief Kellan, of course. The high school principal, though, he wrote a letter to the editor saying Darnell had been a bad influence on teens, he kind of implied that he had known all along. Frank would not put it in the paper since Darnell is not around to defend himself."

Before she hung up, Kim said, "I'm just going to send this check to your last-known address in Minneapolis."

Another Phone Call

"So that brings me up to the present."

"That's the last time you spoke with Kim Joseph?"

"That's right. I've told you everything about how I got that story, but I don't know who sent it to you."

"The only documentation the Indiana Silverton committee received with it was a handwritten note signed by Kim Joseph. She was your direct supervisor?"

"Right. I answered to Kim because we both worked the two-to-eleven shift. Frank was both the editor and the publisher."

"I can't get over the fact that the chain let him do both jobs. We want to draw attention to what went wrong. This kind of—"

"Complete breakdown of journalistic integrity?"

"The *Daily-Observer* isn't the only paper where conditions are ripe for something like this. But the committee is divided. That's why I had to talk to you. The entry form was not filled out. We just got a Xerox copy of the story. We almost threw it out. The headline had been written in pen."

"Yep, black Sharpie."

"The only thing with it was that note. But it had been signed by Kim Joseph, and if she was your primary editor, it qualifies."

"I would never . . . I mean, I would love to be considered for a Silverton, but I would never send you a jerry-rigged Xerox with a headline written in pen. I have the deepest respect for the Silverton Prize."

"Here's the thing: We can't reward this kind of—"

"Complete abdication of journalistic responsibility?"

"Do you always finish other people's sentences?"

"It's a bad habit. I'm working on it."

"We can't reward this kind of behavior."

"But you're saying I would have been considered? Thanks for calling and telling me that. Given my situation, any little bit of encouragement helps."

"Perhaps I haven't made myself clear. You are being considered. We're trying to figure out if you do win, whether we can award you the Silverton personally. Can you honestly say that most of your reporting for this story was done on your own time?"

"Frank wouldn't let me do enterprise work on the clock. He put his foot down after I wrote about how one of the drowning victims changed after his parents divorced. Frank just wanted spot news stories."

"We've got a lawyer going over the rules. My position, and I think I have the other committee members with me on this, is that we need to send a message to other newspapers that this kind of breakdown can't happen. The only thing the lawyer has found so far that would disqualify you is the residency requirement. The winner has to be a resident of Indiana. I understand you're between jobs now. That's a real shame, a reporter like you—"

"Norm Wassle said the same thing."

"I knew Norm Wassle. I didn't realize he was in such bad shape."

"He didn't let on how sick he was."

"What I'm trying to ask is, do you have a friend, someone you could stay with in Indiana? For the residency requirement?"

"Yes, I've got friends in Indiana."

Epilogue

Sandra gave me a bone-crushing hug when I stepped onto her porch. "I know there's a lot to catch up on," she said, "but I need a favor."

She said she was headed out the door to Blue's staking-in ceremony.

I said, "I can watch Matthew, sure."

"Matthew I've got covered. I need you to babysit me. Other than funerals, this is the first Riv'nego anything I've gone to since I joined the church."

"Why are you making the exception now?"

"This is really big. The old aunties have been pushing for someone to stake in for years. Blue's going to commit to getting federal recognition for the tribe. I think he's doing it to tell the oldest ones it's okay for them to die. He'll make it his life's work to keep the culture alive. And to seek reparations."

"For the village being flooded?"

"And for the men being shot." Sandra shuddered. "It was government officials that did that."

Sandra said she was not sure she would be able to drive herself home. "I get really upset when they dredge that stuff up."

Her tone was so plaintive, even though I had been on the road for hours, I got in her car. And truth be told, despite my complicated emotions about Blue, I wanted to witness it. I had seen two of the old aunties at the disastrous bachelor auction. Dora Mayfield, of course, was my main source on the cocaine story. To see them in their colors, as my old anthropology professor would describe it, would be to see them in an entirely different light.

Driving slower than the speed limit, Sandra explained again how she was related on her mother's side to Blue and Dora and the elderly women at the bachelor auction. She said she was so angry at how they had acted after her mother's suicide that it was easier to just stop seeing them. But she made an exception for Blue. "Matthew needed a male role model."

"I don't think you could have picked a better one."

Sandra must have still been thinking about the aunts because out of nowhere, she said, "Those old ladies can be very bossy."

"If you don't like them, why are you going?" I asked. "The way you describe it, this ceremony is more for them than for Blue."

She turned and looked at me as if I had asked her, "Why is there air?" She said, "They are family. There are only nine of us that anyone knows of. When you're in a club that small, you've got to pay your dues."

"And you haven't kept up with yours?"

Sandra winced. I don't know what she thought I meant, but she brushed off my apology. "They want Mattie. They've got Scooter Mayfield. Dora is close to the old ones. She can tolerate them."

"But you can't."

"I didn't cut Mattie off from them completely. I let them babysit him sometimes when he was little."

"But?"

"But if they had their way, he'd be staking in with Blue tonight. He's not old enough to make a choice like that." Her face reddened. "Shouldn't he have a future," she asked, "outside this county?"

I understood too well. "That's what broke up Blue and me. He cannot leave."

Sandra's expression changed to such familiar compassion that I thought it might be hereditary.

I laughed in sad recognition when Sandra turned into the parking lot. It was the game lands. *Right back where we started.*

One of the old aunties came up to Sandra's door. "Where's the boy?" she demanded.

Sandra fingered the cross on her necklace. She seemed unsure whether she should get out at all. "He's too young," Sandra said through the open window.

The tiny old woman stood with her arms crossed tight against her chest. Sandra opened the door gingerly, but the old woman would not move, and the car door brushed against her calico skirt, leaving a print. The old woman bent down and beat the dust off of the fabric, then she glared at me.

"I know somebody who's too young," she muttered. "Piss or get off the pot."

Sandra leaned across the stick shift. "Did I mention they can be difficult?"

As we got out of the car, I saw the pair of elderly women who bid on Blue at the bachelor auction unloading a station wagon. I could hear them murmuring in another language. When they greeted Sandra in English, one of them asked about Matthew.

Sandra clenched her jaw. "He's only ten years old." That didn't seem to satisfy them.

I tried to start over with these two. When I walked around to them, one spit on the ground, but the other took my hand. She smelled like tobacco and a little bit like urine. If I had to guess her age, I'd say she was in her eighties.

I said, "You probably don't remember me, but I sat near you at the firefighters' fundraiser."

The one who spat said, "We remember you."

I suppose they had reasons not to like me. I had, after all, thwarted their plans to marry Blue off all summer.

The four old women gathered in a circle, heads shaking. I could not understand anything they were saying, but Sandra did. She whispered, "This is not about you, so don't take it personally, but one of them wants you to leave. You're my guest and, to the extent we have traditions anymore, hospitality is one of them—"

"But it would be easier if I waited in the car?"

Sandra said, "There's an old deer hunting blind. They built it close to the road for disabled hunters. If you sat in there you could see the whole thing."

At that moment, Blue came out from a break in the trees. I felt a lump in my throat. He was wearing the same ribbon shirt he had worn to the bachelor auction. He walked over to their circle and put an arm around two of the old aunties.

Sandra went over to him and pointed to me. "I hope it's all right that I brought Hallie."

Blue turned to me. "Of course it's all right. Thanks for coming, caterpillar."

I think he saw how that word tore at me, because he quickly turned back to Sandra. I could hear her explaining about the deer blind, but Blue would have none of it.

"If she's your guest, she's my guest."

I was standing there with my heart half out. It felt so strange to see Blue, but not touch him. I said, "I don't mind, really," and walked to the edge of the parking lot. One of the old women shot me a dirty look. I could hear her say, "I suppose she thinks we're going to make her an honorary shaman."

I wanted to disappear.

I walked back to the grove with the two birch trees where I had spied on Blue a lifetime ago. The leaves that were just unfolding then were dead now, crisp and waiting to fall. I could hide my tears behind those shaking yellow leaves.

God, how I wanted to see Blue run again, see the wind in his hair.

Through the leaves I saw him scan the people in the parking lot.

"Where's Matthew?" I heard him ask.

Sandra faced him head on. "This is too heavy." She said it louder than necessary.

Blue said, "You're the mom," and wrapped a hug around her.

I felt left out. I might have whimpered. Blue looked up. I could feel his eyes on my hiding place. But then a drum started, steady and slow, and Blue turned and walked into the woods, following two old women who carried baskets covered with dish towels.

"Hallie?" Sandra called into the trees and I came back out. "I'm sorry they're so—"

I think she was starting to say bitchy. Sandra didn't swear much, and when she did, she always paused first. I didn't want to hear that word applied to these women. Not today.

I said, "They've been through a hell we can't even imagine. Let's just sit in the back."

Sandra laughed. "It's just Scooter and Dora and you and me in the audience. They're going to know you're here. Blue says they can deal with it." As she said that, the beat quickened. "Come on."

We sat on a fallen log next to Dora and Scooter. I could see the scars on Scooter's neck and hand. He seemed uncomfortable around me, but Dora reached out and put a hand on my shoulder.

"Thank you for the story," she said.

I said, "No, thank you. Without that interview—"

Dora cut me off. "I know what you gave up to get it in the paper. None of the other reporters followed through. You're the reason Conrad Kellan had to step down."

Even though I wasn't entirely welcome at the ceremony, I saw that I played a small part in what they were trying to do.

I think Sandra was also thinking about how she fit in. Looking at her profile, I couldn't tell if her fidgeting with the chain on her neck was meant to break it or if she just needed to reassure herself that it was there.

She saw me studying her. "I don't know why I'm so emotional, it's just a ceremony."

But Dora, in that same calm voice in which she had explained to me how the police trucked cocaine into Chicago, said, "It is emotional. We're going to get the tribe re-recognized in this lifetime."

In this lifetime. The words danced in the air. This wasn't some eighth-grade confirmation. Blue was going to vow to make re-recognition his life's work. As if fighting fires and exposing a murderously corrupt police department weren't enough.

Looking at him as he walked into the trees, I saw how his back pushed against his ribbon shirt, confident that he was strong enough for the undertaking.

Dora said, "Maybe there are more kids than just Matthew and Scooter. Maybe if we get re-recognized, more Riv'nego will come out of the woodwork."

Sandra said, "They will, if there's a check from the government."

Dora gave a weary sigh. "Don't hold your breath waiting for reparations."

Sandra seemed a little embarrassed about what she had said. "I know that's not the reason you're doing it." Then she corrected herself. "We. That's not why *we're* doing it."

Dora took Sandra's hand. "It means a lot that you're here, cousin. Matthew should be here, too."

Sandra relaxed her shoulders and almost at once her tears started.

She turned to me. "With his father dead and now his grandmother, he needs normalcy. He's a tough kid to parent, you know. He has to know everything. If I explained even a little of that history, he would need to know everything. It's too heavy."

I said, "He's smarter than you think."

Dora said, "He needs family. Nobody's going to tattle to your church folks if you two come to a sweat lodge now and then."

That made Sandra's tears come faster. I reached around her shoulders to hold her. Dora did the same from the other side.

Sandra said, "I could let him. Maybe next time."

Then it started. One of the women said something in their language.

Blue appeared again from between some trees a few yards in front of us and replied. Dora leaned over and said, "She asked, 'Where did you come from?' Blue said he comes from the river."

Sandra sighed. "We all come from the river," she said, and Dora pulled her so close their foreheads touched. I could see tears falling freely between them and then the drumming changed. The old women chanted, words coming fast to keep up with the beat. Finally, Blue joined in, the single bass in the lopsided choir.

I could almost feel the breath of the old women, an entreaty to a spirit world that had never been explained to me, and yet at that moment, I believed in it. I imagined we were all connected to people who must have sung the same way generations ago.

When the singing stopped, the oldest woman got up from the drum and stood next to Blue. She shook her head slowly.

"We've buried them in our hearts many times."

Dora rocked on the log. All of the old women were weeping. Sandra dabbed her eyes with a Kleenex.

The oldest woman continued, looking at Scooter and then Sandra. "We tell this story in English because we need the young ones to understand. What we kept secret doesn't have to be secret anymore."

Just then, car wheels crunched on the gravel in the parking lot.

Sandra whispered to Dora, "Who comes out here?"

I volunteered to see who it was. It was public property, but it would be wrong for some random bird watcher to stumble through.

In the parking lot, a flustered-looking teenager was getting out of a beat-up Pontiac.

"What's the problem?" I asked.

"I can't handle the little rat," she said, pointing to the back seat.

I peered into the back. Matthew was kicking the seat, his head tilted like he was going to yell bloody murder at any moment.

"Has he been—"

"He's been screaming his frickin' head off. His mother told me if there was an emergency, this is where she would be."

"What's the emergency?" I asked.

"I'm about ready to strangle him."

It made me angry that she talked that way in front of Matthew, but I kept my tone even. "What does Sandra owe you?"

"Not a cent if she never calls me again. I can't take this. Really."

I tried to assess what was going on with Matthew. He wasn't actually doing anything wrong, but tension was coiled tight in him, I could see that.

I opened the back door of the car. "Honey, it's okay. You're mad, aren't you?"

Matthew said, "You better believe I'm mad."

"Can you count, Mattie?"

"How high?"

"How high do you have to count for one hour?"

"Duh. At one number per second, which is the rate at which I count, it's three-thousand six hundred."

"Well, that's what I want you to do. If you can count to three-thousand six hundred, you can stay here and watch the ceremony with me."

"Really?"

"Only if you count very quietly."

He agreed and got out of the Pontiac.

The babysitter looked at me like I was some sort of snake charmer.

I pointed at the clearing. "His mom's right there. It's okay for you to leave." She didn't bother to confirm it. Her tires spit gravel as she fled.

"You're better off here, Mattie." I took his hand and we tiptoed along the side of the road toward the deer blind, Matthew counting the whole time.

"Super quiet," I reminded him.

Matthew nodded. Then he confided, "I don't have to count. You remember at the truck factory? I wasn't counting when the bad guy came in, but I was mad then, too."

"You can be mad. That babysitter was a loser."

He said, "She was a fart trapped in a turd."

"She's gone now. And we're going to get a chance to see something neither one of us may ever get another chance to see in our lifetime. So can you just postpone being mad?"

Mattie said, "Rain check." It was just like his uncle Blue would have said it. But I didn't allow myself to linger with that thought. If Mattie could keep it together, I could, too. I sat on a stump in the deer blind and lifted him up on my knee so he could see the ceremony.

"Do you know your cousin Scooter?" I asked him.

"He's the kid who got bit by Cujo."

"He's right there on the other end of the log from your mother. Can you see he's mostly healed?"

Matthew said, "This is like when my grandmother was in the hospital and Mom didn't think I could handle it, isn't it?"

I said it was the opposite. "Your mother decided you *could* handle it today. You know your uncle Blue?"

Matthew said, "Duh," like it was the stupidest question he'd ever heard. "On my mom's side, I have one uncle, one cousin, one aunt, and four other aunts who call themselves aunties, but they're really great-aunts. And on my dad's side I have one uncle. And I had one grandmother. One really awesome grandmother."

"Did any of those great-aunts ever teach you any songs?"

"One taught me songs, but they were in another language."

"Does your mother know?"

"Auntie told me not to tell her. She said Mom would not like it."

"I think you might get to sing some of those songs today."

The chanting stopped and the oldest woman walked to the center of the clearing. She described what happened before the village was flooded: The men of the tribe staked in, hoping they could stop the dam.

"We had heard President Hoover was a Quaker," she said. "We knew Vice President Curtis was half K'aw. We thought our letters would stop the dam, but we were wrong. Every man was shot.

"Some people ran away as soon as they heard what happened. They were scared. We never heard from them again. Hattie and the rest of us up here, and your grandmother," she gestured to Dora, "we went back for our men. Their bodies were by the river. Someone had stolen the wedding rings from their fingers." She choked up. "Teeth with gold fillings had been pulled out of their mouths.

"We were nearly blind with tears, but we saved what we could from the hogans. Blankets. Pots. A teakettle. The water rose five feet every day. Our village was gone in less than a week. There was nothing for us to do with our grief."

Matthew sat rapt. I asked him, "Do you understand this?"

He said he did. When I asked him if it was scary to him, he whispered, "No. My auntie told me. She said all the men were shot, but one day we would tell the story. She said even though I never met them, I should always remember those great-grandfathers and be strong and brave like them."

"You are strong and brave," I whispered.

Matthew kicked at a stick on the floor of the deer blind. "My mom doesn't think so."

"Give her another chance."

The old woman at the center said the people in town acted as if nothing happened that day. "But we couldn't forget. I found a baby rattle in the rushes that grew up on the new shoreline. Letters addressed to my husband still came to the P.O. But our hopes, our dreams, everything we had built, got stuck in the mud at the bottom of that reservoir." The old woman's voice caught on the last word. Even where I was sitting with Matthew, I could hear how heavy her breath was as she grasped for a present that wasn't so painful.

"That calm water," she choked out. "The new people have no idea what's under the surface."

Blue had been sitting on a stump near the drum. He got up and put his arm around the woman. Holding her, he said, "It was too terrible. We lost so many from my mother's generation. To alcohol. To the numbness that just can't fathom how people could do something like that. But they didn't kill us all. And you didn't give up. You taught us the old games, the old songs."

Blue looked at her as he said, "Thank you for keeping that music in our hearts while you waited for a time to try to be a tribe again. We want our grandfathers' names to be known. We want the sons of the people who killed them to walk with that shame."

Dora made a noise. I think it was a word in their language, and then all the others said it, Mattie too.

"What does that mean?" I asked him.

"It means we're angry and we won't forget."

Up front, the oldest woman approached Blue with precise steps. "Are you sure you want to do this?" she asked Blue. "Do you know what it means?"

With great formality, Blue said, "When a Riv'nego stakes in, he tells the world he will fight until he wins or until he dies. Aunties, Sandra, Dora, and Scooter, you are my people. I can count the next generation on one hand, and that makes us all sad. But one day, this forest will ring with the laughter of a hundred children, our children. We will teach them our songs."

He said something that sounded like "*Ndapnamen*," which Matthew couldn't translate. Then Blue gestured to Scooter, and the teen got up and stood beside him. One of the aunties reached into a basket and pulled out a long strip of leather. Another got out a stake.

"Are you sure?" the oldest one repeated.

"I won't leave you," Blue vowed.

The women at the front clasped their hands together and stretched their arms out straight. One looked up at the sky with a smile from an entirely different century.

Matthew asked, "Why are they so happy?"

I said, "You know how your grandmother said you should remember your great-grandfathers? That's been a terrible secret in their lives for a long time. Blue is taking that burden from them."

"What does 'burden' mean? It sounds like burro."

I said, "A burden is something heavy that you have to carry. Your uncle Blue is saying he'll carry the story for them."

"So they can die?" Matthew asked. "Are they going to die?"

"We're all going to die. I think Blue is also saying that these women can die in the traditional way. Someone will take care of them. Someone will sing them the Riv'nego songs."

"I can sing those songs."

"You might help then, when you're older."

Mattie shouted, "I want to help now!"

Everyone looked back to the deer blind.

"It's okay," Sandra waved. "Come sit with me."

Matthew ran out of the structure. His feet crunched on the twigs as he traveled the fifteen feet to the log where Sandra and Dora sat.

Peering through the sight holes of the deer blind, I looked from face to face to see how the interruption had registered. Blue was beaming. So were the women at the drum.

Matthew jumped into his mother's lap, and she wrapped her arms around him.

Up at the front, Blue ran his hands through his lustrous hair and started again. Facing the old aunt, he said, "You can lay down your burden, your quest for justice. I will carry it."

Just as he carries people out of burning buildings, I thought.

Then Blue threw his arms straight up and let out a yell I had never heard before. It didn't need translation. With that one syllable, he was calling for the power of what is right to enter him.

Dora got up. She knotted the leather tether around Blue's waist. With a large, smooth stone, Dora pounded the stake through the other end of the tether and into the ground.

The three aunts at the drum moved close to Blue and spoke to him in their language. He nodded as if he understood every word. One by one, the old women walked out of the clearing weeping. Then the last one, the oldest, held a pair of sewing shears in her outstretched hands and approached him.

Blue nodded and said, "I'm sure," again.

She walked behind him, pulled all of that beautiful hair together in a pony-tail, and lopped it off.

Matthew gasped.

Sandra hugged him tight for as long as he would let her. I could hear part of what she told him. "That's to tell us he won't quit. Uncle Blue is not going to have long hair anymore. Not until we're a tribe recognized by the government."

After the last aunt left the clearing, Dora stood with her arm around Scooter. Blue walked to the end of the tether and knelt in front of Sandra and Matthew.

I couldn't hear what he said to her, but she nodded, and Matthew got off her lap and walked, holding Blue's hand, to the place where the stake stuck in the ground.

Sandra made them pose for a picture. I'd never seen a bigger smile on Matthew's face.

When they were done, Blue yelled, "Caterpillar," loud enough to wake the dead. "I can't go very far, but I can make you come out."

He picked up a small rock and threw it at the deer blind, then another and another.

"Okay, okay," I called, not knowing what I was surrendering to.

⚊▲▲

Dora said she and Scooter were living outside the county until she gave her testimony in the case against the police chief, but she felt safe leaving Scooter with Blue this one night.

Sandra and Matthew and I were like the guests who stay to pick up after a wedding reception. An entirely different kind of conversation was possible.

Matthew asked Blue, "How long are you staked in for?"

Blue smiled. "It doesn't matter, Mattie." Blue tousled Matthew's hair and then gazed at Scooter. "It doesn't matter because I can see forever."

"Back to reality," Scooter said. "How long do you have to stay tied to that stake?"

"Nobody's done this ceremony in almost seventy years. None of the aunties could remember all the details. But I think staying here overnight is about right. I want you to camp out with me here, protect me from bears."

Scooter said there were only black bears, and he wasn't afraid of them. Then Blue looked at Sandra and asked, "Can Mattie camp with us?"

Matthew exclaimed, "Camp? Like real Indians?"

Sandra said, "You are a real Indian." And then to Blue, "Make him count if he starts to drive you crazy."

"He won't drive me crazy."

I started for Sandra's car.

Blue grabbed my arm. "It wouldn't be a real Indian ceremony without an anthropologist observing."

"That was my minor."

⏜⏝

We all stretched out on the clover. Blue told the boys everything he knew about the tribe. I lay with my head on Blue's belly and Matthew nestled under my arm as we looked up at the clear night sky. "You see the Big Dipper?" Blue asked him, "And Orion, the archer? I want you, whenever you're out on a fall night, to look up at Orion and know that your great-grandfather hunted with a bow. He was a smart man, a trader and a fiddler.

"Scooter, your grandfather was a lot older than Grandma Mayfield. He was the one who got the men to agree to stay. They didn't have time for a ceremony, but they staked in. I think your mom had that in mind when she decided not to pull you out of school after Darnell sicced Cujo on you."

Scooter said, "When we talked about it, she told me that story. I'd heard it before. I know who my grandfather was. She said she could take me out of school, but I was a man, and it was my decision. When she asked me what I wanted to do, I said, 'I'm staking in with you, Mom.'"

—

The cicadas started and we fell silent. I could feel Matthew's breath slowing down. Once he and Scooter were asleep, Blue whispered a thank you.

"For what?" I asked.

"For coming down for my staking-in ceremony."

"I'm going to be here for a while," I said. "I need an Indiana address to be eligible for the Silverton."

"You won?"

"I'm a finalist. Thanks for mailing it in."

"When I went to pack up your stuff for you, I couldn't leave your dream behind."

"Oh God, that makes you one of those Indian dream catchers."

Blue laughed, then caught himself, worried he would wake the boys. There were questions we couldn't discuss with the kids sleeping so close, but that night, I knew what it felt like to belong.

About the Author

Photo by Curt Chandler.

Cynthia Simmons is an award-winning political reporter who teaches in the Bellisario College of Communications at Penn State. She has long considered creative writing to be a way to examine truths that are too big for daily journalism. *Wrong Kind of Paper* is her first novel.

Simmons is a co-author of *The Jury and Democracy*, which examines the life-changing experience of serving on a jury. Her short stories have appeared in the Licton Springs Review. In 2015 she won a Center for American Literary Studies award for nonfiction for an essay about getting a migraine and temporarily losing her vision while reporting inside the Penitentiary of New Mexico.

Simmons grew up near Cleveland, Ohio. During high school she spent a year as an exchange student in Finland. She graduated from Macalester College with a B.A. in cultural anthropology. She later earned an M.A. in journalism from the University of Wisconsin-Madison. She has reported for daily newspapers, city magazines, United Press International, The Associated Press, and public radio stations WHA in Madison and KUNM in Albuquerque. She also worked as the news director at the Madison community radio station WORT. In her 40s, she earned a J.D. from the University of Washington. She taught media law in the journalism program at the University of Washington before moving to Penn State.

In her spare time Simmons enjoys Moth-style storytelling, stand-up paddle boarding, and exploring the woods with her dog.